MiSTER MONDAY

A flash of light suddenly distracted Arthur from his slow, counted breaths. It hit the corner of his eye and he swung around to see what it was. For a moment he thought he was blacking out again and was falling over and looking up at the sun. Then, through half-shut eyes, he realised that whatever the blinding light was, it was on the ground and very close.

In fact, it was moving, gliding across the grass towards him, the light losing its brilliance as it drew nearer. Arthur watched in stunned amazement as a dark outline became visible within the light. Then the light faded completely, to reveal a weirdly dressed man in a very strange sort of wheelchair being pushed across the grass by an equally odd-looking attendant.

The Keys to the Kingdom series

MISTER MONDAY*
GRIM TUESDAY
DROWNED WEDNESDAY
SIR THURSDAY

Also by Garth Nix

Sabriel*
Lirael
Abhorsen

*Also available on audio

Praise for Sabriel

"Sabriel is a winner, a fantasy that reads like realism. I congratulate Garth Nix." Philip Pullman

"Fast pace, drama, vivid descriptions, excitement and humour... What more could you want?" *Guardian*

www.garthnix.co.uk

MISTER MONDAY

GARTH NIX

ILLUSTRATED BY TIM STEVENS

HarperCollins *Children's Books*

First published in the USA by Scholastic Inc 2003
First published in Great Britain by Collins 2004
HarperCollins *Children's Books* is a division of HarperCollins*Publishers* Ltd
77-85 Fulham Palace Road, Hammersmith, London, W6 8JB

The HarperCollins *Children's Books* website address is:
www.harpercollinschildrensbooks.co.uk

1

Copyright © Garth Nix 2003
Illustrations by Tim Stevens 2003

ISBN-13: 978 0 00 725639 6
ISBN-10: 0 00 725639 6

Garth Nix asserts the moral right to be identified
as the author of the work.

Printed and bound in Great Britain by
Bookmarque Ltd, Croydon, Surrey

To Anna and Thomas,
and to all my family and friends.

PROLOGUE

They had tried to destroy the Will, but that proved to be beyond their power. So they broke it, in two ways. It was broken physically, torn apart, with the fragments of heavy parchment scattered across both space and time. It was broken in spirit because not one clause of it had been fulfilled.

If the treacherous Trustees had their way, no clause of the Will would ever be executed. To make sure of this, all seven fragments of the Will had been hidden with great care.

The first and least of the fragments was fused inside a single clear crystal, harder than diamond. Then the crystal was encased in a box of unbreakable glass. The box was locked inside a cage of silver and malachite, and the cage was fixed in place on the surface of a dead sun at the very end of Time.

Around the cage, twelve metal Sentinels stood guard, each taking post upon one of the numbers of a clock face that had been carved with permanent light in the dark matter of the defunct star.

The Sentinels had been specially created as guardians of the fragment. They were vaguely human in appearance, though twice as tall, and their skins were luminous steel. Quick and flexible as cats, they had no hands, but single blades sprang from each wrist. Each Sentinel was responsible for the space between its own hour and the next, and their leader ruled them from the position between twelve and one.

The metal Sentinels were overseen by a carefully chosen corps of Inspectors, lesser beings who would not dare question the breakers of the Will. Once every hundred years one of these Inspectors would appear to make sure that all was well and that the fragment was safely locked away.

In recent aeons, the Inspectors had become lax, rarely doing more than appear, squint at the cage, box and crystal, salute the Sentinels, and disappear again. The Sentinels, who had spent ten thousand years in faithful service marching between the chapters of the clock, did not approve of this slipshod attention to duty. But it was not in their nature to complain, nor was there any means to do so. They could raise the alarm if necessary, but no more than that.

The Sentinels had seen many Inspectors come and go. No one else had ever visited. No one had tried to steal or rescue the fragment of the Will. In short, nothing had happened for all of that ten thousand years.

Then, on a day that was no different from any of the more than three and a half million days that had gone before, an Inspector arrived who took his duties more seriously. He arrived normally enough, simply appearing outside the clock face, his hat askew from the transfer, his official warrant clutched firmly in one hand so the bright gold seal was clearly visible. The Sentinels twitched at the arrival and their blades shivered in anticipation. The warrant and the seal were only half of the permission required to be there. There was always a chance the watchwords delivered by the previous Inspector would not be uttered and the Sentinels' blades would at last see blurring, slicing action.

Of course, the Sentinels were required to allow the Inspector a minute's grace. It was not unknown for a transfer between both time and space to briefly addle the wits of anyone, immortal or otherwise.

This Inspector did seem a bit the worse for wear. He wore a fairly standard human shape, that of a middle-aged man of rapidly thickening girth. This human body was clad in a blue frock coat, shiny at the elbows and ink-stained on the right cuff. His white shirt was not really very white, and the badly tied green necktie did not adequately disguise the fact that his collar had come adrift. His top hat had seen much service and was both squashed and leaning to the left. When he raised it to acknowledge the Sentinels, a sandwich wrapped in newspaper fell out. He caught it and slipped it into an inside pocket of his coat before speaking the watchwords.

"Incense, sulphur and rue, I am an Inspector, honest and true," he recited carefully, holding up the warrant again to show the seal.

The Twelve O'Clock Sentinel swivelled in place in answer to the watchwords and the seal. It crossed its blades with a knife-sharpening noise that made the Inspector tremble and waved a salute in the air.

"Approach, Inspector," intoned the Sentinel. That was half of everything it ever said.

The Inspector nodded and cautiously stepped from the transfer plate to the curdled darkness of the dead star. He had taken the precaution of wearing Immaterial Boots (disguised as carpet slippers) to counteract the warping nature of the dead star's dark matter, though his superior had assured him that the warrant and the seal would be sufficient protection. He paused to pick up the transfer plate because it was a personal favourite, a large serving plate of delicate bone china with a fruit pattern, rather than the more usual disc of burnished electrum. It was a risk using a china plate because it could be easily broken, but it looked nice and that was important to the Inspector.

Even the Inspectors were not allowed to pass the inner rim of the clock face, where the feet of the numerals were bordered by a golden line. So this Inspector gingerly trod past the Twelve O'Clock Sentinel and stopped short of the line. The silver cage looked as solid as it should, and the glass box was quite intact and beautifully transparent. He could easily see the crystal inside, just where it was supposed to be.

"All, ah, seems to be in order," he muttered. Relieved, he took a small box out of his coat pocket, flicked it open, and with a practised movement transferred a small pinch of snuff to his right nostril. It was a new snuff, a present from a higher authority.

"All, ahhh, ahhh, in order," he repeated, then let out an enormous sneeze that rocked his whole body and for a moment threatened to overbalance him over the gold line. The Sentinels leaped and twisted from their regular positions, and the Twelve O'Clock Sentinel's blades came whisking down within an inch of the Inspector's face as he desperately windmilled his arms to regain his balance.

Finally he managed it, and teetered back on the right side of the line.

"Awfully sorry, terrible habit!" he squeaked as he thrust his snuff box securely away. "I'm an Inspector, remember. Here's the warrant! Look at the seal!"

The Sentinels subsided into their usual pacing. The Twelve O'Clock Sentinel's arms went back to its sides, the blades no longer threatening.

The Inspector took out a huge patched handkerchief from his sleeve and mopped his face. But as he wiped the sweat away, he thought he saw something move across the surface of the clock face. Something small and thin and dark. When he blinked and removed his handkerchief, he couldn't see anything.

"I don't suppose there *is* anything to report?" he asked nervously. He hadn't been an Inspector long. A decade short of four centuries, and he was only an Inspector of the Fourth Order. He'd been a Third Back Hall Porter for most of his career, almost since the Beginning of Time. Before that—

"Nothing to report," said the Twelve O'Clock Sentinel, using up the rest of its standard vocabulary.

The Inspector politely tipped his hat to the Sentinel, but he was concerned. He could feel something here. Something not quite right. But the penalty for a false alarm was too horrible to contemplate. He might be demoted back to being a Hall Porter or, even worse, be made corporeal – stripped of his powers and memory and sent somewhere in the Secondary Realms as a living, breathing baby.

Of course, the penalty for missing something important was even worse. He might be made corporeal for that, but it would not be as anything even vaguely human, or on a world where there was intelligent life. And even that was not the *worst* that could happen. There were far more terrible fates, but he refused to contemplate them.

The Inspector looked across at the cage, the glass box and the crystal. Then he got a pair of opera glasses out of an inner pocket and looked through those. He could still see nothing out of order. Surely, he told himself, the Sentinels would know if something had gone amiss?

He stepped back outside the clock face and cleared his throat.

"All in order, well done, you Sentinels," he said. "The watchwords for the next Inspector will be 'Thistle, palm, oak and yew, I'm an Inspector, honest and true.' Got that? – excellent – well, I'll be off."

The Twelve O'Clock Sentinel saluted. The Inspector doffed his hat once more, swivelled on one heel and set down his transfer plate, chanting the words that would take him to the House. According to regulations, he was supposed to go via the Office of Unusual Activities on the forty-fifteenth floor and report, but he was unsettled and wanted to get straight back to the twenty-tenth floor, his own comfortable study, and a nice cup of tea.

"From dead star's gloom to bright lamp's light, back to my rooms and away from night!"

Before he could step on the plate, something small, skinny and very black shot across the golden line, between the legs of the Twelve O'Clock Sentinel, across the Inspector's left Immaterial Boot and on to the plate. The blue and green fruit glazed on the plate flashed and the plate, black streak and all, vanished in a puff of rather rubbery and nasty-smelling smoke.

"Alarm! Alarm!" cried the Sentinels, leaving the clock face to swarm around the vanished plate, their blades snickering in all directions as the sound of twelve impossibly loud alarm clocks rang and rang from somewhere inside their metal bodies. The Inspector shrank down before the Sentinels and started to chew on the corner of his handkerchief and sob. He knew what that black streak was. He had recognised it in a flash of terror as it sped past.

It was a line of handwritten text. The text from the fragment that was supposedly still fused in crystal, locked in the unbreakable box, inside the silver and malachite cage, glued to the surface of a dead sun and guarded by metal Sentinels.

Only now none of those things was true.

One of the fragments of the Will had escaped – and it was all his fault.

Even worse, it had touched him, striking his flesh straight through the Immaterial Boot. So he knew what it said, and he was not allowed to know. Even more shockingly, the Will had recalled him to his real duty. For the first time in millennia he was conscious of just how badly things had gone wrong.

"Into the trust of my good Monday, I place the administration of the Lower House," the Inspector whispered. "Until such a time as the Heir or the Heir's representatives call upon Monday to relinquish any such offices, properties, rights and appurtenances as Monday holds in trust."

The Sentinels did not understand him, or perhaps they

could not even hear him over the clamouring of their internal alarms. They had spread out, uselessly searching the surface of the dead star, beams of intense light streaming from their eyes into the darkness. The star was not large – no more than a thousand yards in diameter – but the fragment was long gone. The Inspector knew it would already have left his rooms and got into the House proper.

"I have to get back," the Inspector said to himself. "The Will will need help. Transfer plate's gone, so it will have to be the long way."

He reached into his coat and pulled out a grimy and bedraggled pair of wings that were almost as tall as he was. The Inspector hadn't used them for a very long time and was surprised at the state they were in. The feathers were all yellow and askew and the pinions didn't look at all reliable. He clipped them into place on his back and took a few tentative flaps to make sure they still worked.

Distracted by his wings, the Inspector didn't notice a sudden flash of light upon the surface of the clock, or the two figures who appeared with that flash. They wore human shapes too, as was the fashion in the House. But these two were taller, thinner and more handsome. They had on neat black frock coats over crisp white shirts with high-pointed collars and very neat neckties of sombre red, a shade lighter than their dark silk waistcoats. Their top hats were sleekly black, and they carried ornate ebony sticks topped with silver knobs.

"Where do you think you're going, Inspector?" asked the taller of the two new arrivals.

The Inspector turned in shock, and his wings drooped still further.

"To report, sir!" he said weakly. "As you can see. To... to my immediate superiors... and to... to Monday's Dawn, or even Mister Monday, if he wants..."

"Mister Monday will know soon enough," said the tall gentleman. "You know who we are?"

The Inspector shook his head. They were very high up in the Firm, that was obvious from their clothes and the power he could sense. But he didn't know them, either by name or by rank.

"Are you from the sixty-hundredth floor? Mister Monday's executive office?"

The taller gentleman smiled and drew a paper from his waistcoat pocket. It unfolded itself as he held it up, and the seal upon it shone so brightly that the Inspector had to shield his face with his arm and duck his head.

"As you see, we serve a higher Master than Monday," said the gentleman. "You will come with us."

The Inspector gulped and shambled forward. One of the gentlemen swiftly pulled on a pair of snowy white gloves and snapped off the Inspector's wings. They shrank till they were no larger than a dove's wings and he put them in a buff envelope that came from nowhere. He sealed this shut with a sizzling press of his thumb. Then he handed the envelope to the Inspector. The word EVIDENCE appeared on it as the Inspector clutched it to his chest and cast nervous glances at his escorts.

Working together, the two gentlemen drew a doorway in the air with their sticks. When they'd finished, the space shimmered for a moment and then solidified into an elevator doorway, with a sliding metal grille and a bronze call button. One of the gentlemen pressed the button and an elevator car suddenly appeared out of nowhere behind the grille.

"I'm not authorised to go in an executive elevator, not up past Records by any means, stair or lift or weirdway," gabbled the Inspector. "And I'm definitely not... not authorised to go down below the Inking Cellars."

The two gentlemen pushed back the grille and gestured for the Inspector to step into the elevator. It was lined with dark green velvet and one entire wall was covered in small bronze buttons.

"We're not going down, are we?" asked the Inspector in a small voice.

The taller gentleman smiled, a cold smile that did not reach his eyes. He reached up and his arm clicked horribly as it stretched, growing an extra couple of yards so he could press a button on the very top right-hand side of the lift.

"There?" asked the Inspector, awed in spite of his fear. He could feel the Will's influence working away inside of him, but he knew there was no hope of trying to help it now. The words that had got away would have to fend for themselves. "All the way to the top?"

"Yes," said the two gentlemen in unison as they clanged shut the metal grille.

CHAPTER ONE

It was Arthur Penhaligon's first day at his new school and it was not going well. Having to start two weeks after everyone else was bad enough, but it was even worse than that. Arthur was totally and utterly new to the school. His family had just moved to the town, so he knew absolutely no one and he had none of the local knowledge that would make life easier.

Like the fact the seventh grade had a cross-country run every Monday just before lunch. Today. And it was compulsory, unless special arrangements had been made by a student's parents. In advance.

Arthur tried to explain to the gym teacher that he'd only just recovered from a series of very serious asthma attacks and had in fact been in the hospital only a few weeks ago. Besides that, he was wearing the stupid school uniform of grey trousers with a white shirt and tie, and leather shoes. He couldn't run in those clothes.

For some reason – perhaps the forty other kids shouting and chasing one another around – only the second part of Arthur's complaint got through to the teacher, Mister Weightman.

"Listen, kid, the rule is everybody runs, in whatever you're wearing!" snapped the teacher. "Unless you're ill."

"I am ill!" protested Arthur, but his words were lost as someone screamed and suddenly two girls were pulling each other's hair and trying to kick shins, and Weightman was yelling at them and blowing his whistle.

"Settle down! Susan, let go of Tanya right now! OK, you know the course. Down the right side of the oval, through the park, around the statue, back through the park and down the other side of the oval. First three back get to go to lunch early, the last three get to sweep the gym. Line up – I said line up, don't gaggle about. Get back, Rick. Ready? On my whistle."

No, I'm not ready, thought Arthur. But he didn't want to stand out any more by complaining further or simply not going. He was already an outsider here, a loner in the making, and he didn't want to be. He was an optimist. He could handle the run.

Arthur gazed across the oval at the dense forest beyond, which was obviously meant to be a park. It looked more like a jungle. Anything could happen in there. He could take a rest. He could make it that far, no problem, he told himself.

Just for insurance, Arthur felt in his pocket for his inhaler, closing his fingers around the cool, comforting metal and plastic. He didn't want to use it, didn't want to be dependent on the medication. But he'd ended up in the hospital last time because he'd refused to use the inhaler until it was too late, and he'd promised his parents he wouldn't do that again.

Weightman blew his whistle, a long blast that was answered in many different ways. A group of the biggest, roughest-looking boys sprang out like shotgun pellets, hitting one another and shouting as they accelerated away. A bunch of athletic girls, taller and more long-legged than any boys at their current age, streamed past them a few seconds later, their noses in the air at the vulgar antics of the monkeys they were forced to share a class with.

Smaller groups of boys or girls – never mixed – followed with varying degrees of enthusiasm. After them came the unathletic and noncommitted and those too hip to run anywhere, though Arthur wasn't particularly sure which category they each belonged to.

Arthur found himself running because he didn't have the courage to walk. He knew he wouldn't be mistaken for someone too cool to participate. Besides, Mister Weightman was already jogging backwards so he could face the walkers and berate them.

"Your nonparticipation has been noted," bellowed

Weightman. "You *will* fail this class if you do not pick up your feet!"

Arthur looked over his shoulder to see if that had any result. One kid broke into a shambling run, but the rest of the walkers ignored the teacher. Weightman spun around in disgust and built up speed. He overtook Arthur and the middle group of runners and rapidly closed the gap on the serious athletes at the front. Arthur could already tell he was the kind of gym teacher who liked to beat the kids in a race. *Probably because he couldn't win against other adult runners,* Arthur thought sourly.

For three or maybe even four minutes after Weightman sped away, Arthur kept up with the last group of actual runners, well ahead of the walkers. But as he had feared, he found it harder and harder to get a full breath into his lungs. They just wouldn't expand, as if they were already full of something and couldn't let any air in. Without the oxygen he needed, Arthur got slower and slower, falling back until he was barely in front of the walkers. His breathing became shallower and shallower and the world narrowed around him, until all he could think about was trying to get a decent breath and keep putting one foot approximately in front of the other.

Then, without any conscious intention, Arthur found that his legs weren't moving and he was staring up at the sky. He was lying on his back on the grass. Dimly, he realised he must have blacked out and fallen over.

"Hey, are you taking a break or is there a problem?" someone asked. Arthur tried to say that he was OK, though some other part of his brain was going off like a fire engine siren, screaming that he was definitely not OK. But no words came out of his mouth, only a short, rasping wheeze.

Inhaler! Inhaler! Inhaler! said the screaming siren part of his brain. Arthur followed its direction, fumbling in his pocket for the metal cylinder with its plastic mouthpiece. He tried to raise it to his mouth, but when his hand arrived it was empty. He'd dropped the inhaler.

Then someone else pushed the mouthpiece between his lips and a cool mist suddenly filled his mouth and throat.

"How many puffs?" asked the voice.

Three, thought Arthur. That would get him breathing, at least enough to stay alive. Though he'd probably be back in the hospital again, and another week or two convalescing at home.

"How many puffs?"

Arthur realised he hadn't answered. Weakly, he held out three fingers and was rewarded by two more clouds of medicine. It was already beginning to work. His shallow, wheezing breaths were actually getting some air into his lungs and, in turn, some oxygen into his blood and to his brain.

The closed in, confused world he'd been experiencing started to open out again, like scenery unfolded on a stage. Instead of just the blue sky rimmed with darkness, he saw a couple of kids crouched near him. They were two of the walkers, the ones who refused to run. A girl and a boy, both defiantly not in school uniform or gym gear, wearing black jeans, T-shirts featuring bands Arthur didn't know, and sunglasses. They were either super-hip and ultra-cool, or the exact opposite. Arthur was too new to the school and the whole town to know.

The girl had short dyed hair that was so blonde it was almost white. The boy had long, dyed-black hair. Despite this, they looked kind of the same. It took Arthur's confused mind a second to work out that they had to be twins, or at least brother and sister. Maybe one had to repeat a grade.

"Ed, call 999," instructed the girl. She was the one who had given Arthur the inhaler.

"The Octopus confiscated my phone," replied the boy. Ed.

"OK, you run back to the gym," said the girl. "I'll go after Weightman."

"What for?" asked Ed. "Shouldn't you stay?"

"Nope, nothing we can do except get help," said the girl. "Weightman's got a phone. He's probably already on his way back. You just lie here and keep breathing."

The last words were directed at Arthur. He nodded feebly and waved his hand, telling them to go. Now that his brain was at least partially functioning again, he was terribly embarrassed. First day at a new school and he hadn't even made it to lunch time. It would be even worse coming back.

He would be seen as a total loser and, after a month of the new term, would have no chance of easily catching up or making any friends.

At least I'm alive, Arthur told himself. He had to be grateful for that. He still couldn't get a proper breath, and he was incredibly weak, but he managed to prop himself up on one elbow and look around.

The two black-clad kids were showing that they could run when they wanted to. Arthur watched the girl sprint through the gaggle of walkers like a crow dive-bombing a flock of sparrows, and vanish into the tree line of the park. Looking the other way, Arthur saw Ed was about to disappear around the high, blank brick wall of the gym, which blocked the rest of the school from view.

Help would be coming soon. Arthur willed himself to be calm. He forced himself up to a sitting position and concentrated on taking slow breaths, as deep as he could manage. With a bit of luck he would stay conscious. The main thing was not to panic. He'd been here before, and he'd come through. He had the inhaler in his hand. He'd just stay quiet and still, keeping panic and fear securely locked away.

A flash of light suddenly distracted Arthur from his slow, counted breaths. It hit the corner of his eye and he swung around to see what it was. For a moment he thought he was blacking out again and was falling over and looking up at the sun. Then, through half-shut eyes, he realised that whatever the blinding light was, it was on the ground and very close.

In fact, it was moving, gliding across the grass towards him, the light losing its brilliance as it drew nearer. Arthur watched in stunned amazement as a dark outline became visible within the light. Then the light faded completely, to reveal a weirdly dressed man in a very strange sort of wheelchair being pushed across the grass by an equally odd-looking attendant.

The wheelchair was long and narrow, like a bath, and it was made of woven wicker. It had one small wheel at the front and two big ones at the back. All three wheels had metal rims, without rubber tyres, or any sort of tyre, so the wheelchair – or wheel-bath, or bath chair, or whatever it was – sank heavily into the grass.

The man lying back in the bath chair was thin and pale, his skin like tissue paper. He looked quite young, though, no more than twenty, and was very handsome, with even features and blue eyes, though these were hooded, as if he was very tired. He had an odd round hat with a tassel on his blond head and was wearing what looked to Arthur like some sort of kung fu robe, of red silk with blue dragons all over it. He had a tartan blanket over his legs, but his slippers stuck out the end. They were red silk too, and shimmered in the sun with a pattern that Arthur couldn't quite focus on.

The man who was pushing the chair was even more out of place. Or out of time. He looked somewhat like a butler from an old movie, or Nestor from the Tintin comics, though he was nowhere near as neat. He had on an oversized black coat with ridiculously long tails that almost touched the ground, and his white shirt front was stiff and very solid, as if it was made of plastic. He had knitted half-gloves that were unravelling on his hands, and bits of loose wool hung over his fingers. Arthur noticed with distaste that his fingernails were very long and yellow, as were his teeth. He was much older than the man he pushed, his face lined and pitted with age, his white hair only growing on the back of his head, though it was very long. He had to be at least eighty, but he had no difficulty pushing the bath chair straight towards Arthur.

The two men were talking as they approached. They seemed entirely unaware of Arthur, or uninterested in him.

"I don't know why I keep you upstairs, Sneezer," said the man in the bath chair. "Or agree to your ridiculous plans."

"Now, now, sir," said the butler-type, who was obviously called Sneezer. Now that they were closer, Arthur noticed that his nose was rather red and had a patchwork of broken blood vessels shining under the skin. "It's not a plan, but a precaution. We don't want to be bothered by the Will, do we?"

"I s'pose not," grumbled the young man. He yawned widely and closed his eyes. "You're sure that we'll find someone suitable here?"

"Sure as eggs is eggs," replied Sneezer. "Surer even, eggs

not always being what one might expect. I set the dials myself, to find someone suitably on the edge of infinity. You give him the Key, he dies, you get it back. Another ten thousand years without trouble, and the Will can't quibble cos you *did* give up the Key to one in the line of heredity, as it were."

"It's very annoying," said the young man, yawning again. "I'm quite exhausted with all this running around and answering those ridiculous inquiries from up top. How should I know how that bit of the Will got out? I'm not going to write a report, you know. I haven't the energy. In fact, I really need a nap—"

"Not now, sir, not now," said Sneezer urgently. He shaded his eyes with one dirty, half-gloved hand and looked around. Strangely, he still seemed unable to see Arthur, though he was right in front of him. "We're almost there."

"We are there," said the young man coldly. He pointed at Arthur as if the boy had suddenly appeared out of nowhere. "Is that it?"

Sneezer left the bath chair and advanced on Arthur. His attempt at a smile revealed even more yellow teeth, some of them broken, but all too many of them sharp and doglike.

"Hello, my boy," he said. "Let's have a bow for Mister Monday."

Arthur stared at him. *It must be an unknown side effect*, he thought. *Oxygen deprivation. Hallucinations.*

A moment later, he felt a hard bony hand grip his head

and bob it forward several times, as Sneezer made him bow to the man in the bath chair. The shock and unpleasantness of the touch made Arthur cough and lose all his hard-won control over his breathing. Now he really was panicking and he couldn't breathe at all.

"Bring him here," instructed Mister Monday. With a languid sigh, he leaned over the side of the bath chair as Sneezer dragged Arthur effortlessly over, using only two fingers to pick the boy up by the back of his neck.

"You're sure this one will die straight away?" Mister Monday asked, reaching out to lift Arthur's chin and look at his face. Unlike Sneezer, Monday's hands were clean and his nails trimmed. There was hardly any force in his grip, but Arthur found he couldn't move at all, as if Mister Monday had pressed a nerve that paralysed his whole body.

Sneezer rummaged in his pocket with one hand, not letting go of Arthur's neck. He pulled out half a dozen scrunched-up pieces of paper, which hung in the air as if he'd laid them on an invisible desk. He sorted through them quickly, smoothed one out and held it against Arthur's cheek. The paper shone with a bright blue light and Arthur's name appeared on it in letters of gold.

"It's him, no doubt at all," said Sneezer. He thrust the paper back in his pocket, and all the others went back in as if they were joined together on a thread. "Arthur Penhaligon. Due to drop off the twig any minute. You'd best give him the Key, sir."

Mister Monday yawned again and let go of Arthur's chin. Then he slowly reached inside the left sleeve of his silk robe and pulled out a slender metal spike. It looked very much like a thin-bladed knife without a handle. Arthur stared at it, his mind and sight already fuzzy again from lack of oxygen. Somewhere in his head, under that fuzziness, the panicked voice that had told him to use his inhaler was screaming again.

Run away! Run away! Run away!

Though the weird paralysis from Monday's touch had gone, Sneezer's grip did not lessen for a moment, and Arthur simply had no strength to break free.

"By the powers vested in me under the arrangements entered into in the blah, blah, blah," muttered Mister Monday. He spoke too quickly for Arthur to make out what he was saying. He didn't slow down until he reached the final few words. "And so let the Will be done."

As he finished, Monday thrust out with the blade. At the same time, Sneezer let Arthur go and the boy fell back on the grass. Monday laughed wearily and dropped the blade into Arthur's open hand. Instantly, Sneezer made Arthur wrap his fingers around it, pushing so hard that the metal bit into his skin. With the pain came another sudden shock. Arthur found that he could breathe. It was as if a catch had been turned at the top of his lungs, unlocking them to let air in.

"And the other," said Sneezer urgently. "He has to have it all."

Monday peered across at his servant and frowned. He also started to yawn, but quashed it, taking an angry swipe across his own face.

"You're very keen for the Key to leave my possession, even if only for a few minutes," said Monday. He'd been about to take something else out of his other sleeve, but now he hesitated. "And to give me boiled brandy and water. Too much boiled brandy and water. Perhaps, in my weariness, I have not given this matter quite the thought..."

"If the Will finds you, and you have not given the Key to a suitable Heir—"

"If the Will finds me," mused Monday. "What of it? If the reports be true, only a few lines have escaped their durance. I wonder how much power they hold?"

"It would be safer not to put it to the test," said Sneezer, wiping his nose on his sleeve. Anxiety obviously made his nose run.

"With the complete Key in his possession, the boy might live," observed Monday. For the first time he sat up straight in his bath chair and the sleepy look was gone from his eyes. "Besides, Sneezer, it seems odd to me that you of all my servants should have come up with this plan."

"How so, sir?" asked Sneezer. He tried to smile ingratiatingly, but the effect was repulsive.

"Because generally you're an idiot!" shouted Monday in a rage. He flicked a finger and an unseen force struck Sneezer and Arthur, sending them tumbling roughly across the grass. "Whose game are you playing here, Sneezer? You're in league with the Morrow Days, aren't you? You and that Inspector, and the Will safe as ever? Do you expect to take over my office?"

"No," said Sneezer. He slowly stood up and began to advance upon the bath chair. With each step, his voice changed, becoming louder and clearer, booming into the distance. Trumpets sounded as he trod, and Arthur saw letters of sharp black ink form upon his skin. The letters danced and joined into lines of type that rushed across Sneezer's face like living, shining tattoos.

"Into the trust of my good Monday, I place the administration of the Lower House," said both the type and the booming voice that came out of his mouth, but was not Sneezer's. "Until—"

Arthur couldn't believe the languid Monday could move so fast. He drew something from his sleeve, a glittering object which he pointed at Sneezer as he shouted deafening words that sounded like thunderclaps, the vibration of them smashing through the air and shaking the ground where Arthur lay.

There was a flash of light, a concussion that shook the earth and a stifled scream, though Arthur did not know who it came from, Sneezer or Mister Monday.

Arthur shut his eyes. When he opened them again, Monday, bath chair and Sneezer had disappeared, but there was still black type running in a thread through the air, moving too quickly for him to read the words. The letters twirled above Arthur into a spiral, a whirlwind of shiny letters. Something heavy materialised between the lines of type and fell down, striking him sharply on the head.

It was a book, a slim notebook, no bigger than Arthur's hand. It was bound in green cloth. Arthur absently picked it up and slid it into his shirt pocket. He looked up and around again, but the lines of type were gone. They had slowed down just long enough for him to make out only four words: *Heir, Monday* and *The Will*.

Arthur could see Mister Weightman sprinting towards him now, a phone at his ear, and the school nurse running much more slowly from the direction of the gym, a resuscitation kit in her hand. Behind Weightman came the whole of Arthur's gym class. Even the walkers were running.

Arthur looked at them and would have groaned if he could have forced any air out of his lungs. Not only was he going to die, it would be in front of everybody. They would all be interviewed on TV and say things that sounded sort of nice but really meant they thought he was a stupid loser.

Then he noticed that he *could* breathe. For a while there his brain had been tripping out from lack of oxygen, with visions and everything, but the inhaler had worked sufficiently well to get him over the worst. He could breathe a bit, and it was worth the pain in his hand—

Arthur looked at that hand. It was still clenched in a fist, with a trickle of blood running out below his little finger.

He'd thought he was clutching his inhaler, but he wasn't. He was holding a weird strip of metal, sharp-pointed on one end with a circular loop on the other. It was heavy and was made of silver with fancy gold inlay, all swirls and curlicues.

Arthur stared at it for a second before he realised what it was. It was the minute hand of some sort of antique clock. It was real and so was the notebook in his pocket. Mister Monday and Sneezer had been there. It wasn't all an oxygen-deprivation dream.

Weightman and the nurse would be on him in a minute. Arthur looked around wildly, trying to think of somewhere he could hide the clock hand. It would be taken away from him for sure.

There was a patch of discoloured grass a few paces away. Arthur crawled over to it and plunged the minute hand into the earth, until only the hollow circle remained, hidden by some tufts of yellow grass.

As soon as he let the hand go, he felt his chest tighten. That catch had snapped shut again and there was no more air. Arthur rolled over, trying to put some distance between himself and the minute hand. He didn't want anyone else to find it.

He'd come back to get it as soon as he could, he thought. If he lived.

CHAPTER TWO

Arthur was still in the hospital twenty-four hours after the strange events of Monday morning. He had spent most of that time unconscious and still felt dazed and confused. Though he was breathing reasonably well again, the doctors wanted to keep him in for a few more days because of his history.

Fortunately Arthur's mother was a very important medical researcher who worked for the government, so not only did the whole family have the best medical insurance, doctors all around the country knew Dr Emily Penhaligon and her work. Arthur always got good treatment and was kept in the hospital even when they made other sicker people leave. He usually felt bad about that later, but when he was actually in the hospital he was too ill to think about it.

Arthur's father was a musician. He was a very good musician, but not always a very commercially minded one. He wrote brilliant songs and then forgot to do anything with them. He'd been the guitar player in a famous band called The Ratz thirty-five years ago, and sometimes people still recognised him. He'd been called Plague Rat then, but had long since gone back to his original name, Robert "Bob" Penhaligon. He still got a lot of money from his time in The Ratz since he'd written most of the songs, some of which were multiplatinum sellers. They still got played on some radio stations quite a lot and new bands used samples from them, particularly Bob's guitar parts.

These days, Bob Penhaligon looked after the family and noodled away on one of his three pianos or one of his twelve guitars, while Emily Penhaligon spent more time than she wanted to in her laboratory doing things with DNA and computers that benefited the whole human race but took her away from her own family.

Arthur had six brothers and sisters. The eldest three, two boys and a girl, were from Bob's liaisons with three different women when he was on tour with The Ratz. The fourth was from Emily's first marriage. The next two were both Bob and Emily's.

Then there was Arthur. He was adopted. His birth parents had both been doctors who worked with Emily. They'd died in the last really big influenza epidemic, the one that had finally been controlled by a new anti-flu drug they'd helped to discover – as part of Emily's team. Arthur had only been a week old when they died. He'd lived through the flu, but he was probably an asthmatic because of it. Besides his parents he had no immediate family, so Emily and Bob had been successful in their application to adopt.

It didn't worry Arthur that he was adopted. But every now and then he would leaf through the photo album that was almost all he had to remember his birth parents. The other thing was a short video from their wedding, which he found almost unbearable to watch. The influenza plague had killed them only eighteen months later, and even to Arthur they looked ridiculously young. He liked that as he got older he looked more like both his birth parents, in different ways. So they lived on in him.

Arthur had known he was adopted since he was little. Bob and Emily treated all the children the same way, and the children considered themselves all brothers and sisters. They never introduced one another as "half-brother" or "half-sister" and never explained the fact that there were twenty years between the eldest, Erazmuz (born in Bob's rock music heyday), and the youngest, Arthur. They also didn't explain the difference in looks, skin colour, or anything else. They were simply all part of the family, even if only the youngest three were still at home.

The four eldest were Erazmuz, who was a major in the army and had children of his own; Staria, a serious theatre actress; Eminor, a musician, who'd changed his name to Patrick; and Suzanne, who was at college. The three at home were Michaeli, who was at a local college; Eric, who was in his last year of high school; and Arthur.

Arthur's father, Michaeli and Eric had already been to see him the night before, and his mother had popped in early in the morning to check that he was OK. Once she was sure of that, she lectured him about it being better to look like a total loser in everyone's eyes than to be dead.

Arthur always knew when his mother was approaching because doctors and nurses would appear from all over the place, and by the time she arrived, Emily would be trailing eight or nine white-coated people behind her. Arthur was used to her being a Medical Legend, just as he was used to his father being a Former Musical Legend.

Since all of his family in town had already visited once, Arthur was surprised when two more people came to see him early on Tuesday afternoon. Children his own age. He didn't recognise them for a second, since they weren't wearing black. Then he realised who they were. Ed and the girl who had helped him use the inhaler. This time they were in regular school uniform, white shirts, grey trousers, blue ties.

"Hi," said the girl from the door. "Can we come in?"

"Uh, sure," mumbled Arthur. What could these two want?

"We didn't meet properly yesterday," said the girl. "I'm Leaf."

"Leith?" asked Arthur. She'd pronounced it strangely.

"No, Leaf, as in *from a tree*," said Leaf reluctantly. "Our parents changed their names to reflect their commitment to the environment."

"Dad calls himself Tree," said the boy. "I'm supposed to be Branch but I don't use it. Call me Ed."

"Right," said Arthur. "Leaf and Ed. My dad used to be called Plague Rat."

"No!" exclaimed Leaf and Ed. "You mean from The Ratz?"

"Yeah." Arthur was surprised. Normally only old people knew the names of the individual members of The Ratz.

"We're into music," said Leaf, seeing his surprise. She looked down at her school uniform. "That's why we were wearing real clothes yesterday. There was a lunch time appearance by Zeus Suit at the mall and we didn't want to look stupid."

"But we missed it anyway," said Ed. "Because of you."

"Uh, what do you mean?" asked Arthur warily. "I'm really grateful to you guys—"

"It's OK," said Leaf. "What Ed means is we missed Zeus Suit because we had something more important to do after we... I mean I... saw those two weird guys and the wheelchair thing."

"Wheelchair thing? Weird guys?" Arthur repeated. He'd managed to convince himself that he'd flipped out and imagined everything, though he hadn't wanted to put it to the test by checking his school shirt pocket for the notebook. The shirt was hanging up in the closet.

"Yeah, really weird," said Leaf. "I saw them appear in a flash of light and they disappeared the same way, just before we got back to you. It was mighty strange, but nobody else blinked an eye. I reckon it's because I've got second sight from our great-great-grandmother. She was an Irish witch."

"She was Irish, anyway," said Ed. "I didn't see what Leaf said she saw. But we went back to have a look around later. We'd only been there five minutes when these guys came out of the park and started saying, 'Go away. Go away'. They were plenty weird."

"Kind of dog-faced, with jowly cheeks and mean-looking little eyes, like bloodhounds," interrupted Leaf. "And they had really foul breath and all they could say was 'Go away'."

"Yeah, and they kept sniffing. I saw one of them get down on the ground and sniff it as we were walking away. There were lots of them – at least a dozen – wearing kind of... Charlie Chaplin suits and bowler hats. Weird and scary, so we took off and I reported them to the office for trespassing on the school grounds, and the Octopus came out to check. Only he couldn't see them, though we still could, and I got a week's detention for 'wasting valuable time'."

"I only got three days' detention," said Leaf.

"The Octopus?" asked Arthur weakly.

"Assistant Principal Doyle. 'The Octopus' because he likes to confiscate stuff."

"So what's going on, Arthur?" asked Leaf. "Who were those two guys?"

"I don't know," said Arthur, shaking his head in mystification. "I... I thought it was all a hallucination."

"Maybe it was," offered Ed. "Only both of you had it."

Leaf punched him hard on the arm. Ed winced. *Definitely brother and sister,* thought Arthur.

"Of course, that doesn't explain why the Octopus couldn't see the guys with the bowler hats," Ed added quickly, rubbing his arm. "Unless all three of us were affected by something like a gas or weird pollen."

"If it wasn't a hallucination, then there will be a small notebook in my shirt," Arthur said. "Hanging up in the closet."

Leaf quickly opened the closet, then hesitated.

"Go on," said Arthur. "I only wore the shirt for a couple of hours and I hardly ran in it."

"I wasn't worried about the smell," said Leaf. She reached in and felt the pocket. "It's just that if there is a notebook, then I *did* see something, and those dog-faced guys were scary, even in daylight with Ed there—"

She stopped talking and withdrew her hand. The notebook was in it, held tightly. Arthur noticed she had black nail polish on, with red streaks. Just like his father used to wear years ago in The Ratz.

"It feels strange," Leaf whispered as she handed the book to Arthur. "Kind of electric. Tingly."

"What does it say on the cover?" asked Ed.

"I don't know," replied Leaf. There were symbols on the cover, but they didn't make sense. She didn't seem able to focus on them somehow. At the same time, she felt a strong urge to give the notebook to Arthur. "Here, it's yours."

"Actually, it fell out of the sky," said Arthur as he took it. "Or kind of out of a whirlwind made out of lines of letters... type... swirling in the air."

He looked at the notebook. It had hard covers, bound in green cloth that reminded him of old library books. There was some type embossed on the cover. Golden letters that slowly swam into focus and rearranged themselves. Arthur blinked a couple of times as the letters climbed over one another and shoved others out of the way to make room so the words would be spelled properly.

"It says *A Compleat Atlas of the House and Immediate Environs*," Arthur read aloud. "The letters all moved around."

"Hi-tech," said Ed, but he didn't sound very convinced, or convincing.

"Magic," said Leaf, very matter of fact. "Open it up."

Arthur tried to open the book, but the covers wouldn't budge. It wasn't as if they were stuck together. He could see the pages rippling a bit between the covers like they were free, but he simply couldn't open the book. Even when he applied so much force that he would have ripped the covers off any normal book.

The sudden effort made him cough, and then it was hard

to get his breath back. He could feel another asthma attack coming on, that sudden tightening of the lungs. The monitor that was checking the oxygen level in his blood began to beep, and there was the sudden sound of a nurse's hurrying footsteps in the corridor outside.

"Uh-oh, I guess that our set's over," said Leaf.

"Did you see if the dog-faced men found anything?" Arthur wheezed hurriedly. "A piece of metal?"

"Like what?"

"The minute hand of a clock," Arthur gasped out. "Silver, with gold inlay."

Ed and Leaf both shook their heads.

"All right, visiting time is over," said the nurse as she hurried over. "We can't get Master Penhaligon overexcited."

Arthur grimaced at being called *Master Penhaligon*. Ed and Leaf mirrored his reaction and Leaf made a gagging sound.

"OK, Arthur," said the nurse, who was no fool. "Sorry about that. I was on the children's ward all morning. Now get going, you two."

"We didn't see anything like you mentioned," Ed said. "And the dog-fay... the dogs were gone this morning. But the whole oval had been dug up and then the turf replaced. They did a good job; you couldn't tell from a distance. I couldn't believe they did it so quickly."

"The whole oval?" asked Arthur. That didn't make sense. He'd buried the clock hand somewhere in the middle. Surely as soon as they found it they'd stop digging? Or were they just covering up what they were doing?

"Out!" said the nurse. "I have to give Arthur an injection."

"All of it," confirmed Leaf from the door. "We'll come back and see you later!"

"Tomorrow," said the nurse firmly.

Arthur waved goodbye, his mind racing. He hardly paid attention as the nurse instructed him to roll over, lifted his ridiculous hospital gown and swabbed the area she was about to inject.

Mister Monday and Sneezer. Who could they possibly be? From what they'd said, the minute hand was part of some Key that Mister Monday had given to Arthur in the expectation that he would die. Then Monday would take it back. And the whole plan had been set up by Sneezer, but there was some double-cross involved. At the end, Sneezer was under the power of something else. Those glowing words. The same ones that had given him the notebook. The *Compleat Atlas* that he couldn't open, so it didn't really matter how "compleat" it was.

Arthur had taken the minute hand – he would call it a Key, he decided – and he hadn't died. So whatever it was, he felt as if he still owned it. Though the dog-faced men in the bowler hats probably worked for Mister Monday. If they'd dug up the whole oval, then they would have found the Key for sure and taken it back to him.

Maybe that would be the end of the whole mystery, but Arthur didn't think so. He felt a deep certainty that something was only just beginning. He'd been given the Key and the Atlas for a reason, and he would find out what it was. Everyone in his family said that he was too curious about everything. This was the biggest thing he'd ever encountered to be curious about.

I'll get the Key back, for starters, he thought fiercely, thrusting his hands under his pillow as the prick of the needle brought him back to the immediate reality.

As he felt the injection going in, Arthur stretched out his fingers – and touched something cold and metallic. For an instant, he thought it was the bed frame. But the shape and feel were completely different. Then Arthur realised what it was.

The minute hand. The Key. It definitely hadn't been there only a few minutes before. Arthur always put his hands under the pillow when he lay down. Perhaps it materialised when Leaf handed him the Atlas? Like the magical objects in stories that followed their owners around?

Only in the stories, most things like that were *cursed*, and you couldn't get rid of them even if you wanted to...

"Stay still," commanded the nurse. "It's not like you to flinch, Arthur."

CHAPTER THREE

Arthur went home on Friday afternoon, with the Key and the Atlas securely wrapped up in a shirt inside a plastic bag. For some reason Ed and Leaf never returned to the hospital. Arthur had thought of trying to call them, but since he didn't know their last name, that had proved impossible. He'd even asked Nurse Thomas if she knew who they were. But she didn't, and the hospital had got busier and busier through the week. Arthur figured that he'd see them Monday at school.

His father picked him up and drove him home, humming a tune under his breath as they cruised through the streets. Arthur looked out idly, but his thoughts, as they had been the whole week, were on the Key, the Atlas and Mister Monday.

They were almost home when Arthur saw something

that snapped him straight out of his reverie. They were coming down the second-to-last hill before their street when he saw it. Down in the valley ahead, occupying a whole block, was an enormous, ancient-looking house. A huge building made of stone, odd-shaped bricks of different sizes, and ancient timbers of many kinds and colours. It looked as if it had been extended and added to without thought or care, using many different styles of architecture. It had arches, aqueducts and apses; bartizans, belfries and buttresses; chimneys, crenellations and cupolas; galleries and gargoyles; pillars and portcullises; terraces and turrets.

It looked totally out of place, dropped into the middle of what was otherwise a modern suburb.

There was a reason for that, Arthur knew.

That huge, crazy-looking house had not been there when he left for school last Monday.

"What is that?" he asked, pointing.

"What?" asked Bob. He slowed down and peered through the windshield.

"That place! It's huge and it... it wasn't there before!"

"Where?" Bob scanned the houses he saw. "They all look pretty much the same to me. Sizewise, that is. That's why we went a bit further out. I mean if you're going to have a garden, you've got to have a real garden, right? Oh, you mean the one with the Jeep out front. I think they painted the garage door. That's why it looks different."

Arthur nodded dumbly. It was clear that his father

couldn't see the enormous, castle-like building that they were driving towards. Bob could only see the houses that used to be there.

Or maybe they are still there, Arthur thought, *and I'm seeing into another dimension or something*. He would have thought he was going insane, but he had the Atlas and the Key, and his conversation with Ed and Leaf to fall back on.

As they went past, Arthur noticed that the house (or House, as he felt it should be called) had a wall around it. A slick, marble-faced wall about ten feet high, that looked smooth and very difficult to climb. There was no visible gate, at least on the side they drove along.

Arthur's own new home was only another mile or so, on the far side of the next hill. It was in a transition area between the suburbs and the country. The Penhaligons had a very big block, most of which was a fairly out-of-control garden. Bob said he loved gardening, but what he really loved was thinking and planning things to do with the garden, not actually doing them. He and Emily had bought the land and established the garden several years before, but had only decided to build a house and move quite recently.

Their house was brand-new, notionally finished a few months before. There were still plumbers and electricians coming back every few weeks to fine-tune various bits and pieces. It had been designed by a famous architect and was on four levels, cut into the hill. The bottom level was the biggest, with garage, workshop, Bob's studio and Emily's home office. The next level was all living spaces and kitchen. The next was bedrooms and bathrooms: Bob and Emily's and two guest rooms. The top level was the smallest and had bedrooms for Michaeli, Eric and Arthur, and one bathroom that they either fought over or were locked out of and had to go downstairs.

No one was home when Arthur and his father returned. A screen on the refrigerator door in the kitchen had the latest posts and e-mails from the various members of the family. Emily was held up at the lab, Michaeli was simply "out" and would be back "later", and Eric was playing in a basketball game.

"Do you want to go out for dinner? Just the two of us?" asked Bob. He was humming again, a sure sign of imminent song composition. It was a sacrifice for him to offer to go out when it was obvious he was itching to get at a keyboard or a guitar.

"No thanks, Dad," said Arthur. He really wanted to be alone so he could check out the Key and the Atlas. "I'll grab a snack later, if that's OK. I might just check out my room. Make sure the others didn't trash it while I was gone."

They both knew that was just Arthur being kind and letting Bob go and work on his song. But that was also OK with both of them.

"I'll be in the studio, then," said Bob. "Buzz me if you need anything. You've got your inhaler?"

Arthur nodded.

"We might get a pizza later," Bob called out as he headed down the stairs. "Don't tell Mum."

Arthur went up to his own room, taking the stairs slowly. He was breathing fine, but was weak after five days of lying around in the hospital. Even a few flights of stairs was hard work.

After locking the door in case his older siblings returned, Arthur put the Atlas and the Key on the bed. Then, without knowing why, he turned off the light.

Moonlight shone through the open window, but it was quite dark. It would have been darker, but both the Key and the Atlas glowed with a strange blue light that shimmered like water. Arthur picked them up, the Key in his left hand and the Atlas in his right.

Without any effort on his part, the Atlas flipped open. Arthur was so surprised he dropped it back on the bed. It stayed open, and Arthur watched in amazement as it grew, becoming longer and wider, until it was about the same size as his pillow.

The open pages were blank for a moment, then lines began to appear, as if an invisible artist was hard at work. The lines were strong and sure, appearing faster and faster as Arthur stared. It only took a few seconds before he realised he was looking at a picture of the House he had seen. A picture so well drawn that it was almost like a photograph.

Next to the picture a handwritten note appeared:

The House: An Exterior Aspect as Manifested in Many Secondary Realms.

Then another few words appeared, written much smaller. Arthur craned forward as the writing appeared, with an arrow that pointed to an inked-in square on the outer wall.

"Monday Postern," Arthur read aloud. "What's a postern?"

There was a dictionary on the bookshelf above his desk. Arthur pulled it out, while keeping an eye on the Atlas in case it did something else interesting.

It did. Arthur had to put the Key down to get the dictionary out, as it was too jammed in with other books. As soon as he dropped the Key on the desk, the Atlas slammed shut, scaring the life out of him. In less than a second, it had also shrunk back to its pocket notebook size.

So you need to have the Key to open the Atlas, thought Arthur. He left the Key where it was and looked up *postern* in the dictionary.

postern *n.* **1.** a back door or gate. **2.** any lesser or private entrance.

So there was Monday's gate in the otherwise seamless wall. Arthur put the dictionary back and thought about it.

The picture of the House and the indication of an entrance was clearly an invitation of sorts. Someone... or something... wanted him to go into the House. But could he trust the Atlas? Arthur was pretty certain that Mister Monday and Sneezer were enemies, or – at the very least – not friends. He wasn't sure about the whirling type, the words in the air that had taken over Sneezer and then given him the Atlas. He supposed those words had given him the Key too, or at least had tricked Mister Monday into doing it. But what was their... *its* purpose?

There was only one way to find out. He would take a look at the House as soon as he could, either tomorrow or on Sunday, and try to get in through Monday's Postern. Depending on what he saw there, he'd tell Ed and Leaf and get their help. They would probably be able to see the place, he thought. After all, they'd seen the dog-faced searchers when the assistant principal couldn't.

In the meantime, he would hide the Key and the Atlas in the best hiding spot he knew. In the belly of the life-size ceramic Komodo dragon that sat on the rooftop balcony just above his bedroom. The dragon – a huge lizard really – was hollow, but its mouth wasn't open enough for anyone with hands larger than Arthur's to reach inside.

No sooner was this mission accomplished than his mother came home, immediately transforming the place from a quiet retreat into a family home. After checking on Arthur, she insisted that Bob emerge from his studio so the three of them could have dinner together. Emily was happy and relaxed, because Arthur was OK and because for the first time in ages she was not working frantically to develop a vaccine or cure for some new influenza strain. Winter was coming, but it looked to be a reasonably quiet one from the point of view of sickness.

Arthur's plan to go look at the House failed its first test when he was not allowed out of his own house.

"You have to take it easy," his mother instructed him. "Reading, television or the PC, that's it. At least for the next few days. We'll take another look at the situation next week."

Arthur frowned, but he knew better than to argue. It was going to drive him crazy thinking about the House just waiting there, but he knew he had no choice. If he sneaked out now, he would be grounded for a month. Or a whole year.

"I know it's hard not doing anything active," Emily said as she gave him a hug. "But it's only for a while. Give yourself a chance to get stronger. I think a day at school will be tough enough for you on Monday."

Forbidden to do anything useful, the weekend dragged for Arthur. His two elder siblings were busy with their usual mysterious activities, Bob was still composing, and Emily was called back to work to check out some strange admissions at the local hospitals. She was regularly called whenever there was a rise in patients exhibiting unusual symptoms. Arthur always felt tremendous relief when she came home and said it wasn't serious. Losing his birth parents as he had, Arthur was acutely aware of the potential tragedy in every report of a new flu strain or potential virus outbreak.

By Sunday morning, Arthur couldn't resist the temptation to get the Atlas and the Key back out of the Komodo dragon. Once again he held the Key and the Atlas open to the same double-page spread with the picture of the House. Though there were no details and no other writing besides the note about Monday's Postern, Arthur spent hours looking at it, trying to work out how it was all put together and what it must look like inside.

Finally it was Sunday night. Arthur restored the Key and the Atlas to the lizard's innards and went to bed early, in the hope that sleep would come and make the time go quickly. But of course it didn't. Arthur tossed and turned and couldn't fall asleep. He read most of a book and then simply lay there, thinking.

When he did fall asleep, it wasn't for long. Something made him wake up. He didn't know what it was for a second. He turned his head and saw the digital clock, red in the darkness. 12:01.

One minute after midnight, on Monday morning.

There was a noise at his window. A scratching noise, like a tree branch scraping. But there was no tree in the garden tall enough or close enough to reach Arthur's bedroom window.

Arthur sat up and snapped on the light, his heart suddenly pounding. His breathing began to get more difficult, his breaths shorter.

Control, thought Arthur desperately. *Calm. Breathe slowly. Look at the window.*

He looked and jumped back, falling down behind his bed. There was a winged man hanging in the air a few feet from the window and easily fifty feet above the ground. An ugly, squat man with a jowled face like a bloodhound. A dog-faced man. Even his rapidly beating wings, though feathery, looked ugly and unkempt, dirty grey in the light that spilled out from Arthur's room.

He was wearing a very old-fashioned dark suit and carried a bowler hat in his hand. He was using the crown of the hat to tap on the window.

"Let me in."

The voice was distorted through the glass, but it was low and husky and full of menace.

"Let me in."

"No," whispered Arthur, thoughts of every vampire film he had ever seen flashing through his head. This was no vampire, but it was asking to be let in, so maybe the same principle applied. It couldn't get in unless it was invited. Though in the films, they normally hypnotised someone to let them in—

The bedroom door opened.

Arthur felt as if his heart had stopped cold in his chest.

Someone had been hypnotised already! They would let the dog-faced thing in...

A long forked tongue flickered around the door, tasting the air. Arthur picked up the dictionary, which he'd left by the bed, and raised it above his head.

A scaly head followed the tongue, and a clawed foot. Arthur half lowered the dictionary. It was the ceramic Komodo dragon from the balcony. No longer ceramic, or maybe it still was, but alive and moving swiftly.

Slowly, Arthur climbed back on to the bed and pressed himself against the wall, keeping the dictionary ready to throw. Whose side was the Komodo on?

"Let me in."

The big lizard hissed and ran forward, shockingly fast, to rear up in front of the window. It opened its mouth and brilliant white light shot out, powerful as a searchlight. The dog-faced man screamed and threw up his arms, his bowler hat flying through the air. Still screaming, he hurtled backwards, wings thrashing, and disappeared in a coiling puff of coal-black smoke.

The lizard shut its mouth with a snap and the intense light disappeared with it. Then the reptile slowly stepped back from the window and ponderously trod to the end of Arthur's bed, where it stopped and settled into its usual stance. Its skin rippled as if every muscle was suddenly galvanised, then it was still. Totally ceramic once more.

Arthur dropped the dictionary, picked up his inhaler and

took several puffs. As he went over to shut his door, he was surprised to find that his legs were trembling and could barely support him. On the way back, he patted the Komodo dragon on the head and briefly considered putting his hand in to check that the Key and the Atlas were still there. But that seemed like something that could best wait for morning.

Back in bed, Arthur looked at the clock again as he pulled up the covers. Surely it was no accident that this had happened first thing on Monday.

It's going to be an interesting day, he thought. Deliberately he turned away from the window, so he wouldn't be tempted to look at it, and closed his eyes.

He left the light on.

CHAPTER FOUR

Arthur was not looking forward to school that Monday morning, to a much greater degree than usual. After the events of the early morning he had enjoyed only brief moments of sleep. He'd woken up every hour or so in incipient panic, his breathing ragged, only to find that his light was still on, the night was quiet and there was no trouble. The Komodo dragon stayed immobile at the foot of his bed, and with sunshine filling the room it was hard to believe that the lizard had come alive and beaten back the horrid thing that had flown up to his window.

Arthur wished he could dismiss it as a nightmare, but he knew it had been all too real. The Key and the Atlas were proof of that. He thought about leaving them behind, inside the ceramic lizard, but after breakfast he took them out and put them in his school backpack. Then he checked the garden carefully through the window before running out to join his mother in her car.

In their previous town, Arthur had walked to school. Here, he would eventually ride his bike. But his parents insisted it was too soon for him to exert himself and his mother said she would drive him to school before going to the lab.

Normally Arthur would have made some show of independence, particularly in front of his brother Eric, who he looked up to. Eric was both a basketball and a track star. He'd had no trouble adapting to the new school. He was already on his way to being a stand-out player for the school's top basketball team. He had his own car, bought with the proceeds of a weekend job as a waiter, but it was assumed that he wouldn't take Arthur to school in it unless there was a real emergency. Being seen with his much younger brother was bad for his image. Despite saying this, he had intervened at various important stages in Arthur's life in their old city, putting bullies to flight in the mall or rescuing him after bicycle mishaps.

Arthur was glad to go with his mother that morning. He had a strong suspicion that the bowler-hatted dog-faced men – or manlike creatures – would be waiting at the school. He'd spent quite a few wakeful hours earlier worrying about how he could protect himself against them. It would be particularly difficult if adults couldn't see them, which seemed possible from what Ed had told him.

The trip to school was uneventful, though once again they passed the bizarre castle-like monstrosity that had replaced several suburban blocks. To test whether his mother could see the House, Arthur commented on its size, but just as with his dad, his mother could only see the normal buildings. Arthur could remember what the area used to look like, but try as he might, no matter how he squinted or suddenly turned his head to look, Arthur could only see the House.

When he looked directly at the House, he found that it was too cluttered, complex and strange to reveal its many details. There were simply too many different styles of architecture, too many odd additions. Arthur got dizzy trying to follow individual pieces of the House and work out how they all fitted together. He would start on a tower and follow it up, only to be distracted by a covered walkway, or a lunette that thrust out of a nearby wall, or some other strange feature.

He also found it very difficult to look at exactly the same place twice. Either the House was constantly changing when he wasn't looking at it, or the car was going past too quickly and the complexity and density of all the various bits and pieces made it impossible for his eyes to regain their focus on any particular part.

After they passed the House, Arthur was put off guard a bit by the normality of the rest of the drive to school. It seemed just like any other morning, with the usual traffic and pedestrians and children everywhere. There was no sign of anything strange as they drove up the street the school was on. Arthur felt relieved and comforted by just how boringly normal it seemed. The sun was shining; there were people everywhere. Surely nothing could happen now?

But as he stepped out of the car at the front entrance and his mother drove away, he saw five bowler-hatted, black-suited men suddenly rise like lifted string puppets between the cars in the teachers' parking lot, off to his right. They saw him too and began to move through the ranks of cars towards him. They walked in strange straight lines, changing direction in sudden right angles to avoid pupils and teachers who obviously couldn't see them.

More of the dog-faces appeared to the left. Arthur saw them issue out of the ground, as dark vapours that in a second solidified into dog-faced, bowler-hatted, black-suited men.

Dog-faces to the left. Dog-faces to the right. But there were none straight ahead. Arthur ran a few steps, his breath caught, and he knew he couldn't run and risk another asthma attack. He slowed down, his eyes darting across at the two groups of approaching dog-faces, his mind rapidly calculating their speed and direction.

If he walked quickly up the main promenade and the steps, he would still get inside before the dog-faced men caught up with him.

He did walk quickly, ducking around loitering groups of

students. For the first time, he was grateful nobody knew him at this school, so no one said, "Wait up, Arthur!" or tried to stop him to talk, which would have happened for sure at his old school.

He made it to the steps. The dog-faces were gaining on him, were only ten or fifteen yards behind, and the steps ahead were crowded, mainly with older students. Arthur couldn't push through them, so he had to zig and zag and weave his way through, calling out, "Sorry!" and "Excuse me!" as he went.

He was almost at the main doors and what he hoped would be safety beyond when someone grabbed his backpack and brought him to an abrupt halt.

For an instant, Arthur thought the dog-faces had caught him. Then he heard words that reassured him, despite the threatening tone.

"You knock the man, you pay the price!"

The boy who held Arthur's bag was much bigger, but not really mean-looking. It was hard to look ultra-tough in a school uniform. He even had his tie done up properly. Arthur picked him instantly as a would-be tough guy, not the real thing.

"I'm going to throw up!" he said, holding his hand over his mouth and blowing out his cheeks.

The not-so-tough guy let go of Arthur so quickly that they both staggered apart. Because Arthur was expecting it, he recovered first. He jumped up the next three steps at one go, only a few yards ahead of a swarm of bowler-hatted dog-faces. They were everywhere, like a flock of ravens descending on a piece of meat. Pupils and teachers got out of their way without realising why they were doing so, many of them looking puzzled as they suddenly stopped or stepped sideways or jumped aside, as if they didn't know what they were doing.

For a second, Arthur thought he wouldn't make it. The dog-faces were at his heels and he could hear them panting and snorting. He could even smell their breath, just as Leaf had said. It stank of rotten meat, worse than an alley full of rubbish at the back of a restaurant. The smell and the sound of their slathering lent him extra speed. He lunged up the last few steps, collided with the swing doors, and fell through.

He was up again in an instant, ready to run, his breath already shortening, lungs tightening. Fear gripped him, fear that the dog-faces would come through the doors and that he would have an asthma attack and be powerless to resist them.

But the dog-faces didn't come through the school's main entrance. Instead they clustered at the doors, pressing their flat faces against the glass panels. They really did look like a cross between bloodhounds and men, Arthur saw, with their little piggy eyes, pushed-in faces, droopy cheeks and lolling tongues that smeared the windows. Kind of like Winston Churchill on a very bad day. Strangely, they had all taken their bowler hats off and were holding them in the crook of their left arms. It didn't help the look of them, for their hair was uniformly short and brown. Like dog hair.

"Let us in, Arthur," rasped one, and then another started and there was a horrible cacophony as the words all got mixed up. "Us, In, Let, Arthur, Arthur, Us, Let, Let, Arthur, In, In—"

Arthur blocked his ears and walked away, straight down the central corridor. He concentrated on his breathing, steadying it into a safe rhythm. Slowly, the baying calls from outside receded.

At the end of the corridor, Arthur turned around.

The dog-faces were gone, and once again pupils and staff were pouring through the doors, laughing and talking. The sun was still shining behind them. Everything looked normal.

"What's with your ears?" asked someone, not unkindly.

Arthur blushed and pulled his fingers out of his ears.

The dog-faces obviously couldn't get him here. Now he could focus on surviving the usual problems of school, at least till the end of the day. And he could try to find Ed and Leaf. He wanted to tell them what had happened, to see if they could still see the dog-faces. Maybe they could help him work out what to do about it all.

Arthur had expected to see them at the gym in preparation for the cross-country run. He had a note excusing him, but he still had to go and give it to Mister Weightman. First he had to suffer through a whole morning of maths, science and English, all of which he was good at when he wanted to be, but couldn't focus on today. Then when he went to the gym, making sure to go through the school rather than across the quadrangle, he was surprised to find that the class was only two-thirds the size of the previous week. At least fifteen children were missing, including Ed and Leaf.

Mister Weightman was not pleased to see Arthur. He took the note, read it and handed it back without a word, turning his head away. Arthur stood there, wondering what he was supposed to do if he didn't go on the run.

"Anyone else got a note?" Weightman called out. "Has some class been held back? Where is everybody?"

"Off sick," mumbled a kid.

"All of them?" asked Weightman. "It's not even winter! If this is some sort of prank, there will be serious repercussions."

"No, sir, they really are ill," said one of the serious athletes. "A lot of people have got it. Some sort of cold."

"OK, I believe you, Rick," said Weightman.

Arthur looked at Rick. He was clearly a clean-cut athletic star. He looked like he could have stepped out of a television advert for toothpaste or running shoes. No wonder Weightman believed him.

Still, it was strange for so many pupils to be off sick at this time of year. Particularly since biannual flu vaccinations had become compulsory five years ago. It was only two months since everyone should have had the shots, which usually offered total protection against serious viruses.

Arthur felt a small familiar fear grow inside him. The fear that had been with him as long as he could remember: that another virus outbreak would take away everyone he loved.

"All right, let's get started with some warm-up exercises," Weightman called out. He finally looked at Arthur and summoned him over with a crook of his finger.

"You, Penhaligon, can go and play tiddlywinks or whatever. Just don't cause any trouble."

Arthur nodded, not trusting himself to speak. It was bad enough when other kids made fun of him, but at least there was a chance he could get back at them, or make a joke out of it or something. It was much harder to do that with a teacher.

He turned away and started walking out of the gym. Halfway to the door, he heard someone run up behind him and then there was a touch on his arm. He flinched and half crouched, suddenly afraid the dog-faces had got in. But it was only a girl, someone he didn't know. A girl with bright pink hair.

"You're Arthur Penhaligon?" she asked over the laughs and giggles from the rest of the class, who'd seen him flinch.

"Yes."

"Leaf sent me an e-mail to give to you," she said, handing

him a folded piece of paper. Arthur took it, ignoring the catcalls from the boys behind her.

"Ignore those mutants," the girl said in a loud voice. She smiled and ran back to join her particular clique of tall, bored-looking girls.

Arthur put the paper in his pocket and left the gym, his face burning. He wasn't sure what made him more embarrassed: getting told to go and play tiddlywinks by Weightman or getting a note from a girl in full view of everyone else.

He took refuge in the library. After explaining to the librarian that he was excused from gym and showing her his note, he took a good look around, then decided to sit at one of the desks on the second floor, next to a window that overlooked the front of the school and the street.

The first thing he did was build some walls on the desk out of large reference books, to make a private cubbyhole. Unless someone came up and looked over his shoulder, nobody would be able to see what he was reading.

Then he took the Key and the Atlas from his bag and laid them down with Leaf's note on the desk. As he did so, he caught the flash of movement out of the corner of his eye. He looked out the window and, as he had more than half expected, there were the dog-faces. Sliding out from between parked cars and trees. Slinking forward to gaze up at his window. They knew exactly where he was.

Arthur had hoped he would feel more secure if he could

actually see them. That he would feel braver for having exposed himself at the window. But he didn't. He shivered as they congregated into a mob, all of them staring wordlessly up at him. So far, none had shown wings like the one that had flown to his window the night before. But perhaps that was only a matter of time.

Forcing himself to look away, he imagined that he was a white mouse tearing its gaze away from a hooded cobra. That having done so, he would be able to escape.

He felt a very strong desire to flee into the deeper parts of the library, to hide between the stacks of comforting books. But that wouldn't help, he knew. At least here he knew where the dog-faces were. What they were was another question, one of the many Arthur was making into a mental list.

Arthur unfolded the print out of Leaf's e-mail and read:

To: pinkhead55tepidmail.com
From: raprepteam20biohaz.gov

Hi Allie

This is me, Leaf. can you pass this message on to arthur penhaligon? boy who flaked on the run last Monday? kind of thin + pale, about ed's height hair like gary krag v. important he gets this. gotta run. thanx

Leaf

hi art

sorry we didn't c u at hospital. ed got sick tues. nite, and then
mum + dad did + aunt mango (not real name). i'm not sick,
tho our house is quarantined. many doctors cops all over our
place, in biohazard suitz, v. scary pigface. They think new flu
and shots DON'T WORK. no one really, really sick yet but when
I go near ed or the others I smell the same revolto smell that
the DOG_FACED GUYS had like they're connected, you know
but the doctors can't smell it they're in suits and neither can
ed or parents, tho so much snot coming out that;s no surprise.
docs have machine that smells 4 them, and it says e'thing OK
when obviously not. no one believes me.

i think the virus from dog-faces I REALLY HOPE you can see
them you have to work it out I'M DEPENDING ON YOU.

feds cut off net and phone I think afraid of big panic. this from
one of the docs palmtops which
I STOLE and they'll figure it out real soon.

im afraid

CHAPTER FIVE

Arthur stared at the last words for a few seconds: *im afraid.*

He shivered, folded the print-out and put it back in his pocket. He felt his breathing catch again and concentrated on a steady, slow rhythm. Breathe in slowly, hold it, breathe out slowly. But all the time his mind was racing. This was even worse than he thought.

All the fears he had managed to keep under control were threatening to break free and send him into total panic. The old fear of a new outbreak. And a new fear, of the dog-faces and Mister Monday, and even of the Key itself.

Breathe, thought Arthur. *Think it through.*

Why had he been given the Key... and the Atlas? Who... or what... were Mister Monday and the dog-faces? Were they really connected to this sudden outbreak of drug-resistant influenza? Was it an outbreak? Maybe only Ed and Leaf's family was affected...

Arthur looked out the window at the dog-faces again and accidentally touched the Key and the Atlas on the desk. As he did so, he felt a sharp electric shock and the Atlas flipped open with a bang, making him jump like a startled cat. As it had done before, the Atlas grew in size till it filled nearly all the desk space in between his rampart of books.

This time, the Atlas didn't display a drawing of the House. Instead it rapidly sketched one of the dog-faces, though without the bowler hat, dirty shirt and black, old-fashioned suit. This one was wearing something like a sack, but there was no mistaking the face.

Words appeared next to the picture, written by some unseen hand. The words were in a strange alphabet that Arthur didn't recognise, let alone have a chance of reading, but as the boy watched he saw that the earlier letters were changing into the normal alphabet and the words were rearranging themselves into English, though the type was still weird and old-fashioned. Every now and then a blot of ink would appear partway through a word, to be hastily wiped away. Then words stopped appearing, and Arthur started to read what was there.

The House was built from Nothing, and its foundations rest upon Nothing. Yet as Nothing is for ever and the House is but eternal, these foundations slowly sink into the Nothing from which the House was wrought, and Nothing so impinges upon the House. In the very deepest cellars, sinks and oubliettes of the House, it is possible to draw upon Nothing and shape it with one's thought, should such thought be strong enough. Forbidden in custom, if not in law, it is too often essayed by those who should know better, though it is not the high treason of treating with the Nithlings, those self-willed things that occasionally emerge from Nothing, with scant regard for Time or reason.

A typical shaping of Nothing is the Fetcher, as illustrated. A Fetcher is a creature of very low degree, usually fashioned for a particular purpose. Though it is contrary to the Original Law, these creatures are now often employed in menial tasks beyond the House itself, in the Secondary Realms, for they are extremely durable and are less inimical to mortal life than most creatures of Nothing (or indeed those of higher orders from within the House). However, they are constrained by certain strictures, such as an inability to cross thresholds uninvited, and may be easily dispelled by salt or numerous other petty magics.

Perhaps one in a million Fetchers may find or be granted enlightenment beyond its station, and so gain employment in the House. For the most part, when their task is done, they are returned to the primordial Nothing from whence they came.

Fetchers should never be issued with wings or weapons, and must at all times be given clear direction.

Arthur thought again of that hideous face at the window, pressed against the glass, its wings fluttering furiously behind it. Somebody had ignored the advice about not giving Fetchers wings. Arthur would not be surprised if the ones waiting outside had weapons as well, though he didn't want to think about what kind of weapons they might be given.

Arthur tried to turn the page of the Atlas to see if there was any more information, but the page wouldn't turn. There were lots of other pages in the book, but they might as well have all been glued into a single mass. Arthur couldn't even get his fingernail between the leaves of paper.

He gave up and looked out the window again and was surprised to see that the Fetchers had moved in the short space of time he'd been looking at the Atlas. They had formed into a ring on the road and were all looking up. A couple of cars had stopped because of them, but it was obvious the drivers couldn't really see what was in their way. Arthur could distantly hear one of them shouting, the angry words faint through the double glazing, "Get that heap of junk outta here! I haven't got all day!"

The Fetchers gazed up at the sky. Arthur looked too but didn't see anything. Part of him didn't want to see, because the fear was rising in him.

Don't look, part of his mind said. *If you don't see trouble, it doesn't exist.*

But it does, thought Arthur, fighting down the fear. *Keep breathing slowly. You have to confront your fears. Deal with them.*

He kept looking, until an intense white light flashed just above the ring. Arthur shut his eyes and shielded his face. When he looked again, black spots danced everywhere in his vision and it took a few seconds for them to clear.

The empty space in the middle of the ring was no longer empty. A man had appeared there. Or not really a man, since he had huge feathery wings spreading from his shoulders. Arthur kept blinking, trying to focus. The wings were sort of white, but dappled with something dark and unpleasant-looking. Then they folded up behind the apparition's back and in an instant were gone, leaving only a very handsome, tall man of about thirty. He was dressed in a white shirt with chin-scraping collar points, a red necktie, a gold waistcoat under a bottle-green coat, and tan pantaloons over glossy brown boots – an ensemble that had not been in fashion for more than a hundred and fifty years.

"Oh, my!" exclaimed someone from behind Arthur. "The very spit of how I've always imagined Mister Darcy. He must be an actor! I wonder why he's dressed up like that."

It was the librarian. Mrs Banber. She'd crept up on Arthur while he wasn't paying attention.

"And who are those strange men in the black suits?"

continued Mrs Banber. "Those faces can't be real! Are they making a film?"

"You can see the dog-faces?!" exclaimed Arthur. "I mean the Fetchers?"

"Yes..." replied the librarian absently, still staring out the window. "Though now that you mention it, I must be overdue for an eye checkup. My contact lenses don't seem to be quite right. Those people are rather blurry."

She turned around and for the first time looked properly at Arthur and his battlements of books.

"Though I can see you all right, young man! What are you doing with all those books? And what is that?"

She pointed at the Atlas.

"Nothing!" exclaimed Arthur. He slammed the Atlas shut and let go of the Key, which was a mistake. The Atlas shrank immediately into its pocketbook size.

"How did it do that?" asked Mrs Banber.

"I can't explain," said Arthur rapidly. He didn't have time for this! The handsome man was walking towards the library, with the Fetchers following. He looked a bit like Mister Monday, though much more energetic, and Arthur wasn't at all sure that the same strictures that kept the Fetchers from crossing thresholds would apply to him.

"Have you got any salt?" he asked urgently.

"What?" replied Mrs Banber. She was looking out the window again and smoothing her hair. Her eyes had gone unfocused and dreamy. "He's coming into the library!"

Arthur grabbed the Atlas and the Key and stuffed them into his backpack. They glowed as he put them away, shedding a soft yellow light that momentarily fell on Mrs Banber's face.

"Don't tell him I'm here!" he said urgently. "You mustn't tell him I'm here."

Either the fear in his voice or that brief light from the Atlas and the Key recaptured Mrs Banber's attention. She suddenly looked less dreamy.

"I don't know what's going on, but I don't like it," she snapped. "No one is coming into my library without permission! Go and hide behind the zoology books, Arthur. I'll deal with this person!"

Arthur needed no invitation. He hurried away from the window, into the maze of library shelves, walking as fast as he dared. He could feel his lungs tightening, losing their flexibility. Stress and fear were already feeding his asthma.

He stopped behind the zoology shelves and crouched down so that he could see through two rows of shelves to the front door, where Mrs Banber stood guard at the front desk. She had a scanner in her hand and was angrily checking in books, the scanner beeping every few seconds as its infrared eye picked up a bar code.

Arthur tried to breathe slowly. Perhaps the handsome man couldn't come in. If he was waiting out the front, Arthur could escape through the staff entrance he'd seen at the back.

A shadow fell across the door. Arthur's breath stopped halfway in. For an instant he thought he couldn't breathe, but it was only a moment of panic. As he got the rest of his breath, the handsome man stopped in front of the door.

He reached out with one white-gloved hand and pushed the door open. For a hopeful moment Arthur thought he couldn't cross that threshold. Then the man stepped into the library. As he passed the door, the antitheft scanners gave a plaintive beep and the green lights on top went out.

Mrs Banber was out from behind her desk in a flash.

"This is a school library," she said frostily. "Visitors must report to the front office first."

"My name is Noon," said the man. His voice was deep and musical, and he sounded like a famous British actor. Any famous British actor. "I am Private Secretary and Cupbearer to Mister Monday. I am looking for a boy. Artor."

He had a silver tongue, Arthur saw. Literally silver, shining in his mouth. His words were smooth and shining too. Arthur felt like coming out and saying, "Here I am."

Mrs Banber obviously felt the same way. Arthur could see her trembling and her hand rose, almost as if it was going to point to where he was hiding. But somehow she forced it back down.

"I... I don't care," said Mrs Banber. She seemed smaller and her voice was suddenly weak. "You have... you have to report..."

"Really?" asked Noon. "You can't allow a few words..."

"No, no," whispered Mrs Banber.

"A pity," said Noon. His voice grew colder, authoritarian and threatening. He smiled, but the smile was cruel and did not extend beyond his thin lips. He ran one gloved finger along the top of a display stand and held it up in front of Mrs Banber's face. The tip of the glove was stained with grey dust.

The librarian stared at the finger as if it were her eye doctor's flashlight.

"Spring cleaning must be done," said Noon. He blew on the dust and a little cloud of it fell on Mrs Banber's face. She blinked once, sneezed twice and fell to the ground.

Arthur stared, horrified, as Noon carefully stepped over the librarian's body and stalked past the front desk. For a second he thought Mrs Banber was dead, till he saw her trying to get up again.

"Ar-tor," called Noon softly, his silver tongue flickering. He had stopped just past the desk and was eyeing the shelves with obvious suspicion. "Come out, Ar-tor. I merely want to talk to you."

"Ar-tor!"

The voice was commanding, and once again Arthur felt the urge to reveal himself, to run out. But he felt a countervailing force from the Key and the Atlas in his backpack. A soothing vibration, like a kitten purring, that reduced the force of Noon's words. Arthur undid the bag, took the Key in his hand, and slipped the Atlas into his shirt pocket. Both were immensely comforting and Arthur found that he could even breathe more easily.

Noon frowned, a momentary ugliness on that handsome face. Then he reached out with his white-gloved hand and opened a small cupboard that materialised in midair the instant he reached for it. There was a telephone inside. A very old telephone, with a separate earpiece on a cord and a bell-mouth to speak into.

"Mister Monday," said Noon into the mouthpiece.

Arthur could hear someone muttering on the other end.

"This is official business, you fool," snapped Noon. "What is your name and number?"

There was more muttering at the other end. Noon frowned again, then slowly and deliberately hung up the earpiece, let it sit for a moment, then took it up again.

"Operator? Mister Monday. Yes, at once. Yes, I know where I'm calling from! This is Monday's Noon. Thank you." There was a pause as Mister Monday was connected. "Sir? I have the boy trapped."

Arthur clearly heard Mister Monday yawn before he replied. His voice not only came out of the earpiece, it echoed around the whole library.

"Have you the Minute Key? It must be brought back to me at once!"

"Not yet, sir," replied Noon. "The boy is hiding in a... library."

"I don't care where he's hiding!" screamed Monday. "Get the Key!"

"A library, sir," said Noon patiently. "There is a lot of type. The Will could be here too—"

"The Will! The Will! I am so bored with this talk! Do whatever you have to! You have plenipotentiary powers! Use them!"

"I need that in writing, sir," said Noon calmly. "The Morrow Days—"

There was a sound that was a cross between a yawn and a snarl, and a tightly bound scroll flew out of the earpiece. Moving so fast that Arthur didn't see it happen, Noon ducked aside, and as the scroll shot past, he snatched it from the air with his free hand.

"Thank you, sir," he said, and paused. There was no answer from the other end. Just a long snore.

Noon hung up the phone and carefully closed the cupboard. As the door shut, the phone cupboard dissolved into thin air.

Noon unrolled the scroll and read it. This time, a real smile fleetingly moved across his face and a red light flashed briefly in his eyes.

"This is your last chance to come out," Noon said conversationally. "I can bring the Fetchers in now. They'll soon root you out, Ar-tor."

Arthur didn't respond. Noon stood there, tapping the scroll against his thigh. Behind him, Mrs Banber pulled herself up on to the desk and picked up the phone handset. Arthur watched them both, panicked, not knowing what he should do. Should he help Mrs Banber? Should he give himself up? Maybe if he gave Noon the Key then they would leave him alone?

Mrs Banber, her hand shaking so much she could hardly hold the phone, started to punch in a number. The keypad beeped and Noon whirled. His wings exploded out behind and above him. Huge, feathery wings that had once been white and lustrous but now were stained with patches of something dark and horrid, something that might even be dried blood.

Noon's wings cast a dreadful shadow over the librarian as he thrust out his hand and flexed his fingers. A fiery sword appeared in his fist and he struck down at the phone, the flaming blade melting it in an instant, the papers on the desk exploding into flame. Mrs Banber staggered away and collapsed near the front door as smoke billowed to the ceiling.

"Enough!" said Noon. He stalked to the front door, his wings still arched up behind him, and opened it.

"Come in, my Fetchers! Come and find the boy! Come and find Ar-tor!"

CHAPTER SIX

Black smoke rolled across the ceiling. A fire alarm began to clang and clatter outside, followed a second later by the *whoop-whoop* of the evacuation siren. The Fetchers came into the library with the sound, all in a rush, barking with excitement at being invited past the door.

Noon pointed at the shelves and the Fetchers bounded forward, many of them bent over so they could sniff at the floor, their tongues lolling and flat noses twitching. Sniffing for their prey. Arthur.

But Arthur hadn't waited. He was already at the back door. It was locked, but there was a release button inside a glass box, plastered with warning signs about alarms and only being used in the event of fire.

There was a fire. Arthur swung his backpack at the box and smashed the glass. It broke into tiny clumps rather than shattering. He reached in with his left hand and punched the button, because he didn't want to let go of the Key he held tightly in his right hand. Somehow it helped him breathe, and he really needed to breathe properly right now. He could hear the Fetchers behind him, growling and grunting as they raced along the corridors made by the shelves, pausing at each intersection of the Dewey Decimal system to sniff out his path.

Nothing happened after he pressed the button. Arthur's hand trembled as he punched it again. The button pressed in easily enough, but the door didn't open. Arthur kicked the door, but it wouldn't budge. As he kicked it again, a red flame ran around the door frame. The same rich, deep red of Noon's fiery sword.

"The back door, my Fetchers! Ar-tor attempts the back door!"

Noon's voice carried through the fire alarm, the siren, and the Fetchers' barks. Arthur immediately knew that Noon had used his powers to seal the door. But Arthur had his own magic. Or at least he had something that had power, even if he didn't know what it really was or how to use it.

The Key.

Arthur touched the door with the point of the minute hand and shouted, "Open!" There was a flash of white light, a sudden heat upon his face, then the twin leaves of the door flung open and a new alarm joined the cacophonous wail. Arthur ran out on to the fire stairs and jumped down the first two steps. Then he suddenly stopped, whirled and jumped back. He had to close the doors behind him or the Fetchers would catch him for sure. But he had wasted a precious second – could he do it in time?

He threw himself at the doors and slammed them shut, just as two Fetchers leaped at the gap. Arthur was thrown backwards and the doors started to open again, the Fetchers yowling and growling as they tried to grab him. Fingers ripped at his shirt, buttons went flying, but he slashed with the Key and the Fetchers let go, screaming horrible high-pitched screams.

Arthur slammed the doors again and made a wild cut across them with the Key, shouting out, "Shut! Lock! Close!"

Whether it was the cut or the words, the doors stayed shut, though Arthur could hear the thuds as the Fetchers threw themselves against the exit. But he didn't hang around. Arthur knew that no doors would stop Noon.

He'd only made it to the narrow hall between the library and the school refectory when there was an explosion above him. He crouched down and looked back as flames jetted out in all directions, and the doors flew over his head, whistling towards the science block a quarter of a mile away. Noon strolled out on to the fire stairs, black smoke rolling out in coils above his head, with the Fetchers crouched around him. They looked less like men now and more like half-human dogs, their black suits in rags and their bowler hats lost somewhere in the burning library.

Arthur turned to run again. But he had only gone a few yards when he heard the *whoosh* and beat of giant wings above him. A cold shadow passed over his head, and Noon landed right in front of him. His wings were spread wide, his flaming sword had appeared in his hand once more, and it was pointed right at Arthur's throat.

"Give me the Key," instructed Noon calmly.

"No," whispered Arthur. "It was given to me."

"It was a mistake, you foolish boy," said Noon. He looked through a window at the sun and frowned. "Hand it over, circle end first. I haven't got all day."

Something about the frown and the way he said those last words sparked an idea in Arthur's mind. He looked down, pretending that he was thinking about handing over the Key. But he was actually looking at his watch. It was one minute short of one o'clock.

"I don't know," mumbled Arthur. Desperately he looked around. He could hear the Fetchers coming up from behind, and the flaming sword was close enough for him to wince at the heat. Sweat was dripping down his face, stinging his eyes. But at least he could breathe, though he was pretty certain that would stop as soon as he let go of the Key.

"Give me the Key!"

"Come and get it!" shouted Arthur. He spun like a discus thrower and hurled the Key across the hall at the nearest door and threw himself after it.

The very tip of the flaming sword caught him on the left

arm as he ran, burning a line of intense pain from his shoulder to his elbow. Noon shouted something, but the boy didn't hear. His lungs had frozen as he let go of the Key and suddenly he didn't have any breath at all, perhaps not even enough to last a few steps.

He'd expected the Key to bounce off the door for him to pick up, but the clock hand had flown like a thrown dagger straight through the paper-thin gap between the door and the wall. So Arthur crashed into the door instead, and once again his expectations were confounded. It should have been locked, but instead of bouncing off and back into the path of Noon's flaming sword he went slam-bang through it and rolled on to the floor beyond. His open hand fell on the Key and his fingers closed on it as tightly as they could. With the Key in his grasp he felt blessed breath come back and the burn on his arm fade into a dull ache.

"There is really no point to your ridiculous acrobatics," said Noon as he stepped through the doorway. "Give me the Key and I shall allow you to crawl away. Otherwise I shall cut off your hand and take it."

Arthur looked at his watch. The second hand was sweeping towards the twelve. It was almost one o'clock. His watch was very accurate and he had set it only a week or so ago.

Slowly, he began to loosen his grip on the Key, as if he were obeying Noon's instructions. As he let go, he felt his lungs tighten again and the burn on his arm began to return.

"Hurry up!" shouted Noon. He raised his sword and the flames upon it roared into brighter, hotter life.

The second hand was on eleven. Arthur gulped as he realised that he was about to bet his hand – his *life* – on a guess. A guess that Noon could only be here in Arthur's world for the single hour between noon and one.

"No!" shouted Arthur. He snatched the Key back and recoiled, shutting his eyes. The last thing he saw was Noon's eyes reflecting red and the flaming sword hurtling down towards his hand.

But no pain came. Arthur opened his eyes. The second hand of his watch was past the twelve, the hour hand and minute hand on one o'clock. There was no sign of Monday's Noon and the Fetchers were silent, though slavering, just beyond the door. There was a smouldering line of ash along the floor, an inch from Arthur's fingers. He stared at it and wondered how Noon could have missed.

The fire alarm was still ringing and the siren still sounded its steady *whoop*. In the distance, Arthur could hear other sirens growing louder as fire engines converged upon the school.

Arthur slowly got up and looked around. He was in the back of the refectory, in fact in the staff and delivery entrance for the kitchen. There was no one around, though it was clear from all the partly made meals, readied ingredients, still-steaming pots and rotating microwave platters that the kitchen staff had only just left, responding to the evacuation alarm.

He looked back at the Fetchers through the open door. They were silent now, standing in ranks. Somehow they had got their bowler hats back, and their black suits were restored. Once again they looked more like very ugly men and less like dogs.

One of them stepped forward and opened its mouth, showing large canine teeth. Then it made a curious repetitive grunting noise. It took a moment for Arthur to realise it was meant to be a laugh. But what reason could this Fetcher have to laugh?

Then he saw what it was holding in its stubby-fingered, long-nailed hand. The Atlas! Arthur's own hand flashed to his shirt pocket and came away holding a strip of cloth. The pocket had been torn off, back when they'd almost got hold of him at the library. His chest was scratched as well, though he hadn't noticed it at the time. Now it hurt. But not as much as losing the Atlas.

The Fetchers all started to laugh now, if you could call a rising-falling series of grunts a laugh. Arthur recoiled as their stinking, sickening breath gusted out with each grunt. They obviously thought they'd captured something very important and won a victory.

Glumly, Arthur had to recognise they had. If he was ever to make any sense of what was going on, he needed the Atlas. So he had to get it back. What had the Atlas said about the Fetchers? They couldn't cross thresholds and—

Salt! Arthur turned to the kitchen shelves. There had to be salt here, and probably lots of it. It was a commercial kitchen. He ran along the shelves, the Key held fast in one hand while he turned bags around and shifted containers with the other. Sugar, four different sorts of flour, spices of all kinds, other grains, dried fruit... salt! There it was, a big tub of regular salt and a small sack of rock salt.

Arthur hesitated, then slipped the Key through his belt like a dagger. As soon as he let go, he felt his asthma returning. The deep breaths of a moment ago were lost to him. But he still felt some ease from the Key. Perhaps having it close was better than nothing.

He put the rock salt in his backpack, slipped it on again, then picked up the tub of salt and threw away the lid. The tub was two-thirds full of fine white salt. Arthur held the tub by its handle in his left hand and took a fistful of salt in his right.

Then he marched back to the door, wheezing and panting a little, but prepared for battle. If he could surprise them, he thought, throw the salt across the front rank, he might be able to dash out and grab the Atlas when they... well, when whatever the salt did to them happened.

At the back of his mind, a doubting question immediately popped up. What if the salt just annoyed them, and as soon as he jumped out they grabbed him and bit him and scratched him to pieces?

Arthur didn't answer that question. He forced himself to

focus on one thing – getting the Atlas back. Once he had that, he could ask some more questions.

These thoughts were racing through his mind as he came to the end of the shelves. Arthur gulped, took as deep a breath as he could, and jumped out in front of the door, screaming and throwing salt.

"Yahhhhh!"

Chapter seven

Salt sprayed out of Arthur's hand and across the front rank of Fetchers. Their laughter instantly stopped, dissolving into startled yelps and cries. As the salt hit, the Fetchers squealed and fell over one another in a panicked attempt to escape, becoming a tangled mess of shrieking arms and legs and ugly faces that made it even easier for Arthur to throw handful after handful of salt over them.

The salt sizzled on the Fetchers as it struck. Both flesh and the black cloth melted, as if the salt were the most potent acid imaginable. Even a pinchful of salt hitting a Fetcher started a chain reaction that in a matter of seconds reduced the creature to a bubbling pile of nasty-looking scum.

After Arthur threw his ninth or tenth handful of salt, there weren't any more Fetchers. There were only fourteen hubcap-sized mounds of evil-smelling glop that looked like a cross between elephant dung and hot tar.

Arthur stared at the piles, salt still dribbling from his hand. He could feel his lungs tightening even more, so he took the Key from his belt. As soon as he touched it he felt his chest loosen and his breath come back, free and unfettered. He could still feel an asthma attack lurking, but it was held at bay by the strange power of the Key.

The asthma was a reaction to what had happened, he knew. He was shocked by the effect the salt had on the creatures and unpleasantly reminded of salting the leeches that had attached themselves to his legs on a hiking trip last summer.

He was also repelled and disgusted by the idea that he would now have to search through each mound to find the Atlas.

There was no way he was going to touch those piles with his bare hands. Breathing only through his mouth, Arthur gingerly touched the closest pile with the toe of his shoe. But just as he made contact, the pile shivered and turned into a column of smoke as black and shiny as his school shoes. Arthur leaped back as the smoke formed into a small misty replica of the Fetcher. The tiny replica spun around several times – and disappeared!

Moments later, every mound did the same. As Arthur desperately kicked at the remnants with his foot, the last pile of glop vanished in a twisting puff of smoke.

Now there was just the concrete alley floor. No sign remained of the Fetchers at all. And wherever their salted leftovers had disappeared to, so had the Atlas.

The fire alarms and siren were still going strong, which didn't help Arthur's thinking process. There were many additional sirens now as well, and Arthur realised that he could hear helicopters too. The fire must be worse than he'd thought.

Suddenly Arthur remembered Mrs Banber. She'd been unconscious at the front of the library! He'd been so scared getting away from Noon and the Fetchers that he'd forgotten. He had to tell the firemen that she was in there!

He ran out into the hall again and looked up. As he'd feared, there were huge clouds of smoke boiling out of the smashed doors and out of the library roof as well. The fire must have spread with incredible speed.

Arthur started towards the stairs. He figured that if the Key helped him breathe despite his asthma, it might help him breathe even through the smoke. Maybe it would protect him from fire as well, since it had instantly healed the cut from Noon's flaming sword.

He hoped it would protect him.

Arthur could hear the deep bellow of the fire inside as he ran up the stairs. A terrible, frightening sound, made worse by the lurid, leaping colours that shone out the door, lighting up the dark smoke.

Arthur was almost at the top of the stairs when he felt

something grab his ankle. He fell forward, lost his hold on the Key for an instant, and felt the terrible heat and instant panic as his lungs were compressed by a deathly grip. Then he caught the Key again and with it came relief. He gripped it tightly and wriggled around, ready to slash with the Key, expecting that it was a Fetcher who held his leg.

But it wasn't. Arthur saw a bright yellow suit, a red helmet and an indistinct human face behind the visor of a fireman's breathing apparatus.

"It's OK, I've got you!" shouted the fireman, his voice muffled and distant. He lifted Arthur up and over his shoulder. Other firemen edged past, all wearing full suits and breathing apparatus. Some carried axes and extinguishers; others were trailing hoses.

"Mrs Banber!" Arthur coughed, tugging at the elbow of a passing fireman, since he couldn't even see the face of the one whose shoulder he was across. His momentary loss of the Key had let smoke get in his lungs. He could feel it being cleared out, but obviously the Key could only do so much in a short time. "She's at the front desk!"

The second fireman stopped.

"What?" he bellowed, his voice indistinct through the mask.

"Librarian!" shouted Arthur. "At the front desk."

"We've got her out already!" responded the fireman. "Was there anyone else inside?"

"No," said Arthur. He was sure no one else had been

there. Unless they'd been hiding in the shelves, like he'd hidden from Noon. "I don't think so."

"You'll be OK!" shouted the fireman, then he was gone, into the smoke and the glow.

Arthur's fireman carried him down the stairs, along the alley, which was now full of firemen, hoses and other gear, and out around the side of the library to the front of the school. There were even more firemen there, with four fire engines in the street, three ambulances, six police cars – and parked behind them, a whole row of odd-looking buses. It took Arthur a second to realise that the buses had no windows and no markings.

The fireman took Arthur to an area in the parking lot where there were stretchers ready, lowered him on to one, clapped him on the shoulder and smiled. Arthur smiled back and realised that the face he was looking at was a woman's. Then she was gone, back to the fire.

The other stretchers were empty. Arthur guessed that they had already taken Mrs Banber off to the hospital.

Arthur lay on his back on the stretcher. He felt dazed and suddenly very tired. Everything had happened so quickly. He kept a tight hold on the Key, but pushed it up against his leg so it couldn't be seen.

There were three helicopters hanging in the blue sky almost directly above him. He expected them to be television news choppers, but they weren't...

Arthur sat up. One helicopter was dark green and had

ARMY on its belly. The other two helicopters were bright orange and they had large black 'Q's on their sides and bellies.

Q for quarantine.

Arthur looked around and saw paramedics coming towards him, carrying their first-aid gear, marked with bright red crosses. That was normal. But they were wearing full biohazard suits, with breathing apparatus similar to the fire brigade's. That wasn't normal at all.

Arthur felt the fear that was always with him become something else. Now it was a reality, not just a gnawing emotion that he could keep a lid on.

He saw police in their blue biohazard gear, and soldiers as well, in camouflage biosuits. The soldiers were setting up all kinds of equipment, including portable decontamination showers. The police were laying out quarantine tape around the school and directing what had to be the last class to come out of the school on to those windowless buses. All the children were silent and downcast, without any of the usual carrying on and talking that would accompany an escape from the usual school routine.

Arthur recognised everything that was happening. He'd been too young to see it before in real life, but he'd watched lots of documentaries. He'd read books and looked at pictures. Emily had talked to him about it a lot when he was younger, helping him to understand what had happened to his birth parents and to the world.

This was biocontainment and quarantine. The school was being sealed off and everyone in it was being taken away to a secure hospital. That meant that the Federal Biocontrol Authority had declared an outbreak and had formally assumed control over the situation. They must think the virus had originated in the school, or that the school was a major source of carriers.

It also meant that some people must have already died from the unknown virus. Arthur thought of Leaf's e-mail, and of Ed. If Leaf was right and the dog-faces... the Fetchers had brought the virus...

Arthur shut his eyes, remembering what he'd read in the Atlas about the Fetchers.

Less inimical to mortal life than most creatures of Nothing...

Inimical meant harmful, and less inimical only meant they weren't as bad as some other dangers. Like a small earthquake was better than a really big one. Though not if you were right in it. The Fetchers probably *had* brought some terrible disease. A disease that his mum would be working on, trying to find a vaccine or a cure. But she wouldn't have a hope if it really was from somewhere else, from some otherworldly source.

Maybe whatever it was could get through all the protective measures and containment in Emily's lab. Arthur might lose her, lose the only real mother he'd known. Then Bob would get it for sure as well, then his brothers and sisters...

"You OK? Take a breath for me."

Arthur opened his eyes. Another breathing mask visor, another indistinct face and muffled voice.

"Yeah, I'm OK," he said shakily. *Physically at least*, he thought, pushing back the panic that was threatening to overwhelm him. He took a breath, once again surprised by how easy it was with the Key held in his hand.

"Did you breathe in any smoke?"

Arthur shook his head.

"Are you burned anywhere? Do you have any pain?"

"No, I'm OK," said Arthur. "Really. I was outside before the fire got going."

The paramedic rapidly looked into Arthur's eyes, attached some sort of tiny electronic diagnostic device to his neck and checked the skin under his tattered shirt.

"Lift your arm for me. What's that?"

"My metalwork project. If I lose it I'll fail the course."

"Whatever," said the paramedic. "Lift your other arm. Wiggle your fingers. OK. Lift your feet."

Arthur complied with the instructions, feeling a bit like a puppet.

"You're in much better shape than you should be after coming out of that," said the paramedic as he looked at the read-out on the device he'd attached. They both glanced back at the burning library. There was a column of smoke hundreds of feet high coming out of it now. "Some people are just lucky, I guess."

"Though not that lucky," amended the paramedic as a police officer lumbered past, unreeling barrier tape that was marked with fluorescent biohazard trefoils. "I'm afraid to say that your school has been listed under the Creighton Act as a Potential Biohazard Threat—"

"A hot spot," interrupted Arthur. Saying it made it easier for him to wrestle his fear under control. Made it a real problem, something that he could analyse and react to, rather than just a nagging, amorphous fear. "Are we all being taken into quarantine?"

"Yeah, that's right," said the paramedic. "Hang on. I have to read you your rights as a quarantined citizen."

He pulled out a plastic card and squinted at it, holding it close to his faceplate.

"OK, here we go. 'You are hereby detained under the Creighton Act. You have the right to electronic communication while held in quarantine and you have the right to appeal that quarantine. You may not be held in quarantine for more than 365 days longer than the incubation period of the disease or agent for which you have been quarantined without formal extension by a Federal court. While in quarantine, any action that you may undertake that may violate that quarantine or endanger the health of others is a Federal offence for which any penalty up to and including the death penalty may be applied.' Do you understand?"

"Yes," said Arthur slowly. His word seemed to hang in the

air, heavy between them. It was one of the most significant things he'd ever said, Arthur realised.

He'd studied the Creighton Act at school. It was a leftover from the flu epidemics that had killed his birth parents. It had almost been repealed several times since then, as there had been no new outbreaks of any consequence, and because it gave the government tremendous powers over quarantined citizens. The last part about the death penalty was particularly controversial, as it had been used to retrospectively justify shooting people who tried to escape quarantine.

Like me, if I try to get away now. But if he didn't get to the House and find out what was going on, there might never be a cure for the virus the Fetchers had brought with them.

"What are we being quarantined for?" Arthur asked as he slid off the stretcher and stood up.

"We don't know yet," replied the paramedic. He was looking away from Arthur, and his voice was very indistinct through his mask. "It starts like a very bad cold, which lasts for a few days. Then the patient goes to sleep."

"That doesn't sound so bad."

"We can't wake them up," said the paramedic grimly. "Nothing works."

"But sleep is good for you..." Arthur started to say. Half-heartedly, trying to convince himself.

"We can't make them eat or drink, and they don't absorb

anything intravenously as they should," continued the paramedic. "No one knows why."

Arthur stared at the paramedic. Even through the mask, he could see that the man was afraid.

"All of the cases are connected with this school – I shouldn't be telling you this," said the paramedic. "Don't worry about it. The quarantine will work. We'll find a cure."

He doesn't believe it, thought Arthur. *He thinks we're all going to die.*

The medic took the diagnostic unit off Arthur's neck, checked the read-out again, and dropped it into a bin nearby that had the barbed trefoil sign of hazardous biological waste. His hand was trembling as he pointed to the buses.

"Go and report to Sergeant Hu, by the bus there."

"Yes, sir."

Arthur walked slowly over towards the policeman who was with three or four kids by the door of the last bus, thinking furiously. He had to do something. He was the only person who could do anything about this outbreak. But what?

He glanced back at the burning library as he desperately tried to work out a plan. The smoke was still a mighty column, but a wisp of it was curling out to one side, as if it were being pulled like a strand of cotton candy. Then that strand was suddenly twisted and stretched and bent in ways no normal smoke would ever follow.

The smoke was forming letters, Arthur realised.

Complete words. He rapidly looked around and noticed no one else was looking in the same direction. Perhaps, as with the Fetchers, only he could see this happening.

The words were compressed and overlapped one another, so it was a bit difficult for Arthur to work out what they said. Then it became clear.

Arthur. Get near the House and I will help you. Will

"Easy for you to say," muttered Arthur, and the smoky words broke apart and drifted off like regular smoke once more.

It was *much* easier said than done. First of all, Arthur had to get out of quarantine without being shot or stunned. Once he was on that bus, it would be almost impossible to escape.

All sorts of possibilities raced through his head. But most of them were imagined scenes of himself running away from the bus, all the policemen and soldiers shouting and chasing him, one of them finally drawing a gun and then a fusillade of shots...

There had to be another way. Arthur slowed down so he would have more time to think. He was halfway there, he had less than a minute of freedom. There had to be an answer. Could he use the Key in some way?

He looked down at it, keeping it by his side, and realised he had another problem. The police officer was searching all the kids before they got on, and there was a pile of small knives, mace sprays and other stuff by his feet. A lot smaller pile than would have emerged from Arthur's old school, and no guns, but still quite a few deadly weapons.

By the police officer's standards, the Key would not be a metalwork project he needed to keep, but a long, thin and weird-looking knife. It would be taken away from him for sure, and then...

Arthur would have an asthma attack. He had his inhaler, but after his running, fighting, and smoke inhalation, he didn't think it would do any good at all.

He suddenly realised the Key was the only thing keeping him alive.

"Hey, kid! Hurry up!" shouted the policeman.

CHAPTER EIGHT

The policeman's voice was more menacing through his mask, made deeper and buzzy and much less human. The last student had gone on the bus and now the sergeant's full attention was on Arthur.

That shout made up Arthur's mind and a plan suddenly popped into his head. Without further thought, he put it into action.

"I'm..." said Arthur. "I'm..."

He pushed the Key deep into his pocket, the point ripping through the bottom so the metal slid through and touched his leg. Then he let go.

The effect was instantaneous. Though he still had some contact with the Key, his breathing immediately changed. It was as if someone had winded him, reducing the capacity of his lungs by fifty per cent with a single blow.

"Asthmatic!" wheezed Arthur, collapsing to the ground

ten paces from the sergeant. Despite the protection of his biosuit and Arthur's explanation, the sergeant's first reaction was to jump back on to the steps of the bus, as if he were seeing the new virus in immediate action.

Arthur fumbled in his other pocket for his inhaler and brought it to his mouth. He also rolled over so that more of the Key touched his leg. About half of it was through his pocket, the metal cool upon his skin, bringing ease to his lungs. He hoped that the circle on the end of the Key would prevent it from falling out of his trouser leg if he stood up.

"Medic!" shouted the policeman. As he shouted, he undid the strap on his holster and his hand went to the butt of his pistol. "Medic!"

"Asthma!" wheezed Arthur again. He took a couple of puffs, then held the inhaler up so the policeman could see it. Arthur hadn't counted on the man being so afraid of the virus that he might shoot.

The paramedic who'd checked Arthur out a minute before was already running over, as was another paramedic, several policemen and a pair of soldiers. It looked like Arthur's sudden collapse was the invitation to action they'd all been waiting for. He hoped the soldiers weren't as jumpy as the policeman. They both had some sort of hi-tech submachine gun.

The paramedic was the first to reach him. He held the inhaler up and helped Arthur take some puffs, at the same time flipping his bag open and checking through it for something. Though Arthur couldn't see his face through the mask, it was clear he was cross.

"Why didn't you tell me you were an asthmatic?" he asked. "It's OK, Sergeant. He's got asthma, not the Sleepy Plague. Besides, shooting patients would just spread bits of infectious material around, so I wouldn't recommend it."

"S... s... sorry," gasped Arthur.

"OK, just relax," replied the paramedic. He turned to his partner. "We'd better take him. Grab the roller, will you?"

Within a minute, the two paramedics had injected Arthur with something that helped him breathe much more easily, though it made him sleepy and he had to fight against that. Then they bundled him on to a stretcher, ran it across the street and slid him, stretcher and all, into an ambulance.

In three minutes, they were on their way, overtaking the buses as they headed for the designated quarantine hospital. Arthur was counting on it being East Area Hospital, because that was the closest to the school. It was also close to the House, and if he was right they would pass that weird building on the way, though on the other side and several blocks over from the road he took going home.

Arthur was also counting on the promised intervention by "Will", who he supposed was the same person or entity as "The Will" that Mister Monday and Sneezer had talked about, who he presumed was also the giver of the Atlas. He figured that if he could get close to the House, it would do something to help him get inside.

Unfortunately he couldn't see out from inside the ambulance. He was loosely strapped to the stretcher so he couldn't sit up, and there were no windows anyway, except for the one in the hatch at the back.

"Where are we going?" Arthur asked.

"East Area," said the paramedic who was sitting next to him. "Don't talk. Save your breath."

Arthur smiled. At least that part of the plan was working. Now he just had to wait five minutes or so, when they would be driving along Parks Way, which would border the House. Then something would happen, he felt sure.

They drove on, without the siren. As the minutes passed – or what felt like minutes – Arthur began to get anxious. What if he was wrong? It seemed like they must already be past Parks Way, just about to turn into the hospital. He must have been wrong about the Will helping out. Or maybe it had tried and failed. Perhaps Mister Monday's minions were trying some scheme of their own to regain the Key...

Then there was a sudden noise on the roof of the ambulance and it slowed dramatically.

"What in the world!" exclaimed the driver. Except that through his mask it came out as, "Werrin der wold!"

The other paramedic climbed past Arthur to stare out through the front to the windscreen. Arthur took the opportunity to draw the Key from his pocket. As he gripped it firmly, all traces of his asthma vanished.

The ambulance came to a complete stop, the drumming sound of rain now a constant roar on the roof, as if they were parked next to the ocean and the waves were crashing very close.

"Local cloudburst!" shouted Arthur's paramedic to the driver. He kept leaning through to the front, only his waist and legs still in the back part of the ambulance. "We'll just wait it out. The boy's doing fine."

Arthur took a deep breath and touched the Key to the strap at his side.

"Release! Undo! Unlatch!" he whispered. He hoped that would work.

The strap fell away, the click swallowed up by the sound of the beating rain. Arthur quickly whispered the words again and touched the other strap. Then he sat up and repeated the process with the strap over his legs.

Then he threw himself forward, pulled the hatch handle, pushed the door open and half jumped, half fell out into the heaviest rain he had ever experienced. Rain that actually hurt, the drops as big as his fist, so big that when they broke over his face he thought he might drown.

It was so heavy that Arthur couldn't see a thing. Blindly, he waded around the back of the ambulance and struck out in what he hoped was the right direction. The road was already knee-deep in rushing water, the drains totally overwhelmed by the downpour.

Arthur clutched the Key and pushed on, his chin tucked

in to his chest to try to keep the rain out of his eyes, nose, and mouth. Water rushed past him, roaring and gurgling. He dimly heard a shout from the ambulance.

Then, all of a sudden, the rain stopped. Arthur lifted his head and looked around, only to see that the rain had not stopped everywhere. He'd walked out of it. Only a few steps behind him, it was coming down as hard as ever. But the rain was only falling on the road, and the dark cloud above wasn't much bigger than the ambulance.

It was hard to see into this weird, incredibly localised cloudburst, but Arthur saw a blurry shape leap from he back of the ambulance. The paramedic had come after him!

Arthur tensed to run, but the paramedic didn't get very far. The rain intensified even more, so that it was no longer individual drops but more like a solid ocean wave being dumped horizontally from the sky. The paramedic was bowled over and swept away, bobbing like a cork as he was washed down the road. Fortunately, thought Arthur, he couldn't drown in his biosuit, with its independent supply of oxygen.

A moment later the ambulance slid sideways, accompanied by the great groan of rubber letting go, and it followed the paramedic down the road, much more slowly. Arthur watched ambulance and man wash down the street in the strangest flash flood that anybody had ever seen. It wouldn't take them far, but far enough for Arthur to get away. Already the rain was lessening and the cloud was shrinking.

Arthur turned away from the road. As he had hoped and half expected, he saw the cool marble of the wall and looming up above it, the crazy architecture of the House.

Though he had lost the Atlas, Arthur still remembered the map/drawing of the House. He'd stared at it long enough, and he knew exactly where he should find the spot on the map that had been marked as Monday's Postern. Once he was through that, he needed only to walk across to the point that was marked FRONT DOOR in one of the hall-like buildings that occupied the central mass of the House. Through the Front Door and then...

Then what? Arthur had no idea. But he knew he could not turn back. He had to find a cure or at least find out more about the disease the paramedic had called the Sleepy Plague. And he had to find out why he had been given the Key and the Atlas.

All the answers lay inside the House, so it was to the House he would go. Arthur walked right up to the wall, touched the cool stone surface, and – keeping one hand brushing the stone – started to walk along the wall southward towards where he thought Monday's Postern should be.

Arthur reached the southwestern corner of the House's border in ten minutes. He found that while he touched the wall, he couldn't see or hear any traffic on Parks Way, or see any people in the houses or yards across the street. It was as if the street and the houses were a painted backdrop, waiting for the cast to come on that evening.

But if he moved away from the wall and stopped trailing his finger along it, then he could see cars passing by and people going into their homes. He could hear dogs barking and children crying and, most of all, distant sirens and the constant clatter of helicopters. It was clear that the quarantine had been extended past the school.

Mostly Arthur kept touching the wall. He figured that if he couldn't see or hear other people, they wouldn't be able to see or hear him.

Monday's Postern was along the south wall, only a few hundred yards from the western corner. Just before he got to where he thought it would be, Arthur walked away from the wall. But when he looked for a door or a gate or some means of entry, there was nothing. Just the cold marble, smooth and shining.

Arthur frowned and walked closer. He still couldn't see anything. So he raised the Key and touched it to the wall.

This had an immediate effect. The marble where he touched the Key glowed brightly and the dark veins in the stone began to throb and move as if they were living, fluid conduits. Ten or twelve paces away, the dark shape of an open, shadowed doorway appeared.

Arthur didn't like the look of it, but he moved closer, keeping the Key touching the wall. As he moved, the marble quietened where he'd left and quickened where he touched.

The doorway was so black Arthur couldn't work out whether it was open or shut. Somehow it absorbed the light, so it was like looking into the deepest shadow. That shadow could be just an image upon the wall, or it could be a deep, dark entrance to somewhere else.

Arthur felt himself shiver as he moved closer to the postern. A convulsive shiver that he was unable to stop. But he had to pass through that doorway to get to the House proper and to the Front Door.

The first step was to see whether it was open or not.

Hesitantly, Arthur reached out with the Key. He met no resistance, the silver and gold clock hand still shining as it sank into the darkness, though its light did not illuminate the doorway.

There was a faintly electric sensation around his hand and wrist, but it didn't hurt. Arthur leaned forward and extended his arm so that it disappeared up to the elbow in the inky doorway. It still didn't hurt and he couldn't feel anything on the other side. There was no resistance, no hard object for the Key to strike.

Arthur pulled out his hand and inspected it. Both the Key and his arm looked exactly the same as they had before he reached into the doorway. His skin hadn't been transformed or injured or affected in any way that he could see or feel.

Still Arthur hesitated. Not being able to see what was

beyond the open doorway scared him. He'd also lost his backpack and the salt, his weapon against the Fetchers. It was probably still in the ambulance.

But he had the Key and he couldn't help feeling excited as well as afraid. The House and all its mysteries – and answers – lay behind this wall. As far as he knew, Monday's Postern was the only way in.

He had to go through.

Arthur took a very deep breath, something that he wasn't often able to do. He enjoyed the feel of his lungs expanding to their maximum capacity. Then, holding the Key in front of himself like a sword fighter about to duel, he stepped completely into the doorway.

CHAPTER NINE

Arthur stepped through the doorway, but not on to solid ground. Not on to any ground. He screamed as he realised he was falling through space and Monday's Postern was not behind him but above him, a doorway of bright light where all else around was darkness. A doorway that was receding every second as he fell away from it.

Arthur's scream faded as he noticed that he wasn't falling all that fast. It was more like sinking in water, though he didn't feel wet and he had no trouble breathing. He tried kicking to see if it slowed his fall. It was hard to tell, since the distant doorway was his only point of reference, but it did seem as if it wasn't receding quite as fast.

Arthur kicked again and tried a couple of strokes with his free hand. That also appeared to work. He was contemplating putting the Key in his belt and trying some full-on swimming when the Key suddenly jerked in his hand. It jerked again a second later, much harder, like a fisherman's strike setting a hook in a fish. Then the Key absolutely rocketed forward, almost ripping itself out of Arthur's grasp. If he hadn't tightened his grip he would have lost it, to fall once more.

He held the Key as tightly as he could and got his other hand on to it as well, the muscles in his forearms taut from the effort. The Key kept accelerating like a tiny rocket, fortunately without the flaming exhaust, dragging Arthur through the inky blackness.

He still couldn't see anything. Without the sensation of air rushing past, or anything to look at, it was very hard to tell how fast he was travelling. But Arthur somehow felt that the Key was still accelerating, going faster and faster and dragging him along with it. After a while – Arthur could not guess how long – the end of the Key began to glow with a red heat and sparks began to shower from it. Arthur flinched and tried to turn his face away, but the sparks flew out at an oblique angle, as if there was some sort of shield around him, and the end of the Key he held remained cool.

A long time passed. Arthur tried to look at his watch, but it had slipped around his wrist and he didn't dare let go of the Key to move it back. He tried counting seconds and then minutes, but kept forgetting what number he was up to.

Eventually he gave up. At least an hour had passed, he was sure of that. His fingers were very cramped and sore, and his shoulders hurt. But not as much as they should have. Once again he could feel the power of the Key lessening pain and stiffness, in the same way that it helped him to breathe.

Eventually he even became bored and started to look around, peering into the darkness in the hope of seeing something. Anything. But apart from the glow of the Key and the sparks, there was no light. Occasionally, as a spark faded in the distance, Arthur thought he saw just the hint of shapes moving parallel with him, but when he stared even harder he couldn't see a thing.

Then, just as he was starting to be afraid again, thinking that he might never get anywhere, the Key suddenly changed direction. Arthur yelped as his body swung around to follow his outstretched arms and his legs jackknifed wildly.

He could see something ahead now. A pinprick of light that became a dot and then a distinct rectangle. It got closer and closer and closer with alarming rapidity and Arthur saw it was another illuminated doorway – one much, much bigger than Monday's Postern. They were going to smack into it at a very high speed, at least a hundred miles an hour and he would be smashed into a pulp—

Arthur closed his eyes as they hit... and fell over something, going no faster than if he'd tripped walking around his bedroom with his nose glued to a book.

Arthur opened his eyes, flailed his arms and smacked into the ground. He lay there for a second, feeling a tremendous surge of relief as he felt honest to goodness solid matter under his hands. He still held the Key, no longer glowing, and the absence of significant pain suggested no bones were broken or other damage done.

But where was he? He became aware that he was lying on grass – he could see and feel that. Slowly Arthur got to his feet and looked around. The first thing he noticed was that the light was strange. Dim and cool and orange-pink, like a sunset when the sun hung low and orange. But there was no sun in sight.

Arthur stood on a bare, high hill of close-mown grass that looked down upon a sea of white... no, not a sea. A fog bank had settled to the limits of the horizon. And there were buildings in the fog, dim shapes that he couldn't quite make out. Spires pierced the grey-white mist, and towers, but none was close enough for him to see any identifying features.

Arthur looked up next, expecting to see the sky. But he didn't and he instinctively crouched at what he saw instead.

There was no sky. There was a ceiling in its place, a vast domed ceiling of dull silver that stretched for miles in every direction. Its epicentre was about six hundred feet directly above the hill where he stood. Swirls of purple and orange moved across the silver surface of the dome, providing what little light there was.

"Pretty, ain't it?" said a voice behind Arthur. A man's voice, deep and slow. Not threatening, just the sort of remark anyone at a lookout might make to another visitor.

Arthur jumped and nearly fell over again as he twisted around to see who spoke. But all he could see was an enormous freestanding door of dark-oiled wood between tall gateposts of white stone, standing on the crest of the hill. Door was an inadequate word, Arthur thought. It was more a gate, as it was easily three or four times the size of his parents' garage door.

The door was decorated with wrought-iron climbing vines and clever curlicues that formed different patterns and designs depending on where you looked and the angle of view. Rather like a puzzle. In a few seconds Arthur made out a tree, which could also be a sea horse if he tilted his head, and that horse's tail could also be a comet surrounded by stars, with the stars joining together to make a ship...

Arthur blinked and saw completely different shapes and pictures. He blinked again and tore his gaze away. The door was dangerous. He felt that the patterns and shapes could trap him into staring at them for ever.

And where was the person... or whatever it was... who had spoken to him? He looked around, but there was only the strange door and the bare hill. A vast door that appeared to go nowhere, standing stark and alone.

Arthur walked around it and was unsurprised to see that the other side was exactly the same. Perhaps the door was some sort of sculpture, he thought, only meant to make an artistic statement. But deep down, Arthur knew that if the door was to open, he would not see the hill on the other side.

"Shift change in a moment," said the voice. "Then you'll see something worth seeing."

"Where are you?" asked Arthur.

"Where?" asked the voice. It sounded surprised. "Ah. Not exactly... wait a moment... a step to the left..."

The ironwork on the door shimmered and the patterns formed into the shape of a man. Then the shape stepped out of the door. The iron tracery became flesh and blood, and standing in front of Arthur was a tall, calm-looking man who looked about the same age as his father, Bob, though he had long white hair that flowed down and over his shoulders. Like Mister Monday, Sneezer and Noon, he was wearing very old-fashioned clothes. In his case, a blue swallow-tailed coat with gold buttons and a single gold epaulette on his left shoulder, over a snowy white shirt, tan breeches, and shiny knee boots with turned-down tops. He held a scabbarded sword in his left hand, gripping it casually below the hilt. Two golden tassels fell over his wrist. It didn't look like he was about to draw the weapon.

"Pardon me," the figure said. "Sometimes I forget myself. I'm the Lieutenant Keeper of the Front Door. Allow me to salute the bearer of the Lesser Key of the Lower House."

He stood at attention and saluted, then offered his hand.

"Arthur Penhaligon," said Arthur. He automatically shook hands. The Lieutenant Keeper's flesh felt strangely smooth and cool, though it was not repellent. Arthur was careful to switch the Key to his left hand and keep a tight grip on it, as he wondered why this strange character had called it the Lesser Key.

"Where am I?"

"Why, the Lower Atrium of the House," said the Lieutenant Keeper. "On Doorstop Hill."

"Right," replied Arthur. He was about to ask another question but didn't, as his next thought was upstaged by a shaft of brilliant light that suddenly shot up from the foot of the hill, extending all the way to the ceiling of the dome. It was joined a moment later by a beam coming down, and then there was a multitude of beams going up and down, as if hundreds or even thousands of intense up-and-down lights were being switched on. All together they created an illumination that was similar to, but not quite the same as, daylight.

Now Arthur could see through the fog, which slowly began to break up and drift apart. There was a whole city below the hill, a city whose architecture was strikingly reminiscent of how the House looked in his own world, though here the buildings were separate, sitting on broad streets rather then being jumbled all together.

"What... what are those beams of light?"

"Elevators. It's shift change," explained the Lieutenant Keeper. "The end of night, and the coming of the light. Work must be done, and the elevators bring workers from above and below, taking the nightwatchers to their rest and conveying all the matters and moments that must be dealt with in this new day."

"What work? What... who?"

"I haven't time to answer questions," said the Lieutenant Keeper. "Though it is shift change, my relief has not marched up for ten thousand years, nor has the Captain Keeper made his rounds. I must return to my post. It is at shift change that danger often comes and I should be on guard. Though I will offer this counsel: hide the Key from prying eyes. And I will give you my spare shirt and watch cap, so you do not look too much the stranger. Good luck, Arthur Penhaligon."

He saluted again, stepped back into the door and became ironwork once more. A second later, even that man-shape flowed into many different puzzle pictures and Arthur had to force himself to look away before his mind was trapped into following the ever-changing images. He missed the ironwork twisting into a shirt and a knitted cap, which then fell out at the boy's feet.

Arthur put the shirt on over his own clothes. It was white linen, had long tails and was much too big. It also had a weird detachable collar and no buttons on the cuffs, but Arthur had to fold the sleeves back several times anyway. The watch cap was a dark blue circular cap made from some sort of felt material.

Hide the Key from prying eyes. Arthur thought about that. It sounded like good advice, and there was something about the Lieutenant Keeper of the Front Door that he instinctively liked and trusted. But how could he hide the Key if he needed to hold on to it to breathe normally?

Or did he? Perhaps things were different here. Wherever here was, it was certainly not his own world. Arthur hesitated, then experimentally opened his hand and balanced the Key on his palm. He felt no different, though of course the metal was still in contact with his skin.

Arthur went down on one knee, hesitated again, then gently tipped the Key on to the grass. He half expected his lungs to seize up as the Key fell, but they didn't. His breath still came easily and he wasn't struck by any sudden pains or tightness of the chest. He felt just the same. Which, he suddenly realised, was very well. Energetic and full of unusual vigour.

So he didn't need to touch the Key all the time here – wherever here was. Arthur picked it up and, after a moment's thought, pushed it through his belt. With the Lieutenant Keeper's shirt coming down almost to his knees, the shining metal of the minute hand was completely hidden.

That done, he looked down at the town or city that was spread out below. He could see people all over the streets now and could hear the hustle and bustle, though there were no cars or any of the noises of a modern city. The only vehicles he could see – and there were few of them – appeared to be drawn by horses. Or something like horses.

Arthur couldn't be sure from this distance, but he didn't think they looked quite right.

"I suppose the first step is to go down and try to find someone who can tell me something about... about everything," he said to himself. It looked safe enough. The weird beams of light continued to shoot up and down all over the place, but he'd noticed they only emanated from the top of buildings, so even if they were actually huge laser beams or death rays he would be able to avoid them. And from up here, the city and the people looked ordinary, if extremely old-fashioned, without cars or traffic lights or power lines.

He would just have to keep a very wary eye out for Fetchers and Noon and Mister Monday and anyone who showed too much interest in him or looked dangerous. It was a pity he'd lost his backpack, he thought, and the salt in it. But perhaps that wouldn't work here anyway.

Arthur looked round the hill once more, but it was only a delaying tactic. He had to go down to the city because there was no choice. He couldn't go back. Even if he knew how, that wouldn't solve anything. The only way to find a cure for the Sleepy Plague was to forge ahead.

Arthur thought of Leaf and Ed again for a moment. They were the best prospects for friends he'd met in the new school. If they survived the plague. Anything could be happening back home. Arthur thought of the incredibly swift spread of the virus that had killed his birth parents. It had exploded through the population, spreading from a single known carrier to infect more than five thousand people in the first twenty-four hours. By the second day, almost fifty thousand people were sick. When Emily's team found a vaccine only eighteen days after the initial report, and with extreme quarantine in place, almost a million people were dead.

I wish I hadn't remembered that statistic, thought Arthur. But there was no point standing around simply hoping. He had to do something.

"Rock and roll," muttered Arthur, thinking of his father. He punched his fist in the air and set off down the hill towards the closest row of buildings and the cobbled lane that ran behind them at the foot of the hill.

*

Half an hour later, Arthur was deep in the heart of the city and extremely confused. There were people everywhere – at least they looked like people. But they were all dressed in the fashions of more than a hundred and fifty years ago. Every man wore a hat of some kind, every woman too, though they mostly went for bonnets and caps. Even the children – not that there were many of them – wore flat caps or obvious hand-me-downs that were too big for them. There was also incredible variation in the quality of the clothes. Some of the people were dressed in little more than the ragged remnants of what appeared to be several very different and incompatible wardrobes. Others were immaculate, with spotless coats, stiff white shirt-points, flowing cravats, shining waistcoats and gleaming boots. None of the children fell into this latter category. All the kids were dirty and dressed in incredible hodgepodges of second-hand clothing.

Even weirder than the people's clothes was what they were all doing. Arthur had expected that he would find all the usual city activities going on, with shops and restaurants and bars and businesses and people shopping and buying and selling, or just walking around and chatting to one another.

There was none of that. There was tremendous hustle and bustle with people going in and out of the buildings and talking in the streets and carrying boxes and pushing little carts around, swapping loads and exchanging boxes and bags and chests and barrels. There were carts drawn by horselike animals, but they weren't horses. They looked like horses from a distance, but they had three distinct toes instead of hooves, no manes, glittering ruby eyes, and their skin had the sheen of metal rather than horse flesh. Definitely not horses.

But the horses weren't the weirdest thing about the city. Even stranger was the fact that everything being moved around or exchanged (or whatever the people were doing) was either paper, something like paper, or related to writing in some way.

There were men carrying piles of papers, their chins pressed down on the top sheets to make sure they didn't blow away. There were men whose coat pockets were stuffed with rolls of parchment, with wax seals hanging off the rolls. There were people pushing carts loaded with stone tablets that had lines of writing carved into them. There were women exchanging leather document cases. Girls running with string bags full of envelopes and loose papers. Boys struggling with small barrels marked SECOND-BEST AZURE-BLUE INK.

Arthur wandered through a marketplace full of street stalls, but every stall was the same, selling quills and cutting feathers for use as quills, with partially plucked geese running around everyone's feet. A line of men in leather aprons passed carrying bundles that Arthur recognised as papyrus reeds, from his project on ancient Egypt last term. Four women struggled by with a huge sheet of beaten gold that had strange symbols hammered into it.

With all the hustle and bustle and papers and stuff being transported everywhere, there was also an incredibly high level of disorganisation wherever Arthur wandered. It seemed like a lot of the people didn't really know what they were doing and were doing something simply because they were afraid to not be doing something. Everyone was busy, always with paper, or stone tablets, or papyrus scrolls, or pens, or ink, or chisels. Arthur didn't see a single person just standing around, or sitting, or chatting without an armful of papers.

The disorganisation was reflected in many of the

discussions Arthur overheard, which were often arguments. He heard one woman refusing to sign for forty-six assorted descriptions on calfskin, and another hotly disputing that she was responsible for the *Aaah! to Aaar* volume of the *Loose-leaf Registry of Lesser Creations*.

A crowd of men and women at the door of one building were arguing with a very tall man in a blue uniform coat who stood in the doorway and wouldn't let them in as he read from a scroll in his hand about some sort of failure to renew a licence.

Another crowd was picking up the pieces of a huge stone tablet that had apparently toppled out of an upper-storey window, which was itself crumbling away. Two men walked around a pile of dropped papers, both loudly disclaiming any responsibility for them as they blew away down the street. Arthur noticed that these papers were rapidly picked up by some of the more ragged children, but when he tried to see where they went with them, he lost them in the crowd.

Every building appeared to be an office of some kind. At least, every one Arthur looked closely at, hoping to find something else, like a café, a restaurant or a supermarket. Not that he was hungry. He just wanted to see something normal.

All the buildings had bronze plates or small signs on the doors or next to them, but almost all of these were so covered in verdigris that Arthur couldn't make out what they said. The few that were bright and polished made no sense to him. He saw signs that read SUB-BRANCH SECOND DIRECTORATE OF THIRD DEPARTMENT OF INTERIOR RATIOCINATION AND CROSS-CHECKING – LOWER ATRIUM OFFICE and WHAT GOES UP NEED NOT COME DOWN INITIATIVE OFFICE – LOWER ATRIUM ANNEX and INQUISITOR GENERAL'S ELEVENTH DEPUTY ASSOCIATE ASSISTANT IN CHARGE OF WINGS – LOWER ATRIUM INSPECTION OFFICE.

Another aspect of the disorganised bustle was that everyone ignored Arthur. In his too-large shirt and watch cap, he didn't look much different from the other children. But the kids kept their distance from him and he knew it was on purpose.

He tried to talk to a woman who looked less busy than most, but as soon as he went up to her and said, "Excuse me", she jumped into the air, pulled a sheaf of papers from her sleeve and held them up close against her face, reading aloud so rapidly that Arthur couldn't understand a word.

He made his second approach to a very old man who was slowly walking up the street, holding a basket full of tiny gold tablets. Arthur fell in step with him and said, "Excuse me" once more.

"It's not my fault!" exclaimed the old man. "The Lower Supernumary Third Archive deposit hatch is shut and no Archivist on duty these last thousand years. Tell that to your superior."

"I just wanted to ask—" Arthur started to say. But before

he could finish, the old man put on a startling turn of speed and pushed through the crowd. His passage provoked a storm of minor accidents and complaints, and soon the whole street was strewn with dropped papers, people banging their heads together as they tried to pick them up, and others falling over at least a thousand lead pencils that had rolled out of an overturned tub.

Arthur stared at the chaos and decided he needed to think about his next approach. He climbed up the steps of the closest office and leaned back on yet another verdigris-obscured brass plate. As he had done every few minutes, he felt through his shirt to confirm that the Key was still at his side.

Just as he touched it, there was a sudden increase in noise from the street. The angry shouts and cries and arguments suddenly changed tone. There were cries of alarm and genuine fear. Instead of milling around, the crowd parted and fled in opposite directions. Many of them were shouting, "Help!" and "Nithlings!"

Arthur stopped leaning and stood up straight to see what was happening. The street had completely cleared in a matter of seconds. A few sheets of paper drifted across the cobbles and fell into the cracks, and a large ox-hide parchment with red ochre pictograms flapped where it had been abandoned a moment ago.

Arthur could see no reason for the panic, but he could smell something.

A familiar odour. The rotten-meat smell of the Fetchers' breath.

Then he saw that the cracks in the street were slowly spreading and widening, and a thin mist of dark vapour was spraying up, as if oil had been struck under the cobbles.

A whistle sounded in the distance, sharp and shrill. It was answered by others, coming from every direction. As if in reaction to the whistles, the cracks in the street groaned open even wider and more streams of dark vapour fountained up.

The vapour plumes grew till they were six or seven feet high, then the black mists began to solidify into semi-human shapes. Misshapen men and women formed out of the gas, creatures whose faces were on backwards, with double-jointed arms and patches of scales upon their skin. Imperfect copies of the clothing worn by the paper-shufflers of the city formed upon them too – coats with sleeves missing, and hats with no crowns, and trousers where one leg was three feet longer than the other and trailed upon the ground.

The plume Arthur had spotted first was also the first to be fully formed. It became a sticklike sort of man-thing with rubbery arms that hung down past its knees. It had one red-rimmed eye in the centre of its forehead and it wore a single garment rather like a blue straitjacket that was tied at the back, a crushed top hat with a gaping hole in the crown, and spurred boots of different sizes.

Arthur stared at it in horror and the thing stared back, one transparent eyelid slowly sliding up and down across his single red-rimmed eye. Then it opened its mouth to reveal yellowed canine fangs and a forked tongue that flickered in and out.

Arthur realised he should have run when everybody else did. He started down the steps, but the thing was already at the bottom and its six brethren were assuming solid form behind it.

CHAPTER TEN

Arthur retreated until his back was up against the door. He pushed on it with his shoulder, but it didn't move. Without taking his eyes off the creature, he reached behind to frantically twist the doorknob, but it wouldn't turn either. There was no escape that way.

Quickly Arthur looked from side to side, seeking some other way out. But the misshapen creatures had spread out to cover the neighbouring buildings and the one-eyed horror was limping up the steps. It drooled as it came and licked its lips, its one eye looking hungrily at the boy.

"Get back!" shouted Arthur. He pulled out the Key, got it tangled in his shirt for a heart-stopping moment, then held it ready like a dagger.

The one-eyed creature hissed when it saw the Key. It turned its head and its misshapen mouth quivered. It stopped its advance and called out to its companions, who had been spreading out down the street. Arthur wished he didn't understand its guttural speech, but he did.

"Treasure! Danger! Come and help me!"

All of the creatures stopped and turned back towards Arthur. The one-eyed one hissed again and began to slink forward, much more carefully this time, its eye focused not on Arthur, but on the Key. The clock hand was glowing again, Arthur saw, light gathering at the point. The Key was gathering its power as the creature gathered its allies.

The one-eyed creature suddenly crouched and Arthur knew it was about to spring. He pointed the Key at it and shouted, a wild cry that wasn't a word at all, but a mixture of anger and fear.

A stream of what looked like molten gold shot out of the Key, meeting the creature's leap head-on. The thing squealed and hissed like a steam train coming to an emergency stop, twisted aside and fell back to the street. It lay there, twitching and groaning, with smoke rising from a hole in its chest. But there were many more of its kind behind it and, though they had slowed down after seeing the fate of their forerunner, Arthur knew they would get him if they all rushed him at once. He would take out as many as he could, he thought, and pointed the Key at the closest one.

"Hey! Idiot! Up here!"

Something soft hit Arthur on the back of the head. He looked up. A small, grimy face looked down at him over the gutter of the roof, several stories up. Hanging beneath that face and a thin, ragged-clad arm was a rope made of knotted pieces of material. The end of it had just struck him.

"Climb, stupid!"

Afterwards Arthur was never quite sure how he managed to put the Key through his belt, jump about eight feet off the ground and climb most of the way up a four-storey building, all before the creatures could get halfway up the front steps.

"Hurry! Faster! Nithlings can climb!"

Arthur glanced behind as he frantically pulled himself up, hands leaping to each knot with a speed that would have surprised any gym teacher. *If only Mister Weightman could see me now*, Arthur thought.

The creatures could climb. One of them was already on the rope, swarming up even faster than Arthur. Another one was swarming straight up the brick wall. It seemed to be able to stick its narrow fingers in the thinnest of gaps, but it was slower.

Arthur made it to the top and swung himself over. He saw a flash of steel and the rope went flying away, cut through at the top. A cry of pain indicated that the creature climbing it had fallen too.

"Quick! Grab a piece of tile and throw!"

Arthur saw a pile of broken tiles, grabbed a jagged piece and leaned over the gutter to let it fly. His rescuer was throwing too, with considerably greater accuracy. Arthur glanced at him... no... her, out of the corner of his eye as he took another shard and shot it down at the second climber.

He saw a girl about his own age, perhaps younger, though she was dressed as a boy, in the same old-fashioned clothes everyone else wore in this place. A crushed and battered top hat. A coat several sizes too large, mostly dark blue but patched with black. Knee-length breeches striped in several shades of grey, and very odd mismatched long socks or stockings that ended in one ankle-high and one shin-high boot. She had on several shirts of various sizes and colours, and a mulberry-coloured waistcoat that looked, if not new, better kept than the rest of the ensemble.

"Who are you?" asked Arthur.

"Suzy Turquoise Blue," replied the girl, throwing one last complete tile with satisfaction. "Got it!"

With a drawn-out scream, the climbing creature fell back to the street, landing on another one that had started up.

"Come on! We've got to get out of here before the Commissionaires lumber into view!"

"The who?"

"Commissionaires! Hear the whistles? They'll sort out the Nithlings and then they'll want to arrest you for sure. Come on!"

"Hold on!" said Arthur. The whistles were much closer now. "Thanks for helping me and everything, but why shouldn't I just talk to the... the Commissionaires? And who... what are Nithlings?"

"You are an idiot, ain't you?" Suzy said, with a roll of her eyes. "There's no time for quizzing."

"Why should I go with you?" asked Arthur stubbornly. He didn't move.

Suzy opened her mouth, but it was another voice that came out, clearly not her own. It was much deeper, and there was a rasp to it as well. It sounded a lot like Sneezer when he had fought with Mister Monday back at the oval, on that Monday that seemed so long ago.

"The Will has found a way and you are part of the way. This is not the time for whims and obstinacy. Follow Suzy Blue."

"Right," said Arthur, shaken by the sudden deep voice coming from the girl. "Lead on."

Suzy spun on her heel, coat-tails flying, and scampered up the roof. It was steep, but the tiles were rough and stepped so it wasn't too hard to climb. Arthur followed more slowly.

The ridge of the roof was flat, though only a foot wide. Suzy ran along it to a chimney stack, which she skirted around, hanging on to the chimney pot and leaning out in a way that made Arthur's stomach do little flips. It was a long way to the ground.

He got to the chimney and started around it. Suzy was on the other side, looking down at an open balcony thrusting out of the next building. It was about ten feet away and six feet below them.

"You're joking! We're not—"

Suzy jumped as Arthur spoke, landing perfectly on the balcony in a nimble crouch. She didn't wait to see what Arthur did, but was up in a flash and working on the door, either picking the lock or forcing it open.

Arthur looked down. The street was very far away and for a moment he was terribly afraid he'd fall. But that fear disappeared as he was distracted by what he saw. There was a full-scale battle in progress below. The whistles had stopped but were replaced by shouts and cries, howls and screams, yelling and a low rumble like constant thunder.

The creatures who'd appeared from the black vapour – the Nithlings – were bottled up in the middle of the street, completely surrounded by a well-disciplined band of large, burly men who wore shining top hats and blue coats, many of the coats adorned with gold sergeant's stripes on their sleeves. They must be the Commissionaires, Arthur realised. The Sergeants were well over eight feet tall. The ordinary Commissionaires were shorter, around seven feet tall, and they were less fluid in their movements. The Sergeants used sabres that flickered with internal light, and the ordinary Commissionaires wielded wooden truncheons that flashed with tiny bolts of lightning and boomed with thunder as they struck their targets.

Not that the Nithlings were an easy mark. They bit and scratched and wrestled, and every now and then a Commissionaire would reel back through the ranks, blood streaming from his wounds. At least Arthur presumed it was blood. The Sergeants had bright blue blood, and the ordinary Commissionaires' blood was silver, and it flowed like mercury, thick and slow.

"Come on!" shrieked Suzy.

Arthur tore his gaze away from the battle and focused on the balcony. He could do it, he knew. If it wasn't such a long way to fall, he wouldn't think twice about it. But it *was* a long way to fall...

"Hurry!"

Arthur crouched, ready to jump. Then he remembered the Key and drew it out. The last thing he needed was to spear himself with that when he landed.

With the Key in his hand, he felt suddenly more confident. He crouched again, then leaped far into space, and drifted down like a feather to land on the balcony, hardly needing to bend his knees. Suzy Blue was already gone, the door banging behind her. Arthur got up and followed, once more tucking the Key through his belt with his shirt over it.

The room behind the balcony was set up like an old-fashioned office, which didn't surprise Arthur much. There were low, wide desks of polished wood with green leather tops, all strewn with papers. There were bookcases laden with more papers as well as books. What appeared to be gas lanterns burned in each corner, and under one of these lights, on a small table, Arthur saw his first sign of any food at all in the city, a bronze hot-water urn with many taps and spigots, a silver teapot and several china cups.

There were also people at work. They looked up as Suzy and Arthur ran past, but they didn't say anything or try to stop them. Even when Arthur knocked a large pile of parchments off one corner of a desk as he zoomed past, the man behind it remained silent and kept scratching away with his quill – though he did look up and frown.

Suzy bounded out of the office and down the central stairs. At the bottom, she turned away from the main door, went through a narrow hall, opened the door of what appeared to be a broom closet and went in. Arthur followed her and discovered it really was a broom closet. Or a mop closet, to be strictly accurate, as there were several mops sitting in buckets. It smelled dank and musty.

"Shut the door!" whispered Suzy.

Arthur shut the door, and with it went the light.

"What are we doing here?"

"Hiding. The Commissionaires will go through every house in Lost Street after the Nithlings. We'll wait 'em out here."

"But they'll find us for sure!" protested Arthur. "This is a pathetic hiding—"

"You've got Monday's Key, ain't you?" asked Suzy. "Half of it, anyway. Or so I've been told."

"Yes," confirmed Arthur.

"Well, use it!"

"Use it how?" asked Arthur.

"I don't know," said Suzy. "It is a Key, so why not lock the door?"

Arthur took out the Key. It glowed in the dark, this time with a faintly green phosphorescence. He'd used it to lock the library doors on the Fetchers, and to release the straps in the ambulance, but he didn't really know what else he was supposed to do with it.

"How exactly do I—"

"Shhh!" ordered Suzy urgently. Then in that weird deep voice, she added, "Touch the door handle and tell it to lock."

Arthur touched the Key to the curved iron handle and whispered, "Lock!"

At the same time he heard the crash of boots in the corridor outside. His heart hammered in his chest almost as loud as the footsteps that came towards their hiding place. Then the handle rattled once... twice... but did not turn.

"Locked, Sergeant!" bellowed a deep voice. It sounded a bit weird, as if the speaker had a metal funnel stuck on his mouth. *Sort of tinny*, Arthur thought. The footsteps retreated, and a few seconds later Arthur heard several heavyset people going up the stairs.

He opened his mouth to whisper something to Suzy, but she held up her hand – mostly covered by a moth-eaten woollen glove – and shook her head.

Several minutes passed. They stood silently in the closet, listening to the footsteps and occasional shouts. Then there was a clattering on the stairs, a sudden rush, and the handle was tried again.

"Locked, Sergeant!" boomed the same voice. Then the footsteps went away and Arthur heard the front door slam.

"They do near everything twice," said Suzy. "At least the metal ones do, the ordinary Commissionaires. They're pretty stupid. Sergeants are a different trouble. They're not Made, and most of 'em have fallen from up above and been demoted to Commissionaire Sergeants as a punishment. Come on – we should be able to sneak out now. Unlock the door."

Arthur touched the door with the Key and said, "Open."

The door sprang open with sudden violence, slamming against the wall. Suzy stepped out first. Arthur was following when her surprised cry gave him just enough warning to whip the Key behind his back.

"Oh! Sergeant!"

A Commissionaire Sergeant stood in the hall, all eight feet of him, though on closer examination a foot of that was from his top hat. He had a waxed moustache, which he was stroking, and a very sharp, long nose under piercing blue eyes. The gold stripes on his blue sleeves gleamed in the gaslight.

"Well, well, well," he said. His voice was deep, but not tinny like the other Commissionaire. He pulled a notebook out of his coat pocket, flipped it open and took a pencil stub out from a thin sleeve on the side of the notebook. "I wondered why that closet would be locked. What have we here? Your names, numbers, rank and business."

"Suzy Turquoise Blue, 182367542 and a half in precedence, Ink-Filler Sixth Class, on ink-filling business."

Halfway through her answer, Suzy's voice changed into the very deep, scratchy tone Arthur had heard before.

The Sergeant's pencil stopped.

"Your voice. What's happened to it?"

"I've got a bit of a frog in my throat," said Suzy, still in the same deep voice.

"A frog? Where'd you get that?" asked the Sergeant enviously.

"Present," said Suzy in her normal voice. "Floated in nice as you like, 'ardly damaged. Might even last a year if I'm lucky."

"I've never had a frog in the throat," said the Sergeant sadly. "Had a small nose tickle once. Confiscated it from a Porter who had it from a Flotsam Raker. Went for a twelvemonth before it wore out. Very distinctive. Not as flamboyant as a sneeze, but very nice... Where was I? Who's this other lad?"

"Ah, I'm—"

"He's one of our lot," interrupted Suzy. "Arthur Night Black. Got dropped on his head in a pool of Nothing down below a couple of hundred years ago and hasn't been right since. Always getting lost. That's why we was in that closet. I was looking for him—"

"Papers!" ordered the Sergeant, looking at Arthur.

"He's lost them," said Suzy quickly. "Got frightened by the Nithlings, wriggled out of his coat and went hiding. Expect the Nithlings et 'em right up."

"Ate them up," corrected the Sergeant. He peered down at Suzy. "Now I haven't got anything against you Ink-Fillers, but orders is orders. I'll have to take him to the Inquiry Clerk."

"Inquiries!" Suzy snorted. "He could be there for years. They'll dock his pay – and him with a new coat to get and all. Can't we sort this out gentlemanly-like? You ain't written anything yet, have you?"

The Sergeant frowned, then slowly pushed the pencil back into its sleeve and folded his notebook.

"What do you suggest, Miss Blue?"

"This frog," said Suzy. "You want it?"

The Sergeant hesitated.

"Free gift," said Suzy. "And it's not as if you'll get cribbed for it. When was the last General Inspection?"

"Ten thousand years and more," said the Sergeant softly. "But I've made mistakes before. I wasn't always a Commissionaire. Once I was..."

"Go on," said Suzy, her voice even deeper and more authoritative. "Take a look."

She held her hand in front of her mouth and spat into her palm.

"Gross!" exclaimed Arthur, though it wasn't spit that

came out, but a small and very beautiful emerald-green frog. It sat in Suzy's hand and emitted a deep, poignant call.

"Give it a try," encouraged Suzy. She took a rather dirty handkerchief from her pocket and gave the frog a quick polish. It didn't seem to mind.

The Sergeant was quite mesmerised by the frog. He looked around, then reached out and picked it up. He stared at it in his hand, then gulped it down as if he were eating a mint.

His mouth closed and he froze in place.

"That's him sorted," said Suzy in her normal voice. "And me free, so no hard feelings, Arthur, but I was impressed on this duty and I 'ave a very urgent ointment—"

She dashed away on the last word, but the Sergeant's hand shot out and grabbed her coat-tails. Suzy tried to shuck out of her coat, but couldn't manage it before the Sergeant transferred his grip to her neck.

"Ow! Ow! Leave off!"

"The Will has need of you, Suzy Blue," said the Sergeant, but once again it was not his voice, but the deep voice that had previously come out of Suzy. "There may be rewards."

Suzy stopped struggling.

"Rewards? Only *may be* don't sound so certain..."

Arthur stepped forward. "Look, I don't know what's going on here, or what the Will wants with me, but it is very important that I find out what's going on. I think... I think a lot of people might die if I don't. So I need your help, Suzy."

Arthur spoke with passion. He could feel the fear and tension trapped inside him, like steam in a kettle. Back in his world, in his town, the quarantine zone would be expanding. The hospitals would be crowded, possibly overflowing, already unable to cope. Arthur could almost see his mother and her team in the lab, working feverishly... feverishly... perhaps they were already sniffling, sneezing with the colds that marked the onset of the plague...

"People? Die?" asked Suzy. "You mean you really *are* from outside the House? From the Secondary Realms?"

"I'm from outside the House," said Arthur. "I don't know what you mean about the Secondary Realms."

"You're a mortal?" asked Suzy. "A real live mortal?"

"I suppose so," confirmed Arthur.

"So am I, sort of, or I used to be," said Suzy. She hesitated, then said, "Will you help me get back? Help all of us get back?"

"Who?" asked Arthur. "Everyone in the city?"

"No!" replied Suzy scornfully. "Everyone grown belongs here. They're wot's called Denizens of the House. I mean us. The children. The ones that followed the Piper all those years ago."

"That is a trivial matter," intoned the Sergeant, or whatever it was that spoke through him. "Arthur must find a way to bring back the Will. All else will follow."

"I'm not helping unless you help us," said Suzy. "Is it a deal?"

"I suppose so," said Arthur. "I mean, if I can help, I will. Yes."

Suzy smiled and held out her hand. Arthur took it and she shook vigorously.

"Danger," said the Sergeant, cupping a hand to his ear. "Commissionaires approach. There is also a great likelihood that Monday's Noon or Dusk knows Arthur has come through the Front Door and has taken charge of a search. We must be away at once."

"Well, you'd better leave this great lunk behind," said Suzy. "Can't take him with us."

There was no answer, but the Sergeant's mouth opened and the green frog climbed out, leaving the man frozen like a statue. The frog jumped over to Suzy's shoulder and started to climb up to her mouth, but she caught it in her hand and stuffed it in an inside pocket that she buttoned shut.

"Not any more, froggy," she said. "Once caught, twice careful. Come on!"

"Where are we going?" asked Arthur. He felt quite confused. So much had happened so quickly he wondered if he was ever going to get a chance to sit down and ask some questions. Or more importantly, get them answered.

"The Office of the Efficiencer General of the Lower Atrium."

"The where?"

"The Efficiencer General is in charge of making everything work efficiently in the Lower Atrium," explained

Suzy as they exited through a back door into a lane. "Only there ain't one. An Efficiencer General, that is. Apparently the last one never got replaced when he moved up. And there's no staff neither. So that's where I live, off shift, of course."

"Is it far away?"

"Thirty-nine hundred floors," said Suzy, pointing straight up.

CHAPTER ELEVEN

We'll take a goods elevator," Suzy said as they carefully loitered on a street and slipped into place behind a procession of bearers carrying bundles of linen rags that would ultimately be made into paper. "There's one in the Instrumentality for Rapid Dissemination of Excess Records."

"The beams of light," said Arthur, discreetly pointing at one of the nearer ones. "They're elevators?"

"Not exactly," replied Suzy with a frown. "They mark the path of an elevator. When you're inside it's just like being in a little room. Very boring."

"Oh, good," said Arthur. He was relieved that he wasn't going to be turned into a stream of photons or something. Or if he was, he wouldn't know about it.

"Some of them have music," added Suzy. "But only the

big ones that can fit in a few minstrels or a band. We won't be going in one of those. They're for the big nobs."

"The what?"

"The high-ups. The executives. Officers of the Firm."

"The Firm?" asked Arthur as they crossed the street, ducking under a very long rolled-up parchment that was being carried like a carpet between a very short fat man and a very tall thin woman.

"The Firm. The Company. The Business," said Suzy. "Them as wot runs the House and all its... I dunno... business."

"What is the House?" asked Arthur. "And how can all this be inside it?"

"Through here," said Suzy. She looked around, then opened a trapdoor at the base of a nearby wall. "Bit of a crawl."

Arthur followed her into a narrow tunnel that led under the building. It sloped down quite sharply, then levelled out. As they crawled, Suzy answered his question.

"I've never been exactly sure what the House is, cos I was an immigrant so to speak and I never seen much 'cept the Lower Atrium and maybe a dozen other floors. And I ain't had much eddication but what I read and what some folks have taught – *oomph*."

"What?" asked Arthur.

"The House is the Epicentre of All Creation," said a deep voice in the darkness, scaring the life out of Arthur.

"Tarnation!" exclaimed Suzy. She burped and added, "It got out. I mean in."

"Um, er, frog, or whatever you are," Arthur asked nervously, "what do you mean, the Epicentre of All Creation?"

"You may call me the Will, of which I am not an unappreciable fraction. The House is the Kingdom of All Reality and holds the Archive of All Things."

"OK... what does that actually mean? Um, Your Will-dom."

"The House was built from Nothing by the Great Architect of All and was populated with servants to do Her work. Then She made the Secondary Realms, which you would call the Universe. The House and its servants were dedicated to recording and observing this great work, and did so faithfully for uncounted aeons. Then the Great Architect went away, leaving a Will to ensure that Her work, and the work of the House, would continue as it should."

"Right—"

"BUT IT DID NOT!" thundered the voice.

"Ow! It's *my* throat, you know," complained Suzy.

"It did not," said the voice, quieter this time. "The Will was not executed, but broken into seven parts, and the parts scattered across the Secondary Realms, through space and time. The seven Trustees broke their faith and set out to rule the House, and not to just observe and record, but to interfere with the Secondary Realms. To meddle with Creation!"

"Let me guess," volunteered Arthur. "Is Mister Monday one of those guys?"

"He is indeed, though that is not his real name," rumbled the Will. "There is little honour among thieves, but enough that the seven Trustees agreed to divide power in both the House and the Secondary Realms. Monday rules the Lower House. Outside of it, he holds dominion over everything on any given Monday."

"This really isn't the place to talk about this stuff," said Suzy nervously. "How about we wait... *eerg—*"

Her voice was drowned in a gurgle.

"Time moves in the House ever forward, though it be malleable outside," the Will continued. "Even now Mister Monday seeks to retrieve what he has lost. Half of one of the Seven Keys to the Kingdom, the Seven Keys of the House, the Seven Keys of Creation!"

"Half of one of seven Keys don't sound like much," said Suzy. "By my reckoning that's—"

"*From Nothing came the whole House,*" intoned the Will, cutting Suzy off. "Half of one Key is better than nothing. Soon the Rightful Heir will have the other half too, and the first part of the Will shall be done!"

"Hang on!" exclaimed Arthur. "You mean me? I don't want to be the heir to anything. I just want to get a cure for the plague and go home."

"You are *a* Rightful Heir!" bellowed the Will. Then a little more quietly it added, "You are the only one on hand, that is, whether you like it or not. We shall prevail!"

"Bit overconfident, aren't you?" Suzy coughed. In the dim light Arthur saw she was massaging her throat. "A deluded green frog, one mortal visitor and a Ink-Filler Sixth Class ain't much up against Mister Monday and the whole apparatus of the Lower House."

"The what?" asked Arthur.

"Something I heard once," said Suzy. "Sounded good. *The apparatus of the House.* Which means Monday's Noon and his goons, the Elevator Drivers, the Commissionaires in the Atrium, and the Stampers and Sealers. Not to mention Monday's Dawn and her Corps of Inspectors, and Monday's Dusk and whatever special thingummies he commands."

"Winged Servants of the Night," said the Will. "And Midnight Visitors. No... the Winged Servants fall under the aegis of Sir Thursday and his Dusk. I think."

"Now it's not even sure about a minor detail and it wants to take on the Big Bosses," said Suzy. "We're about to come out in the street, Will, so be quiet!"

"I am only a portion of the Will and so my knowledge is incomplete."

"I said be quiet!" hissed Suzy. She stopped and lifted a trapdoor above her head a fraction, poked her head up, and looked around.

"Right. Looks clear. We'll come out in the corner of a shipping office, behind a crate that's lost its label. Been here for a couple of centuries. We'll wait there for a second, then when the bell rings, we run for the goods elevator. Understand?"

"No," said Arthur. "I mean, I get the bit about running for the goods elevator at the bell. It's everything else I'm having trouble with."

"I bet it's going to get even worse," said Suzy gloomily as they climbed out and crouched down behind the crate. "I knew I never should have picked up that cursed frog. Though I suppose anything beats filling up inkwells all day for the next ten thousand years. And I might miss the next time they try to wash between my ears."

"Wash between your ears? You mean behind?" asked Arthur. From what he could see, Suzy could do with a wash behind her ears.

"No, *between*," replied Suzy. "Every hundred years or so all the kids get their minds washed. Dunno why. It hurts likes a toothache, not that I've had a bad tooth here, and you forget most everything except the basics. I've had to learn to read again about... well... a lot of times. 'Cept I never really forgot how I got here, and sometimes I can still sort of remember wot life was like before—"

She was about to add something else when a bell started clattering in the room. Instantly Suzy jumped up, grabbed Arthur's hand and dragged him across the room, pushing through a group of leather-aproned men and women who had just started carrying boxes and crates towards an open goods elevator.

Suzy and Arthur beat them to it, and Suzy rolled the door shut in front of their surprised faces. Though there was something odd about their looks of surprise, Arthur thought as Suzy selected and pressed a button from the hundreds or maybe even thousands of tiny bronze buttons that covered one entire wall of the elevator.

"I do this all the time," said Suzy as the elevator began to move with a series of shudders that slowly became a fluid motion. Arthur felt himself being pushed down by the acceleration and had to bend his knees and grab hold of a polished wooden handrail. It was a lot more acceleration than he'd ever experienced in an elevator before.

"They always look surprised, but I think that's just in case someone from outside is watching," continued Suzy. "Though they might have really been surprised this time, since I always travel alone."

"Won't there be a problem when whatever they're supposed to be delivering doesn't get there?" asked Arthur.

Suzy shook her head.

"Probably no one will even notice. Everything in the Lower Atrium is right stuffed up. Nothing ever gets done shipshape and in proper fashion."

"Why not?"

"I dunno," said Suzy with an expressive shrug. "I've heard

it said Mister Monday won't do anything to fix any problems – *ick*—"

"Sloth," pronounced the Will from Suzy's mouth. "Mister Monday is afflicted with it, and it creeps ever more from him and downward through the Lower House. When the Will is done, sloth shall be banished and vigour will return."

"Can't you get out and talk for yourself?" protested Suzy angrily as she massaged her throat again.

"Yes, please do," said Arthur anxiously. It was very creepy listening to that deep voice emanating from a young girl.

"Very well, since you ask, Arthur," said the Will. As it spoke, Suzy's eyes goggled and she leaned forward, her throat convulsing. A moment later the green frog shot out and landed on the wall with a sticky plop. It hung there for a while, its iridescent eyes swivelling around, then jumped to the handrail near Arthur.

"Concealment is often necessary," said the frog in the same deep voice. "Mister Monday is not without certain powers and his minions are not without perception."

"How long will it take to get to the... I forget the name of the office?" asked Arthur.

"Oh, a minute more or so," replied Suzy. "You never know. Sometimes it's almost straight away, sometimes hours. I was in one elevator that broke down and I was stuck in it for fourteen months. But we're travelling well today."

"Fourteen months! But you'd die."

Suzy shook her head. "It's not easy to die in the House. You can't die from lack of food or water. Though you can get horribly hungry, and you can get killed, but even that's not easy. There's pain all right and you can suffer something terrible, but wounds that should kill don't always, least not for the Denizens and maybe not for us Piper's children neither, though I ain't testing it to find out for sure. The Denizens can even get their heads cut off and, if they can stick it back on again soon enough, they'll come good in a while. But the Commissionaires' weapons can kill, and fire if it's hot enough, and the Nithlings... a festering bite or scratch from a Nithling will dissolve you into Nothing. That's why everyone's afraid of them.

"But you can't die of sickness here, or even get sick. Not real sick, like with a fever or the water runs or the black vomiting. There is a fashion to use colds and sniffs brought in from the Realms. But they're usually in a charm that you can take off, or in something you can eat that only lasts for a while, and you only get the sneezes or the cough or the red eyes. You don't feel sick. No one needs to eat or drink either, though tea is fashionable and everyone eats just for fun or to show off. No trouble neither, since you don't... you know... no toilets in the House, none required."

"How long have you been here?" asked Arthur. He felt his head whirling with everything he'd learned.

"Dunno," replied Suzy with a shrug. "It's the cleaning between the ears. Besides, House Time is different."

"House Time is true Time," intoned the Will. "Time in the Secondary Realms is malleable to a certain degree, at least going backwards. Remember that, Arthur. It may be useful. *Gleep.*"

"What? Gleep?"

"This frog's body was forged from Nothing. Though it is only a copy of a jade taken from your own world, Grim Tuesday himself shaped it, so much of its frogginess and the strength of the original stone were captured. It is a hard shape to inhabit. Remember this too, Arthur—"

"Hang on!" interrupted Arthur. He took a deep breath. "I want to get a few things sorted out. Why did you choose me to be this Rightful Heir? Why did I get the Key and the Atlas – which, by the way, the Fetchers took off with."

"Chance and circumstance," said the Will. "I will relate to you the situation. Twelve days ago, as Time flows in the House, I managed to free myself from the bonds and strictures employed to imprison me on a distant star. I came to the House and managed by ways sneaky and deceitful to enter the mind of Sneezer, Mister Monday's butler and factotum. From within Sneezer, I enticed Monday to give away the Key to a mortal who was soon to die. He thought he could then reclaim the Key, since having given it away once he would have fulfilled the conditions of the Will and so would be safe from any retribution by the powers of Righteousness and Law. That is to say, myself and the other parts of the Will that may yet escape their durance. You know what happened then."

"But why me? And why did you want a mortal to have the Key?"

"It was mere chance you were chosen in particular. It was written by the Architect that only a mortal can be a Rightful Heir," said the Will. "I simply went through the records of those who would die on an easily accessible Monday. I wanted someone who would be mentally flexible. Young and not oversuperstitious or rigidly religious, so that ruled out a great many Mondays throughout what you call history. It had to be a Monday so Mister Monday and myself – as Sneezer, of course – would be able to enter your world."

"I was really going to die?" asked Arthur slowly. This was a new shock. "Of an asthma attack?"

"Yes," said the Will. "But when you took the Key, you changed the record."

"I don't understand."

"It's quite simple, Arthur. Listen carefully. Every record in the House, whether it be on stone or metal, papyrus or paper, is intimately connected with what it records in the Secondary Realms. As whatever it records changes out there, so does the record. If you have the power, you can see what changes are to come and it is possible to intervene. But the reverse is also true. If a record is changed here, then that change will occur to the person, place, object, or whatever is recorded."

"You mean if someone changed my record to show that I died, then I would die?" asked Arthur.

"They'd have to find your record first," interrupted Suzy. "Fat chance of that. I've been looking for mine for centuries. When I remember. So have all the others – the children – and not a one has ever shown up."

"The records are in a sorry state, it's true. But very few inhabitants of the House have the power to change the records anyway," said the Will. "The Keys, of course, can be used to alter almost any records. Some other office holders have lesser powers. Though it goes against the Original Law and the purpose of the House, which is to observe and record the Secondary Realms, and NOT INTERFERE!"

"Ow!" exclaimed Arthur and Suzy together, clapping their hands to their ears.

"Your folk are at least partly to blame," said the Will sadly, pointing one green sticky finger at Arthur. "No one was tempted to interfere when it was just biological soup. But let a few million years go by and those single cells got very interesting. And your people are so creative. If only the Architect hadn't chosen to go away..."

"What would have happened to me if I had died?" asked Arthur.

"You'd be dead," said the Will. "What do you mean?"

"I mean..." Arthur's voice trailed off. He didn't know what he meant. "Where am I now? Is there some sort of life after death? If the Architect created everything..."

"There is no afterlife that I know of," said the Will. "There is Nothing, from which all things once came. There is the House, which is constant. There are the Secondary Realms, which are ephemeral. When you are gone from the Secondary Realms that's it, though some say that everything returns to Nothing in the end. The record marks your passing and is dead too, though it is stored for archival purposes."

"Lost and forgotten, you mean," said Suzy with a snort. "You wouldn't believe how hopeless they are. Hang on – we're slowing down. Almost there. Hold tight!"

Chapter twelve

Arthur grabbed the handrail as the elevator slowed suddenly and went through a series of juddering halts that threatened to throw everyone against the ceiling and then the floor. It ran smoothly for a few seconds after that, long enough for him to relax, then it came to a sudden stop, this time successfully sending Arthur and Suzy against the walls and floor. The Will, courtesy of its sucker-toed frog shape, stayed stuck to the handrail.

Arthur picked himself up a little slower than Suzy, who was already sliding the elevator door open. He expected to see an office like the one they'd run through down in the Atrium, all dark wood, green baize and gaslights. His mouth hung open at what he saw instead.

The elevator door opened out on to a shaded grove of very tall, very thick-trunked trees. They formed a circle around a roughly trimmed lawn, which had the remains of a campfire sitting in a burned patch at its centre. A narrow but beautifully clear stream cut through one corner, burbling gently along. A wooden footbridge crossed the stream, with a paved path leading across to an open summerhouse that was like an old-fashioned bandstand. In the summerhouse were a desk, a lounge chair and some bookcases.

"Here we are," said Suzy. "The Office of the Efficiencer General."

Arthur followed her out, with the Will jumping ahead. The elevator door rolled shut of its own accord behind him and an electric-sounding bell rattled, making him jump. When he looked back he saw the elevator door was in the trunk of one of the vast trees. With the door closed, he could barely see its outline in the bark or the call button that was concealed in a knotted whorl.

"There's sunshine here," Arthur said, pointing to the rays that came through the foliage. He peered between two trunks and saw a distant vista of grasslands beyond, with blue sky above. "And I can see a normal sky and everything. Where are we?"

"We're still in the House," said Suzy. "All that stuff is like a picture. You can't go out past the trees. I've tried. You'll just smack into something. It's kind of an all-round window."

Arthur kept staring. He could see shapes moving in the grass. Huge, reptilian animals. Prehistoric creatures that he had seen in books and museums. Except these weren't grey like in all the pictures, but a pale yellow with faint blue stripes.

"There are dinosaurs out there!"

"They cannot get in," said the Will. "Suzy is correct. There is a panoramic window around this office, which looks out into a particular place in the Secondary Realms. It is unusual that it looks out upon a distant past, as that is most difficult. The greater the distance back from House Time, the more unstable the window."

"Can one of these look into the future too?" asked Arthur. "Can you change where it looks into?"

"It depends what you mean by the future," said the Will. "There are many different relationships between House Time and time in the Secondary Realms. If you mean the future of your world, no. That is closely in step with House Time, so the future is not accessible. But we could look at any time before you came here, if we had the document that describes the window. You see, as it looks out on the Secondary Realms, it is part of them and will have a record somewhere in the House. Perhaps in that desk."

"It doesn't matter," said Arthur. "I just wanted to see... to check what was happening back home. But not if I can't see after I left."

It's probably better not to see, Arthur thought despondently. All it would do was feed the fear and the tension inside him.

"I'll start a fire," said Suzy. "We'll have tea."

We haven't got time for tea! Arthur thought. But he managed not to say it. He had to wait and listen to what the Will had to say in any case. They might as well drink tea while they were listening.

Suzy went over to the burned patch and started assembling a small pyramid of black stones. Arthur followed her. It took him a second to realise that the stones were pieces of coal. He'd never seen any before. Not real coal, so shiny and black. All the pieces of coal were exactly the same shape and size, which he thought couldn't be normal.

"I don't get this place at all," he said. "Why have gaslights and coal fires and the old-fashioned clothes and everything? If this is the epicentre of the universe, couldn't it be all done by magic or whatever? And you could have better clothes."

"It's fashion," said Suzy. "It changes every now and then, dunno why. When it does, everything's different, but there's always the records and rotten jobs and things you want and can't get, like decent clothes. I don't really remember the last fashion. It was more than a hundred years ago. Too much washing between my ears. I do vaguely remember having to wear a pointy hat."

"Robes and cow dung campfires and donkey carts up endless mountains instead of elevators," said the Will. "That was the fashion before I was locked away. I think the Architect liked to take on ideas from the Secondary Realms, at least cosmetically. Doubtless the current fashion is the work of the Trustees."

"Whatever the fashion, it's impossible to get clothes from the official supplies, so you have to get 'em from the smugglers," complained Suzy. "But you've got to have House gold, and that's almost impossible to come by, or something to barter. Course the big nobs always have a supply of coats and shirts and tea and buttered scones and suchlike. Mind you, every now and then they mislays a bag of coal or a tea caddy."

Suzy winked and went to the summerhouse and retrieved a battered, blackened teapot that she filled with water from the stream and hung over the coal fire on a tripod made from three bent pokers and some wire.

"So, froggy, tell us what Arthur is supposed to do," said Suzy. She sat down cross-legged on the lawn and stared at the pop-eyed amphibian. Arthur lay down on his stomach and rested his chin on his hands.

"Arthur. You have the Minute Hand, which is half of the Key that governs the Lower House," said the Will. "It is not as powerful as the Hour Hand that Mister Monday retains, but it is faster to use and can be used more often. You are aware that it can lock and open doors, but it has many other powers that I will explain in due course. Now, as the First Part of the Will, I have chosen you as the Rightful Heir to the House. The Minute Hand is only the very beginning of your inheritance. Your immediate goal is to get the Hour Hand

and complete the Key. With it, you will easily be able to defeat Mister Monday and claim the Mastery of the Lower House. The Morrow Days will protest, of course, but under the agreement they themselves forged with Monday, they will not be able to interfere.

"As soon as Monday is defeated and you have become Master, then we will need to put in train significant changes to the Lower House, in order to have a solid base from which to free the remaining parts of the Will. There is clearly tremendous slackness and stupidity here now and, worst of all, I believe, even interference with the Secondary Realms. You will need to select a cabinet, your own Dawn, Noon and Dusk, of course—"

"Hold it!" exclaimed Arthur. "I don't want to be the Master or whatever. I have to get a cure for the plague and take it back home! I just want to know how to do that."

"I was discussing grand strategy," sniffed the Will, "not tactics. However, I shall endeavour to answer your questions."

It folded its webbed hands together and leaned forward.

"*Imprimis*, you must defeat Mister Monday in order to have any chance of doing anything, including getting a cure for this plague of yours. *Secundus*, you will sneak into Mister Monday's aptly named Dayroom and retrieve the Hour Hand, which is your own lawful property. In fact, once you get in there and call it, using the spell I shall teach you, it will simply fly to your hand, unless Monday is holding it at the time, which is unlikely.

"So there's no way to get a cure for the plague without defeating Monday?" asked Arthur.

"Once you are Master, all manner of things will be possible," said the Will. "You will have full access to the Atlas, for example, a repository of considerable knowledge. I expect there would be a cure for this plague in there."

"I haven't got the Atlas! The Fetchers took it. Wherever they went."

"The Fetchers were banished back to the Nothing from whence they came," said the Will. "The Atlas, however, will be back where it came from, which is the ivory-faced bookshelf behind the tree fern in Monday's Dayroom."

"So there is no other way I can get a cure for the plague and get home?"

"No," said the Will firmly.

"OK, if I have to do this, I have to do it," said Arthur. "How do I sneak into Monday's Dayroom?"

"That is a detail I have not yet grappled with," said the Will. "Suffice to say there are a number of possibilities, including the use of the Improbable Stair, though that is a last—"

He stopped in midsentence, tilted his small green head, and said, "What was that?"

Arthur had heard it too. A distant roaring. He looked questioningly at Suzy.

"I dunno," she said. "I've never heard anything here but the stream and the elevator bell."

The roaring came again, much louder and closer. In the gap through the trees, Arthur saw a yellow and blue striped monster that, apart from its colour, was very reminiscent of every Tyrannosaurus Rex picture he'd ever seen. The creature had to weigh several tons, was forty feet from head to tail and had teeth as long as his arm. It was coming directly at the office, roaring as it loped forward.

"Uh, are you absolutely sure that can't get in?" asked Arthur. "How come we can hear it now?"

"Monday," said the Will hurriedly. "He's used the Hour Key and Seven Dials to connect that reality and this room. So it can get in, and so can Monday! We must flee to fight another day! Do not freely give up the Key, Arthur!"

The little frog immediately jumped in the stream. Suzy almost jumped too, but hesitated, then ran to the elevator and pressed the button. Arthur followed her, drawing the Key from under his shirt.

A few seconds after he'd crossed the footbridge, the huge yellow dinosaur crashed through the trees, sending splinters flying. Its beady eyes focused on the smoke from the fire and it plunged forward, roaring and biting. Red-hot coals scattered under its feet and it roared again, this time with pain, and went into a frenzy, biting and smashing at the smoke and the summerhouse with its bony head.

Arthur and Suzy crouched by the elevator door, close to the tree trunk. Suzy started to reach up to press the call button again, but Arthur held her back.

"Don't move," he whispered. "It thought the smoke was alive, so it must have rotten eyes and can't smell. If we stay still it might go away."

They watched in silent horror as the dinosaur demolished the summerhouse completely, leaving only the foundations. Everything else was smashed and bitten into pieces. Furious at not finding anything edible, and burned by the fire, the dinosaur gave out its loudest roar yet, then crashed its way through the trees and disappeared.

"I ain't never coming back here," whispered Suzy. "Reckon it's all right to move?"

"No," said Arthur grimly. He had just spotted other movement where the dinosaur had first crashed through. A line of men had emerged from the trees. They reminded him a bit of the Fetchers, though these were tall and skinny and somewhat more human-looking, though their eyes were red and sunken, and their faces thin and pallid. They wore black too, all black, with tailcoats, and had long black ribbons around their top hats. They all carried long-handled whips, held tightly in their black-gloved hands.

"Midnight Visitors," whispered Suzy fearfully. "With nightmare-whips and night-gloves."

"Is there any other way out besides the elevator?" asked Arthur urgently.

"No," said Suzy. "There might be a weirdway, but I don't—"

She stopped as the elevator bell rang and they shared a

smile of relief. Both she and Arthur sprang up and gripped the door, sliding it open so quickly it banged against the tree. With the bang came a blinding flash of light. Arthur and Suzy staggered back and fell over on the lawn.

"So here you are," yawned Mister Monday. He stepped out of the elevator car, the Hour Key glinting in one hand and a shooting stick in the other. He yawned again, took a few more slow steps over to the lawn, plunged the shooting stick into the grass, unfolded its narrow seat and sat down.

Behind him came Noon, smiling his perfect smile. At his shoulder was a beautiful woman dressed all in pink and rose, who looked like Noon's sister and so must be Monday's Dawn. Two paces further back was another impossibly handsome man, his face the twin of Noon's. He wore a coat of black dusted with silver, and so must be Monday's Dusk.

Mister Monday was clearly taking no chances. He had gathered all his most powerful supporters. As if the three of them weren't enough, they were followed by a rush of Commissionaire Sergeants, a mass of lumbering Commissionaires and a swirl of other less identifiable people.

"Hurry up!" snapped Monday. "I'm exhausted. Someone get the Minute Key and bring it here."

Dawn, Noon and Dusk looked at one another.

"I'm waiting!"

"The Will—" said Noon cautiously. Like his siblings, his eyes continued to scan the office. All three of them kept their right hands open, as if they were about to draw weapons, though no weapons were in sight.

"The Will cannot face all of us," yawned Monday. "I expect it has already fled. Now get on with it!"

There was another slight pause. No one seemed keen to step forward. Finally Noon gestured and spoke.

"Commissionaire!" ordered Noon, pointing to where Arthur lay on his back on the grass, partially stunned by the blast, only his fluttering eyelids and moving chest indicating that he was still alive. "Take that metal object from the boy."

The Commissionaire saluted and strode forward, his legs stiff at the knees, the metal joints grinding as he moved. He stopped a pace short of Arthur, stamped his feet and came to attention. Then he bent down from the waist and reached for the Key.

It should have come easily from Arthur's hand, as the boy had no strength to hold it. In fact he was only dimly aware of what was going on. But the Key would not move. It seemed to be glued to his palm. The Commissionaire tugged at it, then knelt on one knee and tugged again, pulling painfully at Arthur's arm.

"No," groaned the half-conscious Arthur. "Please, please don't."

"Rip his arm off," ordered Noon. "Or cut it off. Whichever's quicker."

CHAPTER THIRTEEN

The Commissionaire stood back up and slowly unscrewed his right hand. He put this through his belt, then drew a much stranger hand from inside his coat. This one had no fingers, but a single broad blade like a cleaver. He screwed this hand into his wrist. As soon as it was secure, the cleaver began to jitter and move up and down so swiftly that it became a blur of steel.

The Commissionaire bent back down and lowered the knife towards Arthur's wrist. The boy cried out, but before he could do anything, or the knife could touch him, the Key suddenly shot out of his hand like an arrow. It plunged into the Commissionaire's breastbone, came out through his back, and spun once more into Arthur's hand.

There was no blood. A vague look of puzzlement crossed the Commissionaire's face. He stood up and stepped back, and the sound of grinding gears came from his torso. Then his blue coat ripped open from the inside and a spring uncoiled to hang limp and broken down his front. It was followed a moment later with a *pop-pop-pop* as a rain of small cogs tumbled out around the broken spring and fell to the ground.

The Commissionaire slowly bent his head to look at his chest, raised his one normal hand to touch it, then froze in place, with a small stream of silver fluid trickling down from the corners of his eyes and out of his mouth.

There was silence for a moment. Arthur stared at the broken Commissionaire, then at the Key in his hand, then up at his enemies. There was no chance of escape, at least not for the moment. He glanced across to Suzy Blue, but she was lying on her side, facing away, and he could not tell whether she was conscious or not.

Noon frowned and gestured to a Commissionaire Sergeant.

"Send four of your most trusted men and fetch that Key!"

The Sergeant saluted and turned to bellow orders at his metal minions. But before he could speak, Monday's Dusk spoke. Unlike Noon, his tongue was black, not silver, and his voice was a hoarse whisper.

"It is as I guessed – he has now bonded fully with the Key," he said. "So force will not avail us, unless our Master cares to risk the Greater Key against the Lesser?"

Noon looked sourly at Dusk, then over at Mister

Monday, who appeared to have fallen asleep, balanced precariously on his shooting stick. He did not answer Dusk's question, though a faint tic appeared above his right eye.

"No?" continued Dusk. "Why lose more Commissionaires, brother, to no avail? The Grim charges dear for their replacement, does he not?"

"What then? The boy will not hand it over willingly, or from fear. I have tried that."

"Let him keep it, for now," said Dusk. "He does not know how to use it. Let us put him somewhere safe and unpleasant. When he has suffered enough, he will give us the Key."

"What place is safe from the interference of the Will?" asked Noon. "Nowhere I know."

"There is one place the Will cannot go," replied Dusk. "Or dare not. The Deep Coal Cellar. The Old One will not suffer the Will to come there."

"The Old One?" Dawn shivered. Her voice was bright and loud, and her tongue was golden. "We should not meddle with him."

"He is chained." Dusk shrugged. "And he has never interfered with any of the workers in the Cellar."

"But if he can gain the Key?" asked Dawn. "He might free himself—"

"Never," said Dusk. "All the Seven Keys together could not free him from that chain."

"There are often Nithlings in the coal cellars, even in the

Deep," said Noon. "If one of them should gain the Key—"

"How, when we cannot?" whispered Dusk. "I have studied the Keys and I tell you, now it has bonded, it can only be given, not taken. It will protect its wielder from serious harm, though not entirely from pain, and not at all from discomfort. I say put the boy into the darkness and the damp. He will soon see that his only way out is to give us—"

"Me," interrupted Mister Monday, suddenly straightening up. "Give *me* the Key."

Dawn, Noon and Dusk smiled and bowed to Mister Monday before Dusk continued.

"As you say, sir. The boy will soon come to realise that he must give Mister Monday the Key."

"Delays! Difficulties!" complained Mister Monday. "But I see sense in your plan, Dusk. Take care of it. I am going back to take a nap."

"What about me, sir?" Suzy suddenly piped up. "I didn't mean to do it, sir. It was that Will that made me."

Mister Monday ignored her. He slowly stood up, left the shooting stick where it was, and ambled towards the open elevator. The Commissionaires and Sergeants saluted as he passed, and Dawn, Noon and Dusk bowed once more. The elevator door closed, then almost immediately opened again. There was no sign of Monday inside.

"Honest, sir! It wasn't my fault," Suzy continued, to Noon. She knelt down and bowed her head so low it touched the grass, her fingers scrabbling into the dirt in her distress. "Don't send me to the Coal Cellar. Let me go back to work!"

"Where is the Will?" asked Noon. He strode over to Suzy and lifted her up by the hair till she stood on tiptoe, grimacing at the pain.

"It left when the dinosaur came," Suzy cried. "It knew a weirdway out, a small one, too small for us to use."

"What shape has it assumed?" asked Noon. "Where was this weirdway?"

"The Will... the Will looked like an orange cat, but with long ears," sobbed Suzy. "It went up that tree and then... it was gone. I didn't want to do what it said, but it made me—"

Noon dropped her in disgust.

"Do you want this?" he asked Dawn and Dusk, indicating Suzy, who was once again prostrate. This time she had managed to get dirt all over her face, mixing it into mud with her tears.

Dawn shook her head. Dusk did not answer immediately. Then a slight smile flitted across his face, so slight Arthur wondered if he had imagined it.

"You are one of that irresponsible Piper's children, are you not?" asked Dusk. "Once a mortal?"

"Yes, Your Honour," sobbed Suzy. "I'm an Ink-Filler now, Sixth Class."

"An honourable occupation," replied Dusk. "You may

return to your duties, Suzy Turquoise Blue. But first wash your face and hands. This stream looks convenient for that."

Suzy stared up at him suspiciously as she heard her name, then bowed once more and stood up shakily. Only Dusk and Arthur watched her as she went over to the stream and bent down to wash. Arthur had been surprised by her wailing and begging, but now that she had gone to the exact point in the stream where the Will had dived in, he thought differently. She had her back to everyone, using it to block the view of what she was doing with her hands in the water. Which, Arthur hoped, was retrieving the Will. Not that he expected the Will to do anything, not with Monday's three powerful servants at the ready.

"Destroy this office," Noon instructed a Sergeant. He took out a notebook, scribbled something in it with a pen that appeared out of the air, tore out the page, and gave it to the Sergeant. "Use this to close the picture window."

"My Midnight Visitors and I will take Arthur to the Deep Coal Cellar," announced Dusk. He gestured to his funereal followers, and they stepped forward.

"No, they will not," countered Noon. "This is my duty. I still hold our Master's plenipotentiary powers."

"Given for the Secondary Realms, I believe," said Dusk mildly.

"That detail was omitted," replied Noon with a bright smile. He turned to Arthur and said, "Get up, boy. If you come along in a docile manner, I will not be forced to hurt you. Remember that much pain can still be visited upon you, provided we do not try to take the Key."

Dusk looked at Dawn, who shrugged.

"Noon has the right," she said. "I will accompany him."

"As you say. Sister, brother," said Dusk. He clicked his fingers and pointed up. The Midnight Visitors bowed slightly and wrapped their capes around themselves. Then they all slowly rose into the air, standing at attention as they levitated towards the ceiling. At the height of the treetops, they disappeared.

Arthur watched them go, then looked back. Dusk had disappeared and Noon and Dawn were staring back at Arthur.

"Well, boy?"

Arthur sneaked a glance at Suzy. She had stepped back from the stream but would not look at him. He couldn't tell whether she had picked up the Will and was struck by sudden doubt. What if she did only want to wash her hands, both of dirt and any responsibility to him? Or what if she did want to help, but the Will had already gone?

"I guess I don't have a choice," Arthur replied slowly. He got up and lifted his chin to show that he was not afraid. "I'll go with you."

Arthur surreptitiously looked again at Suzy as he spoke. She was still crouched above the stream, but was half looking back at him. Arthur gave her a very slow, sly wink. Suzy tapped her throat and coughed. She clearly had the Will and Arthur took some small comfort from that. Only a small comfort, but at least there was a chance of help somewhere along the line.

Noon gestured again and the Sergeants bellowed orders. A dozen metal Commissionaires marched up around Arthur, boxing him in. They were so close together, and so tall, he could barely see out between them.

"Commissionaires escorting the prisoner, by the left, slooooow march!" shouted a Sergeant. The Commissionaires stepped off, and Arthur had to start marching too, to avoid being crushed or trodden on. Somehow he doubted the Key would protect him from a bruised foot or rib.

Arthur expected at least some of the entourage to peel off before they got to the elevator. In fact he couldn't understand how so many of them had come out of the elevator in the first place. But as they continued to march in, he realised that it was not the elevator he and Suzy had used, though it was in exactly the same place. This elevator was many times larger. It was the size of the school assembly hall and was much fancier too, with highly polished wood panelling on the walls and a parquetry floor.

There was a brass-railed rotunda in the centre of the elevator. Noon and Dawn strode over and climbed up into it, while everyone else arrayed themselves in front of the rotunda, as if they were on a parade ground. Arthur had one last glimpse of Suzy talking to the Sergeant who was going to destroy the office. Then the doors slid shut and a bell sounded.

Now Arthur felt truly a prisoner. Alone among enemies.

Noon touched the air in front of him and a speaking tube appeared. He pulled it to his mouth and said, "Lower Ground twenty-twelve. Express."

Someone or something said something back. Noon frowned.

"Well, reroute it! I said *express*."

The lift suddenly lurched and fell, hurling Arthur into one of the Commissionaires, who remained rock-steady at attention. Noon and Dawn were thrown against the railings of the rotunda. Noon scowled and pulled the speaking tube towards him. Then he reached in with one long, slim finger and tugged at something. There was a stifled scream from the tube, then Noon slowly pulled out a nose he had twisted in his white-gloved fingers, followed by a mouth and chin, then a whole head complete with a battered hat – all of which was impossible for Arthur to believe since the tube was no wider than a can of soup.

A few seconds later, Noon had dragged an entire man out of the tube, dropping him on the floor next to the rotunda. The extracted fellow was short and fat. His coat was too long, its badly mended back brushing the floor.

Noon glowered down at him.

"Elevator Operator Seventh Grade?"

"No, Your Honour," said the little man. Arthur could see he was trying to be brave. "Elevator Operator Fourth Grade."

"Not any more," replied Noon. His notebook appeared in

his hand and he wrote in it quickly. Then he tore out the sheet and let it fall.

"Oh, please, Your Lordliness," said the man miserably. "I've been in grade four a hundred years—"

The paper hit the little man's shoulder and exploded into blue sparks that surrounded his head like a corona. The sparks ate away the man's squashy hat, leaving him bald, then descended to destroy his coat, his shirt and his breeches. Arthur shut one eye, not really wanting to see what might come next, particularly if the man's skin started dissolving or something. But it didn't. Instead the sparks formed into a simple toga-like robe of off-white that settled on the man in place of his former clothes.

"You didn't need to do that as well," said the elevator operator with considerable dignity. "They were hard-won, those fittings."

Noon held the speaking tube over the man's head.

"Count yourself lucky," he said. "Do not cross me again – and get back to work."

The elevator man sighed, rubbed one knuckle to his forehead in a perfunctory gesture of respect and raised his hand. It went easily into the speaking tube, then somehow all the rest of him was sucked up as well, as if the tube were a vacuum cleaner and the man was collapsible.

When he was gone, Noon spoke into the tube again.

"As we discussed. Express and smooth. Lower Ground twenty-twelve. The Upper Coal Cellar Entry."

Arthur suppressed a shudder. That sounded like a long way away from anywhere he knew. With that thought came a wave of negativity. Everything was too difficult, too hard. He might as well give up.

How can I save everyone from the plague? the depressed section of his mind said. *I can't even save myself from imprisonment.*

Stop it! Arthur told this part of himself. *Suzy and the Will are free. I've still got the Key. There will be the chance to do something. There has to be...*

CHAPTER FOURTEEN

The Upper Coal Cellar Entry was a rickety wooden platform on the edge of a blasted plain. A vast panorama of open space, dimly lit by the beams of only three or four elevators. As in the Lower Atrium, there was a ceiling above the platform, but unlike the Atrium the ceiling here was flat, not domed, and it was much higher up.

Arthur was marched out on to the platform within his box of Commissionaires. As his eyes adjusted to the dim light, he saw that the plain beyond the platform was not a totally featureless expanse as he'd thought. There was something in the middle.

A circular patch of total darkness.

A huge hole, at least half a mile in diameter and of a depth unseen and unknowable.

"Yes," said Noon, who had been watching Arthur. "That

pit is the Deep Coal Cellar. Sergeant! March the prisoner to the edge."

There was a pathway from the elevator platform to the pit. It was paved with white stone which repelled the black dust that lay everywhere else, dust that billowed up as they passed. Coal dust, Arthur guessed it was. He hoped he wasn't breathing it in and that it wouldn't still be in his lungs when... if... he ever got back home. He'd really need the Key then, to keep on breathing. There was no way his poor lungs could survive coal dust along with everything else.

As the Commissionaires marched, their legs occasionally squeaking for want of oil, Arthur tried to stay calm. Suzy had retrieved the Will, and surely it would come looking for him. Though Dusk had said that this was one place the Will wouldn't dare go, because it feared the Old One.

That doesn't sound good, whispered the defeatist part of Arthur's mind. *Stuck in a prison pit with some creature called the Old One.*

"You will not be alone down there," said Noon. He looked at Arthur knowingly, as if he had just read his mind. "There are some House Denizens down there, demoted to the most menial of tasks, chipping coal to size and so forth. They will not dare bother you. But there is one other, who you should stay away from if you value your life and sanity. He is called the Old One and he is not to be trifled with. Keep away from him and you will merely suffer from the cold, the damp and the coal dust."

"How will I know the Old One if I see him?" asked Arthur. He tried to sound defiant but it didn't come out that way. His voice sounded squeaky and small. He cleared his throat and tried again, "And how am I supposed to get out of here, if I do want to give Mister Monday the Key?"

"You'll know the Old One," said Noon. He smiled his cold smile, white teeth gleaming. "He's hard to miss. As I said, avoid him, if you can. As for getting out, just say my name three times. Monday's Noon. I'll come and fetch you. Or I'll send someone to take care of the matter."

They arrived at the edge of the pit as Noon finished speaking. The Commissionaires stopped right at the lip, with only inches separating their toes from the void. Arthur peered past them, down into darkness. He could not see how deep the pit was, or any lights below.

Noon took out his notebook and tore out a page. He quickly folded this page into the shape of two wings, serrating the edges with a small knife to give the impression of feathers. Then he wrote a word on each small paper wing and shook them slowly. With each shake they grew bigger, until Noon was holding a pair of feathery wings as tall as Arthur. They were pure white and glowing, but where Noon held them, black ink trickled down from his fingers like blood.

"Let me through," Noon instructed the Commissionaires. They stepped aside to let him pass, but the one closest to the pit thoughtlessly stepped out into nothing. He made no effort to save himself or grab the edge. He just fell into the void without making a sound, save the sigh of the air parting. Arthur didn't hear him hit the bottom.

Noon frowned, shook his head and muttered something about "inferior merchandise". Then he suddenly slapped the wings on to Arthur's back and pushed the boy extremely hard – into the pit!

Arthur felt the wings attach themselves to his shoulder blades. It was a weird sensation. Not exactly painful, but not pleasant. Rather like having a tooth filled at the dentist, with an injection removing the pain but not the vibration. The shock of this sudden attachment, and then the next shock as his wings spread and slowed his fall, took Arthur's mind off the fact that he had just been pushed into an apparently bottomless pit. By the time this had registered, his wings were beating hard and he was falling very slowly, no faster than a spider leisurely descending on her web.

Up above, and far behind him now, Arthur heard Noon laughing, and then the tromp of the metal Commissionaires' boots upon the white pavestones as they marched away.

"I'll never call you," whispered Arthur. He clutched the Key tightly in his hand. His voice came back, strong, angry and loud. "I'll find a way out. I'll sort you out and Mister Monday and the whole lot of you!"

"That's the spirit!" said a soft voice near him in the darkness. Surprised, Arthur lashed out with the Key, but the metal met no resistance. He was still falling slowly, and there was nothing around him but air and darkness.

Or was there? Arthur raised the Key and said, "Light! Shed light!"

The Key shone with sudden bright light, casting a globe of illumination around Arthur and his beating wings. In the light Arthur saw another winged figure, matching the speed of his fall. A man, all in black, his black wings as glossy and dark as a raven's, with not a touch of white.

"Monday's Dusk," spat Arthur. "What do you want?"

"It seems the Key's powers are not all unknown to you, as Noon would have it," whispered Dusk. Arthur could hardly hear him over the beating of both their wings. "As to what I want, I want to help you, Arthur. You have been chosen by the Will. You hold the Minute Key of the Lower House."

"What?" asked Arthur. Surely this was some sort of trick. "Aren't you like Monday's right-hand man or something?"

"Noon sits at the Master's right hand, Dawn at his left. Dusk stands behind, in the shadows. Yet sometimes it is easier to see the light when you stand partly in the darkness. Monday was not always as he is now. Nor were Noon and Dawn. The Lower House was not the shambles it has become. All of this has led me slowly... oh so slowly... to come to the conclusion that something must be done. I helped the Will free itself, by giving an Inspector a box of snuff. Now I will help you by giving you some advice."

Arthur snorted in disbelief. This was so obvious. He'd seen it a million times on television. Good cop, bad cop.

Noon had done the bad cop act, now it was Dusk's turn. He was pretty convincing at it, though.

"You should talk to the Old One. The others forget that while he opposed the Architect, he does not hate Her work. You are one small part of that, and so he will be interested and will not harm you. Ask him about the Improbable Stair. Use the knowledge he gives you."

"Why should I trust you?" asked Arthur.

"Why trust anyone?" Dusk replied, so quietly that Arthur could not hear him and had to repeat his question. Dusk flew closer until his face was close enough to touch, the tips of his ebony wings almost brushing Arthur's snowy ones with every forward beat.

"Why trust anyone?" he said again. "The Will wants its way. Monday wants his way, as do the Morrow Days. But who can say what those ways will lead to? Be cautious, Arthur!"

On the last word, Dusk's wings beat more strongly and he rose, while Arthur continued to fall. Arthur had no control over the wings Noon had made for him. They merely slowed his fall, like a parachute, only better.

Arthur had a long time to think about what Dusk had said. His wings kept beating and he kept falling, until he grew used to the motion and it even made him sleepy. The Deep Coal Cellar was deep indeed, deeper than any pit or mine Arthur had ever heard of in his own world, save the ocean trenches where strange life forms dwelled.

Finally there was an end to the interminable falling. Arthur had a brief warning as his wings suddenly doubled their efforts, beating furiously so he came to a complete stop. Then they detached themselves, dumping Arthur the last three or four feet on to hard, wet ground. He landed with a splash and fell over, soaking himself and almost losing the Key. A second later, two shredded pieces of paper fell next to him, to become lumps of wet pulp.

The water was only a few inches deep. Little more than a puddle, though it was not an isolated one. Arthur held up the Key so its light shed further and saw that there were puddles of water everywhere. Black water, lying stagnant in pools between stretches of marginally drier ground that were a foul, muddy mixture of coal dust and water.

There were also piles of coal. Lots and lots of small pyramids five or six feet high had been laboriously piled up every five yards or so. Arthur took a look at the closest pile. Unlike the perfectly even pieces that he'd seen Suzy use, the coal here was all misshapen lumps of very different sizes. As he walked around, Arthur saw that the pyramids were also of different sizes, and some were much better ordered than others. A few times he saw collapsed pyramids that were just dumps of loose coal.

As Noon had promised, it was cold as well as damp. *At least the water keeps the coal dust down*, Arthur thought, though it billowed up as he moved around. But he had to keep moving because it was too cold to stay still. If Suzy was right and he didn't need to eat, then he supposed he could keep moving all the time.

Except that she hadn't said anything about not needing to sleep and Arthur *was* tired. They had shifts here, he knew, so presumably that meant the people – or Denizens, as they seemed to be called – did sleep.

Hopefully the Key would protect him from getting pneumonia or a cold, if it was possible to catch such things here, despite Suzy's opinion. But it would be a miserable experience trying to sleep on a pile of coal in the cold and wet.

Arthur kept weaving between the piles of coal as he thought about what he was going to do. Should he trust Dusk? One of the last things the Will had mentioned was the Improbable Stair, as a possible means of getting to Mister Monday's Dayroom. Dusk had talked about the Improbable Stair too. Perhaps it was a way out of here as well as a way into Monday's rooms.

But to find out he would need to find the Old One and risk talking to him. Arthur had noted the shiver that had gone through Dawn and the Commissionaire Sergeants when the Old One had been mentioned. They were afraid of him, that was for sure. And the Will must also fear the Old One, Arthur concluded, or Noon and Monday would never have left him down here with the Key.

He couldn't think of an alternative. Which meant that he had to get methodical about finding the Old One. The pit was only half a mile in diameter, though many miles deep. If Arthur kept track of where he'd been, he should be able to search the whole pit in a grid pattern, though it would not be quick work.

The obvious way would be to take a few coals off each pyramid and set them down in a pattern. So whenever he came to a pyramid he would know if he'd been that way before.

Arthur sighed and went to the closest pyramid. He had just reached over to lift off a big chunk of coal from the top when someone sprang up from the other side, brandishing a weapon and squealing.

"Ho! Stop! Unhand my coal, you ruffian!"

CHAPTER FIFTEEN

Those are my coals, villain!" continued the man. Then he saw the Key in Arthur's hand and in midbreath changed his tone, immediately lowering the strange metal implement he was brandishing. "Oh, not you, sir, whoever you may be. I am referring to someone else. There he goes!"

Puzzled, Arthur looked where the man pointed. But there was no one there.

"I'll just get back to work then, sir," added the man. He was dressed in the same basic toga-like robe that the elevator operator had been reduced to, though this one was black as the coal and very tattered. He was also short, a head shorter than Arthur, though he otherwise had the physique of a grown man.

"Who are you?" asked Arthur.

"Coal-Collator Very Ordinary Tenth Grade," reported the man. "Number 9665785553 in precedence."

"I mean what's your name?"

"Oh, I haven't got a name, not any more. Very few of us down here have names, Your Excellency. Not what you would call names, no, sir. May I go now?"

"Well, what *was* your name?" asked Arthur. "And what were you before you were down here?"

"That's a cruel question, and no mistake," said the man. He wiped a tear from his eye. "But there's the Key in your hand, so I must answer. I was called Pravuil, sir, Tenth Assistant Deputy Clerk of Stars. I counted suns in the Secondary Realms, I did, sir, and kept their records. Till I was asked to amend the paperwork pertaining to a certain sun. I... ah... refused and was cast from on high."

"I don't want to... I don't want to upset you," said Arthur. "But what do you do down here?"

"I collate the coal into piles," explained Pravuil. He indicated the pyramids. "Then one of the Coal-Chippers comes and cuts the coals to size and puts them in a request basket, which takes them up to whoever ordered coal, probably so long ago they've forgotten what a fire is and become used to shivering."

"Baskets?" asked Arthur. "What kind of baskets? How do they get taken up?"

"I see your thinking, sir," replied Pravuil. "Escape, that's what you're thinking. Lax procedures. Someone you'll want to punish. But it's not so. The baskets are small and they come with active labels. The labels take them where they're supposed to go. And if you're thinking that a label might be detached and used to transport someone, you'd be wrong, as Bareneck would tell you if he can ever find his head down here."

"Bareneck?"

"That's what we call him. He took a label off a basket and tied it around his neck," said Pravuil with a sniff. "I told him it was stupid, but he wouldn't listen. The label went up, but it didn't take any of Bareneck with it. Cut clean through his neck it did, and the head rolled off somewhere and his body blundered around knocking coal all over the place. I expect he'll find it eventually. His head, I mean. Or someone else will."

Arthur shuddered and looked around, half expecting to see a headless man groping around in the darkness, forever searching for his head. Or even worse, the head lying buried somewhere here, with senses intact, but no way to communicate, immured under the coal.

"I'm not investigating anything," said Arthur. "I have the Key, but I'm not an official of the House. Or a friend of Mister Monday. I'm a mortal, from outside."

"Whatever you say, sir," Pravuil said, with unveiled suspicion. Clearly he thought Arthur was trying to trick him into something. "I'll be getting on with my work."

"Before you go, can you tell me... or show me... where the Old One is down here?"

Pravuil shivered and made a gesture with his hand.

"Don't go near him!" he warned. "The Old One can finish you off permanent-like. Reduce you to Nothing, less than a Nithling, with no chance of coming back!"

"I have to," said Arthur slowly. At least, he thought he had to. There didn't seem to be any other way out of here.

"That way," whispered Pravuil. He pointed. "The coal will not be ordered there. No one dare sweep around the Old One."

"Thank you," said Arthur. "I hope you are restored to your old position one day."

Pravuil shrugged and resumed work. The strange implement he held, Arthur finally saw, was a kind of weird broom and pan combination that formed swept-up coal dust back into irregular pieces of coal, which Pravuil then stacked.

Arthur started in the direction that Pravuil had indicated. A few seconds after the light from the Key had left the Coal-Collator behind, his voice echoed out of the darkness.

"Don't stay past twelve!"

"What does that mean?"

There was no answer. Arthur stopped to listen, but there was only silence. When he retraced his steps to ask again, there was no sign of Pravuil. There was only the pyramid of coal he'd been working on, with a few new pieces on top.

"Excellent," muttered Arthur to himself. "More advice. Don't go near the Old One. Do go near the Old One. Don't stay past twelve. Trust the Will. Don't trust the Will. I wish someone would tell me something straightforward for once."

He paused as if there might be an answer, but of course there wasn't. Arthur shook his head and started off again. To make sure that he could find his way back if he needed to, he took off ten pieces of coal from the first pyramid and stacked it in a pattern at the base. At the next pyramid, he took nine pieces, eight from the next, and so on, till he was down to one, when he started again but also used a separate piece of coal to indicate it was the second progression.

By the time he'd repeated this procedure across one hundred and twenty-six pyramids of coal, Arthur was doubting several things. First, that he would ever find the Old One, second, that Pravuil had shown him the right direction, and third, that the pit he was in was only the size it appeared to be from its above-ground opening.

He was also getting very cold, despite the constant walking. He didn't feel hungry, but he still wished for something to eat, because it would warm him up. At least he thought it would. Certainly it would relieve the boredom of trekking through this freezing, wet, dark dump of a place with nothing but coal everywhere.

Because he was tired, Arthur had been holding the Key lower and lower by his side, so the circle of light it shed around him had grown smaller and smaller, until it was only illuminating the ground around his feet. Beyond that light lay only darkness, until Arthur suddenly caught a glimpse of something that was not illuminated by the Key or a reflection. It was another light. A blue, shimmering light, as if there was a gas fire somewhere ahead.

Arthur raised the Key higher and walked faster. Surely this must be where the Old One lurked. He felt nervous and excited at the same time. Nervous because Dawn and the Commissionaire Sergeants had been genuinely afraid of the Old One, as had Pravuil. Excited, because it was something different from cold puddles and coal. He might be able to get food or, even better, find a way out.

As he got closer to the light, Arthur slowed down and held the Key still higher. He didn't want to be surprised by anything. Every shadow behind a pyramid of coal promised some sort of ambush, but the pyramids were getting fewer, as were the puddles. He was coming to open ground. Drier, higher ground. There was even less of the muddy coal dust beneath his feet and more patches of dry stone.

At the last pyramid of coals, Arthur crouched down to look at what lay ahead. He had to blink a lot, since it was hard to see in the strange combination of light from the Key and the shimmering blue radiance that bathed the area ahead.

He saw a raised circular platform, rather like a low stage made of stone, about sixty feet in diameter. There were Roman numerals set upright around the edge of the platform, and two long pieces of metal issued out from a central pivot, one piece shorter than the other. As Arthur watched, the longer piece of metal moved a little, progressing along the rim.

It was a minute hand, Arthur suddenly realised. The circular platform was a clock face. A giant clock face laid flat. But that wasn't the strangest thing. There were chains leading from the ends of the clock hands that ran through some mechanism of gears and pulleys near the central pivot that he couldn't quite work out. The chains then connected to manacles on the wrists of a man who was sitting near the numeral six. It was the chains that shed the glimmering light. They looked like steel but could not be. No steel shone with such a vivid spectral blue.

Nor was the man precisely a man, Arthur thought, taking in the size of him. He was a giant, easily eight feet tall. He looked like some sort of aged barbarian hero, with overdeveloped muscles along his arms and legs, though his skin was old, wrinkled and partially translucent so you could see the veins. He wore only a loincloth and his head was shaved to a stubble. He seemed to be asleep, though his closed eyes looked kind of strange. The eyelids were raw and red, as if he'd been sunburned. Which was impossible down here. Or anywhere in the House, for all Arthur knew.

This, Arthur figured, must be the Old One, and he was chained to the clock's hands. Arthur gingerly sneaked closer to study the gears and wheels of the chain mechanism. It wasn't easy to work them out, but after watching for a few minutes, Arthur thought that the chains would be quite loose around half-past six, but would be very tight at twelve. In fact, they must drag the giant back almost to the centre of the clock at noon and midnight.

At the moment, the hands were on twenty-five to seven, so the Old One had enough slack to sit next to the numeral six. Judging from the length of the chains at that moment, Arthur guessed the prisoner would not be able to move past the border of the clock face.

There were two trapdoors on either side of the central pivot. Both were the size of regular doors, with arched peaks. Like the doors of a cuckoo clock. Somehow Arthur suspected it would not be cuckoos that came out of these doors.

"Beware!" shouted the Old One suddenly.

Arthur leaped back and tripped over some loose bits of coal. As he scrabbled to get up again, he heard the rattle of chains. Panic rose as he scrabbled on the ground.

But he was too slow. The giant had been holding the chains close against his body, to disguise how much slack he really had, and in an instant the Old One was standing over Arthur. He looked even taller and meaner close up. His open eyes weren't much better than his closed ones. They were red-rimmed and bloodshot. One pupil was gold and the other black.

"Have you seen enough, Key-bearer?" asked the Old One as he casually looped a piece of his chain over Arthur's head and pulled it tight around Arthur's neck. Arthur struck at him with the Key, but it didn't even scratch the giant's flesh.

There was no burst of molten fluid, or electric sparks, or anything. Arthur might as well have hit him with a plastic clock hand.

"Did your masters not tell you that nothing of the House can harm me?" growled the giant. "And nothing of Nothing, save the creatures of this clock, who nightly gnaw and gouge my eyes? But I give you my thanks for the moment of entertainment you shall give me as I rend you limb from limb and consign your essence to the void!"

CHAPTER SIXTEEN

I'm not from the House!" croaked Arthur. "I'm not an enemy!"

The Old One growled and tightened the chain till it hurt. Then he pulled Arthur upright and sniffed the air above his head. After the third sniff he abruptly let out a few links of chain so it wasn't so tight, though it was still around Arthur's neck.

"A mortal in truth," he said in a somewhat friendlier tone. "From a world I know well. You have robbed me of my amusement, manikin. So you must provide by other means. How comes a mortal to bear the Lesser Key of the Lower House?"

"The Will—" Arthur began, but before he could go on, the Old One suddenly lifted the chain over Arthur's head and let it hang slack. A few seconds later both the minute and the hour hand of the clock behind him moved closer to twelve. The chain rattled as it tightened and made him step back.

Arthur gulped. If that loop of chain had still been around his neck it would have strangled him, and he now seriously doubted Suzy's words about the difficulty of dying in the House. Clearly the Old One had the capacity to kill – or easily deliver some sort of final ending that sounded remarkably like death.

"Speak, mortal!" commanded the Old One. "Tell me your name. Fear not, for I was always a friend to your folk. It is the Architect who is my foe. I bear no ill will to the things She has wrought. Indeed, I too had a hand in your making long ago, though the Architect sought to deny my artistry."

"My name is Arthur Penhaligon," said Arthur. He spoke slowly at first, then sped up as he worked it out in his head. "I'm not really sure why I have the Key. The Will tricked Mister Monday into giving it to me, but now he wants it back and that's why I was put down here, till I agree to hand it over. Only before that the Will said I have to get the Hour Hand and take over the Lower House, because that's the only way that I can get home and stop the plague that the Fetchers brought with them..."

"Hold!" commanded the Old One. "This is no simple tale. You will begin at the beginning, go on to the middle, and... already I can see there is not yet an end. First we will drink wine and eat honey cakes."

"I would like a cake," said Arthur. He looked around to see where cakes and wine might come from, but there was no sign of any larder, or kitchen, or waiters, though nothing would have surprised him at that point.

The Old One held out his hand, palm down towards the ground, and intoned:

"Sweet cakes of almond meal, sticky with honey,
A dozen piled on a platter of woven straw.
A pitcher of wine from the sun-kissed hills,
Flavoured with resin from the crack-barked pine."

Arthur felt the floor under his feet shiver as the Old One spoke. Then the stone cracked and groaned apart. In the fissure, a pool of darkness slowly rose, till it lapped out and spread across the floor near Arthur's feet. He stepped back as the darkness changed colour and quickly coalesced into an earthenware jug and a flat-sided basket full of delicious-looking small cakes.

The fissure snapped shut as the Old One bent down to pick up the food and wine.

"Where did they come from?" asked Arthur. He wasn't sure he wanted a honey cake all that badly now.

"Nothing lies close beneath us here," said the Old One. He upended the jug and poured a continuous stream of light-coloured wine into his mouth. "Ahhh! If you have the power, or a tool of power like your Key, many things can be brought forth from Nothing. After all, it is where everything began. Even the Architect came from Nothing, as did I, hard upon Her heels. Here, drink!"

He passed the jug. Arthur took it and tried to pour it as he'd just seen. But it was much harder than it looked and he splashed more wine on his chin than he got in his mouth. When he swallowed, he wished he hadn't got any wine in at all. It tasted horrible, like licorice, and burned his throat.

The honey cakes were much better, though they were very sticky. They had pieces of orange peel all through them and were soft and moist. Arthur ate three of them in quick succession. The Old One ate the other nine with considerable relish.

"Now, tell me your tale," commanded the Old One after he had brushed the last of the crumbs from his chin and chest. "And wet your throat when you have need."

Arthur shook his head at the offered jug. But he told the Old One everything, from the first appearance of Mister Monday and Sneezer. The giant listened carefully, sitting with one knee up and his chin rested upon his fist. Every now and then he moved from this position so that the chains did not jerk him back when the clock hands moved.

When Arthur was finished, the hands stood at twenty to nine and the Old One was kneeling a few feet inside the rim of the clock face, with Arthur sitting by the numeral eight, on the safe side of the minute hand. It was warm on the clock face, a gentle warmth, like that given by the sun on a clear, calm winter's day. Arthur felt much more comfortable... and extremely tired.

"This is a curious tale," rumbled the giant. "One where I must weigh my part. It is true I am the enemy of the Architect whose Will has made you its agent. Yet I am not the friend of Mister Monday or the Morrow Days, whose petty usurpation offends me more than any enmity I have for the Architect. Yet should I help you, hinder you, or simply let be? I must think on it. Rest here, Arthur, till I know my mind."

Arthur nodded sleepily. He was very, very tired and it would be extremely easy to stretch out here and take a nap. But there were those creepy doors at the centre of the clock, and Pravuil's warning... Even if the Key kept him sort of safe, he didn't want to suffer pain.

"Will you promise to wake me before twelve?" he asked. The Old One seemed trustworthy, at least to the extent that he would keep a small promise like that.

"Twelve?" asked the Old One. He too looked at the doors. "I should not ponder for so long."

"Do you promise?" asked Arthur again. He could barely get the words out, his jaw an effort to move, and his eyes so heavy they were inexorably sliding shut.

"I will wake you before twelve," confirmed the Old One.

Arthur smiled and collapsed on to the warm clock face. The Old One watched him, turning his hands so that the chains clanked quietly together.

"But how long before twelve, I do not know," whispered

- the Old One a minute later. He looked at the doors again and hooded his eyes. "Shall I let them have your sight so that I might sleep a single night without torture? Or shall I suffer as I always suffer, and give you what help I can?"

Arthur was woken by a shout, a shout that filled his whole body with sound. It felt like the sound hurled him upright, though it was actually his adrenaline-spiked muscles.

"Wake, Arthur! Run! Run, or they will have you!"

For a frozen moment, Arthur stood dazed and disoriented, the Old One's shout echoing inside his head. Then a tremendously loud bell struck somewhere near, the vibrations almost shaking him off his feet, like an earth tremor. At the same time he heard the two doors near the centre of the clock bang open and a horrid, high-pitched giggle came from whatever was inside.

The next thing Arthur knew he was in full flight, tripping and stumbling off the clock face, then sprinting as fast as he could to the border where the pyramids of coal began.

He was halfway there when the bell tolled again, shaking the ground once more. Obviously it was the clock, striking noon or midnight. After the bell, the horrible giggling continued, accompanied by the sound of clockwork unwinding and the ratchet of moving gears.

Arthur threw himself behind a pyramid of coal at the same time as the clock struck for the third time. Again, both the ground and the air vibrated with the bell, and pieces of coal fell off on the boy's head.

By now thoroughly awake and thoroughly frightened, Arthur's immediate desire was to run like crazy into the coal field. He wanted to get away from the tolling bell, the insane cackling and the zinging sound of clockwork. The fear was so strong that he turned to run, holding the Key high to illuminate his way. But after a couple of steps, he forced himself to stop. What was he running from? Just a noise and nothing more. What if he couldn't find his way back to the clock and the Old One? He still had to find a way out and the Old One offered the best chance of that. He couldn't give up that chance because he was afraid of a noise. Arthur took a deep breath and turned around to see if there actually was anything to be afraid of.

He had to squint because the blue light was shimmering even brighter than before. The Old One's arms were behind his back, held tight by the chains against the hands of the clock, which were both on the twelve. His ankles appeared to be stuck against the hands further down, though Arthur couldn't see any chains or anything else. But it was clear the giant couldn't move at all.

The doors on either side of the central pivot suddenly slammed open. As Arthur watched, a small figure hopped out of each door. One began to move jerkily out towards the numeral nine and the other to the three on the opposite side.

The first figure was a caricature of a woodchopper, a little man in green with a feather in his cap, no taller than Arthur. He held an axe that was almost as big as he was, which chopped up and down haltingly as he moved. The second figure was a short fat woman with an apron and a frilly cap. She held a giant corkscrew, at least two feet long, which she held in front of her, turning it with irregular motions as she advanced across the clock.

Both of them appeared to be made of wood, but looked horribly alive at the same time. Their eyes flickered from side to side and their mouths seemed human, lips curled back every few seconds to let out their awful giggling noise. But their arms were not human at all. They were jointed like a puppet's and moved in fits and starts. Their legs did not bend, but stayed straight, and they proceeded around the clock as if they were on wheels, or being dragged along by hidden wires.

When they reached the nine and the three, they turned towards the Old One and advanced upon him. As the woodsman passed the ten, he began to chop faster. As the woman glided past the two, she started to turn her corkscrew more rapidly.

Arthur watched in horror. The Old One couldn't move at all, couldn't do anything to stop these hideous puppet things. Arthur knew they were intent on doing something horrible. But what could he do? He couldn't just stand and watch.

Arthur looked at the Key, hefted it like a knife and took a step forward.

As he stepped out from behind the pyramid, the clock struck again, perhaps the fifth stroke of its full twelve. As the echoes died, the woodsman and the corkscrew woman stopped just short of the Old One. Arthur took another step and both of the puppet things rotated in place, staring back at the boy.

"No! Don't!"

Someone clutched at Arthur's sleeve. He swung around, the Key ready to strike, but it was only Pravuil. The Coal-Collator gripped Arthur's elbow and tried to drag him back behind the pyramid.

"It is the Old One's punishment. Nothing can be done. They would simply take *your* eyes as well," said Pravuil. "And I do not think yours would regrow with the same facility as the Old One's. Not when taken by the clock-marchers."

"What?" asked Arthur, aghast. "They take out his eyes?"

He glanced back as he spoke and wished he hadn't for the microsecond it took him to look away again. The woodsman and the woman had advanced next to the twelve. They were standing on the Old One's chest, looking down at his face, and both axe and corkscrew were about to descend.

"Let us retreat a little further," said Pravuil anxiously. "They can sometimes leave the clock face, you know! Yes, it is his eyes for now, though for many centuries they took his liver."

"His liver?!"

"It is a punishment laid upon him by the Architect," explained Pravuil as he quickly led the way behind a particularly large pyramid of coals, with constant glances over his shoulder. "Every twelve hours, for ever and ever. He will regrow his eyes by two or three o'clock, only to have them... ah... attacked nine hours later."

"But what did he do to deserve this?" asked Arthur.

"Deserve? I don't know about *deserve*," muttered Pravuil. "Did I deserve to be sent down here? As to what he did, I have no idea. Best not to inquire about that sort of thing. I gather it had something to do with interfering in the Architect's work in the Secondary Realms. She is a jealous creator, you know. Or was."

The clock struck again. Both Arthur and Pravuil flinched at the bell.

"But if the Architect's gone, why isn't the Old One free?"

"Her work inside the House cannot be undone," said Pravuil. "Lesser beings may meddle in the Secondary Realms, but the House is constant. Well, apart from minor decorations and fittings, wallpaper and suchlike. But anything big like the Old One and the clock, that's fixed for ever."

Arthur shivered, not just from the returning cold. He thought again of that chopping axe and the turning corkscrew, and the Old One chained and defenceless, his eyes open... and that would happen every twelve hours for eternity? It was too awful to think about, but he knew he wouldn't be able to not think about it. He had to distract himself.

"Why did you come back to help me?" Arthur asked.

"I had a visit from Monday's Dusk," said Pravuil. He still kept looking over his shoulder, though he seemed a little more relaxed. "Scared the wings off me. Or would have, if I still had any. But he was very nice. He... um... promised me some small luxuries if I assisted you. Is it true you're a mortal? Even though you have the Lesser Key?"

"Yes," said Arthur.

"And you are a Rightful Heir to the Lower House?"

"Well, that's what the Will says," replied Arthur uncomfortably. "Actually, I just want to get home with a cure—"

He faltered as the clock struck again, and Pravuil went down on one knee before him.

"Let me swear my allegiance to the true Master of the Lower House," pledged Pravuil. "Though I am but a mere Coal-Collator, I will serve the Master as best I am able."

Arthur nodded and wondered what he was supposed to do. Pravuil looked up at him eagerly as if he expected Arthur to do something. The clock struck again as Arthur hesitated. He wasn't sure what he was supposed to do, and there was still something shifty about Pravuil. Something that he instinctively didn't trust. But perhaps the Denizen would be more trustworthy if Arthur let him swear allegiance...

As the bell's sound echoed around them, he thought of films he had seen, and knights and kings. He lightly tapped Pravuil on each shoulder with the Key. The clock hand shone brighter as it touched the Denizen and some of its light flowed into Pravuil.

"I accept your allegiance and, um... thank you for it," said Arthur. "You may arise, ah, Sir Pravuil."

"Sir Pravuil!" exclaimed the man as he stood. "That's very fine, thank you, my lord! I like that."

Arthur stared at him. Pravuil had been a little shorter than he was. Now he was several inches taller. He was standing much straighter, but that couldn't explain this gain in height. He also looked less ugly and Arthur realised his rather large nose had shrunk, and most of the caked-on coal dust had fallen off his face.

The clock struck once more. Arthur noticed that the last few chimes had been much closer together. He'd lost count, but perhaps this was the last, the stroke of twelve. It was followed a moment later by the sound of slamming doors.

"Was that... the clock-marchers going back inside the clock?" asked Arthur. He was already wondering when he could go back and ask the Old One about the Improbable Stair. If it was the way out, he wanted to get on it.

"That was indeed their doors closing," said Pravuil. "If they haven't left the clock face, they always return on the twelfth stroke. But it is best not to trouble the Old One till his eyes have regrown. Would you like a cup of tea?"

"Yes," said Arthur. "I would."

"We will have to go a little way, to my... ahem... camp, I suppose you would call it," said Pravuil, with a bow and a sweep of his arm. "Fortunately, Dusk's providence included a little box of the best Ceylon tea and some sugar biscuits. I haven't had a cup of tea for... oh... a century at least."

"How long have you been down here?"

"Ten thousand years, give or take a month," said Pravuil. "Very dull it's been too, my lord."

"I don't suppose you know anything about the Improbable Stair, do you?" asked Arthur as they walked between coal pyramids. "Or the powers of my Key?"

"I fear not, sir, I fear not," replied Pravuil. "I know of the Improbable Stair, at least by hearsay. It is supposed to be the Architect's personal stair and was used by Her to reach all parts of Her creation, both in the House and beyond. But that is all I know. As to the powers of your Key, I was only a cataloguer of stars, and a relatively junior one at that. Such things as the Keys to the Kingdom were well beyond my purview. But the Old One will know, I'm sure, being as how he is the Old One, the oldest save the Architect Herself. A left turn here, sir, and then left again—"

He stopped talking as Arthur stopped walking. Both had heard the same thing. A stealthy step behind them, the soft *zing* of clockwork, and the faint *swish* of air, as if it had been disturbed by something moving up and down.

Something like an axe...

CHAPTER SEVENTEEN

Quick!" Pravuil gasped. "Up the pyramid!"

He leaped forward and was halfway up one of the pyramidal stacks of coal before Arthur could even move. But when the boy tried to follow the Coal-Collator, he went feet first into the pyramid and the whole thing collapsed, almost burying him.

Arthur struggled out from under the collapsed heap, his heart racing. There was coal dust everywhere, in his eyes and all over his face. He couldn't see a thing, but he could hear the zinging clockwork and the chopping noise, and then an axe blade suddenly chopped down right in front of him, heading straight at his wrist.

Somehow, Arthur managed to parry the blow with the Key. But he felt the shock of it all through his arm and the Key didn't do anything magical to defend him. In a flash of fear, Arthur realised that whatever magic it possessed was not strong enough to save him from these monsters. The Key might be the work of the Architect, but so were they, and they were made to gouge out the eyes and liver of someone much more powerful than Arthur.

"They can't climb!" screamed Pravuil, who was teetering on top of another pyramid, his arms outstretched for balance. "Climb up!"

"How?!" screamed Arthur as he rolled out of the way of another blow and sprang to his feet. The woodsman was right in front of him, but where was the corkscrew woman?

Something flashed in the corner of his eye. Instinctively, Arthur jumped away, crashing into another pyramid. Coal cascaded around him as the vicious corkscrew drilled the air where he had been an instant before.

Arthur pushed through the coal and sprinted away. But the woodsman was moving impossibly fast on his right and once again he'd lost sight of the corkscrew woman. Arthur couldn't believe the puppet monsters could move so fast. The woodsman's legs stayed completely stiff and still, but he scuttled swifter than a rat across a kitchen floor. Too fast for Arthur to run away from him.

He jumped at another pyramid as the woodsman hacked at his legs. But once again the coal scattered everywhere and all it did was slow Arthur down. He turned and slashed back at the woodsman with the Key, but it didn't do anything beside scrape across the puppet's wooden skin.

Panic was overtaking Arthur's brain. He ducked under the axe, almost fell as he feinted past the corkscrew woman, and ran again, this time for the biggest pyramid he could see. He had to do something to make it stay together, something to make the pieces of coal stick—

"Coal! Stick together!" screamed Arthur as he jumped, holding the Key out so it struck the coal before he did.

The coal did stick together. Arthur hit the pyramid and bounced off, right back into the path of the woodsman and the corkscrew woman. The axe fell as Arthur rolled aside, right into the path of the descending corkscrew.

Arthur just managed to get the Key in the way and shove the corkscrew aside. It bored into the stone floor with a shower of sparks and the woman's insane giggling became an angry shriek.

Arthur rolled again, got up on all fours and speed-crawled up the now stable pyramid of coal like a lizard up a tree. When he was perched on top, he slowly stood up and looked down, his breath coming in sobs of relief.

The two puppets circled the pyramid. Not only could they not climb, they couldn't look up either. Their necks were as stiff as their legs.

"Well done, my lord!" cried Pravuil, who was several pyramids away. He held a candle in his hand that shed far more light than any candle outside of a movie. Arthur noticed that the whole candle shone, and the flame didn't move. "Now we just have to wait till they go back in."

Arthur sighed and crouched back down, unable to trust his balance.

"How long will that take?"

"They will go in on the hour," said Pravuil. "Or faster, if they catch someone sooner."

"Are there many... um... people down here?" asked Arthur.

Pravuil shrugged. "Perhaps a hundred Coal-Collators, and fifty Coal-Cutters. A few others who have ended up down here without any employment at all."

"We have to warn them," said Arthur. The woodsman and the woman had disappeared out of the circle of light from the Key. They were out there in the darkness now, creeping around. They could easily fall upon some unsuspecting Coal-Collator or Cutter who was intent on work. "We'll have to shout. Sound should carry a long way down here."

"Oh, I shouldn't worry," said Pravuil. "Even if they do run across someone, they'll only gouge out their eyes. While not as robust as the Old One, most of us would grow eyes or a liver back in a month or two. And you forget the pain. They got me once, a long time ago. Of course, they were vultures then. Almost preferable to these clockwork horrors, though they were particularly nasty vultures—"

"I think we should try at least," said Arthur. Judging from the speed with which Pravuil had jumped out of the way of the clockwork figures, he thought the other workers down here would be glad of a warning. "We can shout together. How about, 'Look out! The clock things are loose!' On the count of three. One... two... three!"

"The tock lings are goose!" shouted Pravuil, or something that sounded like it, and he was half a second behind Arthur's shout. The boy frowned and tried again several times, but Pravuil never got it right, or didn't want to. Still, Arthur thought, the noise at least might have warned somebody.

"Do you have friends down here?" he asked after they'd sat in silence for a few minutes. The cold was starting to bite into Arthur again and he knew it was going to get worse.

"Friends? I fear not," sighed Pravuil. "We're forbidden to talk to one another, except upon business, and you never know who might be a spy or a visiting Inspector or suchlike. That's what I thought you were at first, my lord, though of course my superior intelligence soon penetrated your disguise."

"I thought Dusk told you who I was," said Arthur. Pravuil wasn't getting any more likable.

"Well, he did, but I already had more than an inkling as to what was what, what?"

"Tell me about the Secondary Realms," said Arthur. "What are they exactly?"

"Hmmm, very tricky, tough question," replied Pravuil. He took off his tattered hat and scratched his head. "There is the House, you see, which is here. Then there is Nothing, which is not here, but the House is built upon it. Then there are the Secondary Realms, which are out there, outside the House and not connected to Nothing. The Secondary Realms all started as a sort of Nothing that the Architect just threw out there, and this expanded into all kinds of things like stars and planets and so on, and then some of those planets kept developing and living things emerged and we in the House keep the records of them too, along with everything else, but that's all. That's the Original Law. No interference, none permissible! Watch and record only! Well, first of all the Old One went out there and interfered quite a lot, but he was chained up. Serves him right, I say. Then the Trustees interfered just a little bit when the Architect first went away and then a little bit more and I wouldn't be surprised if they've been up to all sorts of things, only I've been trapped down here, so I wouldn't know, but I say if a mortal shows up with the Lesser Key of the Lower House then there must be a lot going on that shouldn't."

Pravuil stopped to draw breath. As he was about to start again, a scream sounded in the distance. A scream that made Arthur shiver and feel sick, for in the scream were two barely identifiable words.

"My eyes!"

"Oh, good," said Pravuil happily. "We can get down now. My camp isn't too far away."

Arthur climbed down reluctantly, though now that he knew how to make the coal stick, he could easily climb another pyramid if necessary. And he knew that whoever had lost eyes would grow them back, but he still couldn't forget that terrible scream. Or the fact that Pravuil couldn't care less what happened to anybody else. He considered that as he followed the Coal-Collator. Arthur thought he was pretty good at figuring out what people would do and what they were really like. Pravuil had refused to do something he wasn't supposed to and had suffered for it. But then he appeared to have his own interests very much at heart. A strange contrast. Though perhaps it could be explained by the fact that Pravuil wasn't really a person. Or he was a person, but he wasn't really human. He was a Denizen. No one in the House was human, except maybe the children like Suzy who had once been mortals. But even they were changed. Arthur wasn't sure exactly what the others were, let alone what the Old One was, or the Architect. He really didn't want to dwell on it, particularly since his thoughts were heading in a direction that he was uncomfortable with. None of his family went to Church and he knew very little about any religion. Now he kind of wished he did and was also kind of glad that he didn't.

Pravuil's camp, when they finally got to it after traversing more freezing coal-strewn wasteland, consisted of a small wooden chest, a threadbare armchair and a weird-looking metal urn about three feet high that had lots of taps, spigots and little drawers. It glowed with a dull heat and Arthur was glad to put his hands near it.

Pravuil explained that the urn was called a samovar and that it was his most precious possession, bequeathed to him by a Coal-Collator who had been reprieved and returned upstairs. According to Pravuil, the samovar, if correctly supplied with raw ingredients, could provide hot tea, mulled wine, coffee or cocoa.

This turned out to be almost true. Pravuil filled one of the drawers rather hesitantly with some of the tea Dusk had given him. But after some spouting of steam and considerable rattling, he was disconcerted to find that every tap and spigot dispensed a rather nasty blend of cocoa and wine. After several attempts to fix this, Pravuil finally ended up with something hot, pale and amber that tasted faintly of apples. He served Arthur some of this in a pewter flagon that was a foot high and had a broken lid.

Arthur drank it gratefully. He was very cold and whatever the fluid was it warmed him up.

"Why don't you conjure up tea from Nothing?" he asked after a few mouthfuls had revived him. "Like the Old One?"

"If only I could," sighed Pravuil with an angry glare at the samovar. "But that is a great magic, to work with Nothing. The Old One is an adept, of course, though limited by his chains. Apart from him, there would be few in the House who can work with Nothing, particularly without assistance from some object of power, like your Key."

"I see," said Arthur. He wondered if he could use the Key himself to conjure something out of Nothing. But common sense told him it would be best not to try without some expert help. What if he called up a whole bunch of Nithlings like the ones who'd come up out of the cobbles in the Atrium?

Thinking of expert help reminded Arthur that he needed to talk to the Old One as soon as possible. He wondered if enough time had passed for the Old One's eyes to grow back, and that led immediately to wondering how much time might have passed back home. Though the Will had said time between the House and the Secondary Realms was flexible, Arthur worried that he had been away too long. If he'd been missing for a day, then his parents would be terribly worried. Unless they had the Sleepy Plague already, in which case every minute was too long to delay getting back with a cure...

"What time is it?" asked Arthur. "Is it safe to approach the Old One?"

"Mmmm, hard to say what time it is for the Old One," replied Pravuil. "Unless we look at his clock. Shall we go and see?"

CHAPTER EIGHTEEN

Pravuil hung back as they approached the clock and then stopped altogether.

"I'll wait here if you don't mind, my lord," he said. He kept his head bowed and he avoided Arthur's gaze. "The Old One can be a little bit tetchy. Though of course he won't be to you, Master."

Arthur looked at him suspiciously. Pravuil hadn't been afraid to go quite a bit closer before. What was he up to?

"What does 'a little bit tetchy' mean?" he asked. "What will he do?"

"That's really quite difficult to say..."

"Well, what sort of things does he do? And what doesn't he like?"

"Well, last time I went up to the clock he threatened to pull my head off and kick it over the rim of the pit. I'd never find it if he did that. I'd be worse off than Bareneck."

"But why?" asked Arthur. "He was quite friendly to me, once he knew who I was."

"You're a mortal and you carry the Lesser Key," said Pravuil. "It's the Denizens of the House the Old One doesn't like. He said he particularly didn't like me for some reason. I can't think why. So I'll just wait here, shall I?"

"Do whatever you like," said Arthur. He thought Pravuil was up to something, but he didn't have time to argue with him and there was no point trying to drag him closer. "Just remember you swore to serve me, Sir Pravuil."

"Oh, yes, a chap couldn't forget that!" said Pravuil brightly, but still he didn't look Arthur in the eye. "I stand by my words. Good luck, my lord. Sir."

Arthur nodded and began to cross the open ground between the coal pyramids and the clock. He could see the Old One now. The giant was crouched in his thinking position, near the numeral two. His chains were still quite tight and it was clear he couldn't move beyond the first quarter of the clock.

Arthur walked slowly towards him. He was glad to see that the doors on the clock were shut, though he only had Pravuil's word for it that the horrid puppet things had gone back inside.

The Old One looked up as Arthur stepped up and on to the clock face. His eyes were red, but they were there. If it weren't for the splashes of dried blood upon his cheeks

Arthur would have doubted that the giant's eyes had been the targets of the woodsman's axe and the woman's corkscrew.

"Greetings, Old One."

The Old One inclined his head in what might be a very restrained greeting. But he did not speak, nor did he smile or show any other sign of welcome. Arthur started to feel nervous. He remembered the feel of the chain around his neck and he wondered if his own head could be reattached if it was severed from his body by the Old One. Somehow he doubted it.

"I've come back to see if you've decided to help me or not," Arthur announced as he took several more slow steps towards the Old One. "You said you wouldn't need that much time to think about it. Then the things came out of the doors—"

"Yes," growled the Old One. "I deliberated too long and almost gave you to them. If you had stayed another second on the clock, they would have taken your eyes."

"They came out and took somebody's," said Arthur, restraining his anger. "Why didn't you wake me earlier?"

"I wished to test myself, to see if I could let a sleeping boy pay terribly for my night's rest," rumbled the Old One. "At the last, I could not. I am pleased that this is so. You have earned some answers, Arthur. Ask me three questions and no more, and I shall answer."

Arthur almost asked the Old One why only three

questions, but bit his lip just in time. That would have counted as a question for sure and then he'd only have two left. He had to think carefully about this.

"You may begin," said the Old One, breaking Arthur's train of thought. "I will give you two minutes, by the hand of this clock."

"Two minutes!" exclaimed Arthur. He thought furiously, then gabbled out, "How can I use the Improbable Stair to get to Monday's Dayroom from here?"

"The Improbable Stair exists everywhere there is somewhere to exist," said the Old One. "You must imagine a stair where there is not one, a stair made of whatever you can see, be it a grass stem broken in three places or a peculiar step-shaped cloud. Then you must jump towards the first step of the stair, making sure you have the Key in your hand. If you believe it is there, it will be – at least it will be for the wielder of the Lesser Key.

"Once upon the stair, you must keep going until you arrive where you want to be. The Improbable Stair has many landings, and upon each landing you may need to find the Stair again. If you do not find the continuation of the Stair quickly, you will be stuck wherever and whenever you have stopped. The Stair winds through all the Secondary Realms, through both time and space, and also through the House, so you must be wary. It is possible to end up somewhere you particularly do not wish to be. It is even likely, for that is part of the Stair's nature. It takes strength of will as well as power to get to where you really want to, using the Stair. You must also beware of other travellers, particularly Nithlings who sometimes manage to find their way on to the Stair."

The long hand of the clock moved, rattling the Old One's chain. A whole minute gone!

"What... how do I use the powers of the Lesser Key?" asked Arthur. He held up the Key as he spoke and its light flared briefly, though it was washed out by the strange blue glow of the Old One's chains.

"The powers of the Lesser Key are numerous," intoned the Old One. "In the hands of its rightful wielder it may do almost anything that is asked of it, though it is generally weaker in the House than in the Secondary Realms, and it may be opposed by both Art and Power. In general it may be used to lock, unlock, bind, unbind, open, close, animate, petrify, illuminate, darken, translate, befuddle, and to perform small diversions or redirections of Time. It will protect you to some degree from both physical and psychic harm, though as you are mortal there are close limits on this power. As to how you might use it, you know already. Ask or direct, and if it is within its powers, the Key will work as you require. You have thirty seconds left."

Arthur looked at the minute hand. It had moved again, halfway to the next mark. But he was sure he hadn't used ninety seconds already! In a panic, he tried to think of a good question, one that might attract a better answer than the last two. Something more direct, more straightforward.

"What is happening back at home? My home?"

"I cannot tell you that," replied the Old One. "The Secondary Realms are forbidden to me and many, many years have passed since I last looked upon anything that happens there. You may ask another question."

"Who can I trust?" Arthur blurted out.

"Those who wish you well," said the Old One. "Not those who wish to use you well. Be a player, not a pawn. And that is three questions and all your time."

He raised his hand and waved Arthur away.

"That's not really an answer. I meant who in particular can I trust?" said Arthur. He refused to back off, though the Old One again gestured for him to go. "Like the Will or Monday's Dusk."

The Old One climbed to his feet, the chains rattling. He made a loop with one chain and flicked it idly in the air. Still Arthur didn't move. He stood there, looking up at the giant, the Key in his hand. *It's just like standing up to a bully,* he told himself, though he felt very shaky inside. *It has to be done.*

"You must decide who to trust yourself," said the Old One. He started to wave Arthur off again, then paused.

"But I will tell you one more thing without a question, Arthur Penhaligon. A mortal who wields the Key will become its tool as much as it is his. It will change you, in blood and bone, remaking you in the image of its maker. The Key does not befit a mortal bearer. In time, it will remake its wielder. Think carefully about that, Arthur. To wield power is never without cost. As you can see here. Now go!"

He roared the last two words and jumped forward, swinging his chain. Arthur ducked the flailing links and sprinted off the clock, his heart pounding.

When he got to the edge of the coal pyramids, Pravuil was nowhere in sight. Looking back, Arthur saw the Old One sitting back down, once again resting his elbow on his knee and his head on his fist. Thinking.

Something Arthur would need to do himself, though his uppermost thought was to use the Improbable Stair to get out of this freezing, dusty pit. But it wasn't as simple as that. Should he risk the Stair when there might be another way out? Where should he go? Straight to Monday's Dayroom, to try to get the Hour Hand? What about the Will and Suzy Blue? And Monday's Dusk?

Monday's Dusk... Arthur suddenly wondered if Pravuil had some means to communicate with Dusk. What exactly had Dusk told Pravuil to do, besides help Arthur and give him a cup of tea?

"Pravuil!"

Arthur's shout echoed around the pyramids of coal, but there was no answer out of the darkness, nor from the blue-lit region around the clock.

"Pravuil! Come here!"

Again there was no answer. *So much for swearing loyalty,* thought Arthur. He looked around and wondered if he could remember how to find Pravuil's camp. He could really do with a hot cup of something, even if the Coal-Collator wasn't there to answer questions. But without having left markers, he knew it was useless. He'd just wander around in the dark, a moving patch of light that would only stumble on the camp by blind good luck.

"Pravuil!"

Silence returned as the echoes died away. But as Arthur took a breath to shout again, he heard something. A faint noise that was hard to pinpoint. It grew louder as Arthur used the Key to stick the coal together and climbed up a pyramid. The light from the Key spread out as he got higher up, but he still couldn't see anything.

Then he recognised the noise and looked up. It was the beating of wings. Someone... something... was coming straight down towards him!

Arthur jumped out of the way as a flapping shape zoomed over his head. As he hit the ground, he heard it crash into one of the pyramids, sending pieces of coal flying everywhere. Whoever it was clearly didn't know how to fly properly.

Before whoever it was could recover, Arthur rushed over, the Key held ready to strike. He didn't think it was Dusk, because the wings had looked white as they streaked past, and somehow he didn't think Dusk or Noon or Dawn would have a problem with their wings.

"That was a facer and no mistake!" declared a familiar voice. Arthur stared down at a blackened shape that was crawling out of a pile of coal. "No one told me the ground could come up as fast as that!"

"Suzy Blue!" declared Arthur. He smiled, put the Key through his belt and bent down to help her up. "What... how did you get here?"

"The Will took over a careless Third Secretary in Charge of Ceiling Maintenance and got me his wings," said Suzy. She stood up shakily and brushed herself off, sending coal dust billowing all around. Her wings were still attached, though they were quite bent at the top. They looked as if they weren't very white to start with, but now there were only glimpses of white beneath the black dust. "Sent me down to find you. Wouldn't come itself. Said it couldn't go near some old geezer. Lucky I aimed at the right light. What's that blue glow over yonder?"

"The old geezer," said Arthur. "I'd stay away if I were you. So Noon did let you go?"

"Sort of," said Suzy. "Least, we gave 'em the slip to start with. It ain't half cold down here. You'd better read this message, then we can clear out."

She reached inside her grimy waistcoat and pulled out an envelope of thick buff paper, sealed with a large blob of wax that was imprinted with what looked like a frog's handprint.

Arthur tore it open. For a moment he couldn't work out where the letter was. Then he realised that the writing was on the inside of the envelope. It was like an old-fashioned aerogram. The letter itself had been folded into an envelope.

The letter was written with beautiful penmanship, in faintly glowing green ink.

To Arthur, Rightful Heir to the Keys to the Kingdom and Master of the Lower House, the Middle House, the Upper House, the Far Reaches, the Great Maze, the Incomparable Gardens, the Border Sea, and those Infinite Territories beyond the House commonly called the Secondary Realms…

Greetings from your faithful servant, Paragraphs Three to Seven of the Will of Our Supreme Creator, Ultimate Architect of All, conveyed to you by the hand of Miss Suzy Turquoise Blue, Ink-Filler, etc, etc.

Sir, I trust this finds you well, and in good time to warn you that on no account must you approach the giant chained to the clock in the region you unfortunately and temporarily occupy. Called by some the Old One, he is extremely dangerous. I repeat, do not approach him or venture near the clock!

I regret your temporary incarceration, but assure you that our plans, though temporarily set back, are still in motion. Our next step, may I suggest, is for you to come at once to Monday's Antechamber, as I fear that his actual Dayroom is now defended more carefully and will need close examination before we can proceed.

How to get from your dank cellar to Monday's Antechamber? I had thought of procuring additional wings for Suzy to bring you, but their use is difficult and I feared an accident. Better and more fitting that you use the Improbable Stair.

"I can't get these stupid flappers off," interrupted Suzy. Arthur stopped reading a description and explanation of how to use the Improbable Stair that was almost identical to the one given to him by the Old One, as if it came out of the same book and both the Will and the giant had memorised it. Suzy was trying to reach over her own shoulder and was struggling with a wing.

"Do you want me to help?" he asked.

"No!" exclaimed Suzy. "They feel like they've grown into my back."

"That's what mine felt like," said Arthur. "But they fell off and turned back into paper just before I hit the ground here."

"Paper wings? They're just temporary, small magic," said Suzy scornfully. "These are real top-class wings, permanent ones. I've seen 'em put on and off and shrunk up and down. There must be a trick to it."

Arthur nodded warily. If there was a trick, it didn't look like Suzy was anywhere near figuring it out. He went back to reading the Will's letter.

By means of the Improbable Stair, come to Monday's Antechamber. I have done a small sketch so that you may visualise your destination. Remember that the Stair is contrary and will stop in many places. Do not let it leave you before Monday's Antechamber!

Arthur looked at the sketch. It was about the size of his thumbnail, but was incredibly fine and detailed, like a really old engraving. It showed the inside of a room, or rather, a tent, because the walls were obviously cloth and there was a pole in the middle. Other than that, there were piles of cushions and a small table with a very tall, thin jug and several wineglasses on it.

Strange-looking antechamber, thought Arthur. He shrugged and went back to the letter.

If all goes as I expect, I will await you there, with whatever allies I can muster. I shall reveal the next stage of my plan when we meet again.

Until then, I remain your obedient and respectful servant.

May the Will be done.

Arthur folded the letter and put it in his trouser pocket. Suzy was still grappling with the wings.

"What did the Will tell you to do?" Arthur asked. "Now that I've got the message?"

"I dunno," said Suzy. She stopped trying to tug her wings off, let her hands fall and thrust her fingers under the armholes of her waistcoat instead. "It didn't say. I suppose I'll go along with you."

"I don't know if you can come with me," said Arthur.

Suzy stared at him angrily. "Oh, fine! I fly all the way down here and then you can't be bothered taking me along for whatever happens next!"

"I'll take you if I can," said Arthur patiently. "I have to go on something called the Improbable Stair, and I just don't know if both of us can go along it, that's all. I'm surprised the Will didn't tell you."

"That Will only thinks of itself," muttered Suzy darkly. "Do this, do that, we must carry out the intentions of the Architect... drove me crazy, it did. Well, let's get on with it then, before Noon's goons catch up with me."

"What?"

"This Improbable Stair. Let's get on it. Where does it start?"

"No, what's this about Noon's goons?"

"Oh, well, it was easy enough to give the slip to the first lot Noon set to follow us from the Efficiencer General's office. But when I came down to the Upper Cellar, there was a whole bunch of Commissionaires on watch around the edge of the pit. I got past 'em, but I guess some of them will have gone and got wings by now. So we'd better get a move on. They might not be able to do anything to you, but they can sure hurt me."

As she spoke, Arthur looked up. At first he couldn't see anything, until he moved the Key aside so its light wasn't in his eyes. Sure enough, there were faint lights up above that had not been there before. Lights that grew brighter and larger as he watched.

"Watch lanterns," said Suzy. "Commissionaire Sergeants, I guess. Half a dozen of them."

Arthur was about to say something when an angry roar echoed out behind them, a roar so loud that Suzy instinctively clutched her hat, even though it was wedged on her head so securely no wind could blow it off. The Old One had also noticed the Commissionaires.

"Take my hand," Arthur instructed Suzy. He held his left hand out, the Key still in his right. Suzy took it reluctantly, holding it as she might a dead rat, with only two fingers.

"No, hold on hard!" said Arthur. "Otherwise you'll get left behind for sure."

Suzy's grip tightened. Arthur hoped that he was telling her the truth. He had no idea whether he could take her along or not. He didn't even know if he could find the Stair, let alone use it himself.

What had both the Old One and the Will said? *Imagine a stair where there isn't one. Focus on something that resembles steps and believe the Stair will be there.*

There in the darkness above that slightly slumped pyramid, Arthur thought. *That's where the Stair will be. It will just continue on from the natural steps of coal that have formed where the side of the pyramid has slipped.*

Yes, he thought. *A broad stair, leading straight up. Steps of white marble, gleaming in the darkness.* He could see it clearly in his head, but was it there in that dark space?

"Halt! Stop where you are!" came a shout from above, but it was faint and still some distance away. It was answered by a bolt of blue lightning that flashed up from the clock, but that too fell short, rebounding as if it had hit a glass ceiling only a hundred yards above the Old One's unusual prison.

Arthur ignored both the shout and the lightning. He could see the Stair now, the marble steps. They were shining there, above the pyramid. All he had to do was jump to that first step—

"Ow!" Suzy exclaimed as Arthur leaped forward without warning. Her wings flapped with the effort to keep up as the boy jumped into the air near the pyramid. But his feet didn't land on the coal. They hit something that Suzy couldn't see, and he jumped again. Suzy's wings beat hard to stay with Arthur, and she shut her eyes. She felt him jump again and shut her eyes even harder, in anticipation of being dragged painfully back to earth, wings or not.

But they weren't. Suzy's feet touched something, but not with the impact of a heavy fall.

Suzy opened her eyes and looked down. White marble gleamed under her dirty boots. She looked to the left and the right, and up. Apart from the steps climbing straight ahead, she could see only light, blazing white light, everywhere else around.

"Look down, at the steps," shouted Arthur. "And come on! We mustn't stop!"

CHAPTER NINETEEN

So how does this work, then?" puffed Suzy after she had dutifully kept up with Arthur for at least two hundred steps, still holding on to his hand. "We keep on climbing steps till we fall over and roll all the way back down?"

"I don't know," replied Arthur. He was tired, but also felt weirdly exhilarated. There was no way he could have climbed so many steps so quickly in the normal world, at least not without the Key. He relished the way the air flowed easily in and out of his lungs, even if his muscles were protesting at the continual effort. "But we have to keep on going. There are Landings every now and then, but I'm not sure what they are. If we get to one, we have to quickly find the Stair again, or we'll be stuck on the Landing. For ever, I suppose."

"Nothing but trouble," grumbled Suzy. "I should have

stuck to my ink pots. Never volunteer for nothing, my old man used to say."

She almost stopped, dragging Arthur back.

"What is it?" he asked sharply, tugging at Suzy's hand to keep her going.

"I remembered!" exclaimed Suzy. "I remembered my old dad, just for a second! Haven't done that for years! Too much washing between the ears. What's that?!"

Arthur had half turned his head to look at her. Now he almost got whiplash as he looked up the steps again. There was something ahead, something colourful emerging from the white glow that surrounded them. At the same time, he had the uneasy sensation that the steps were moving beneath their feet like an escalator. Whatever lay ahead, they were approaching it far faster than walking speed.

"Look out!" cried Suzy, and then the steps were gone and so was the white light. They were standing in knee-deep water, amid lush green plants that looked like house-sized cabbages, and the sun was above them in a clear blue sky.

"A Landing!" exclaimed Arthur. "Quick! We have to find the Stair again!"

A deep bellow answered him and, from behind one of the giant cabbages, a huge reptilian head slowly rose upon an ever extending neck.

"More dinosaurs!" groaned Arthur. This one looked like a plant eater, fortunately, but it was as big as an articulated lorry and could easily crush a couple of children without even meaning to. It was also a sort of swampy blue colour, with mottled patches of a deep purple. Arthur stared at the purple patches and felt an urge to break into hysterical laughter. But he couldn't do that. He had to find something that looked like steps—

The dinosaur bellowed again and moved forward, completely crushing the giant cabbage plant with its chest. Even if it was only curious, it still represented a major danger. They had to get out of its way and back on the Stair.

Arthur looked frantically around, almost swinging Suzy as he turned. Her grip relaxed a little, but Arthur tightened his.

"Don't let go! You'll be left behind! Ah!"

He'd seen something that might be useful. A bunch of tall reeds. Arthur ran over to them dragging Suzy, who wasn't ready for the sudden rush. If he could bend one of the reeds into the shape of steps, that might be enough. Without thinking further, he thrust the Key through his belt – and his lungs stopped on half a breath and he felt the familiar tightness in his chest.

He'd forgotten. He wasn't in the House any more. They were out in the Secondary Realms, perhaps even in the distant past of his own world, and he needed to hold the Key to be able to get his breathing a hundred per cent. But there wasn't time!

Arthur quickly bent the reed at half a dozen regular points, let the whole thing hang out at an angle and snatched the Key out again. He stared fiercely at the bent reed. There, there were the steps, coming off the top of the reed towards the sky. Arthur stared at the thin outline of reed steps and imagined them merging into much more three-dimensional marble ones.

A wave splashed against his back, thrown up as the dinosaur plunged closer. Suzy gasped or stifled a scream, and then Arthur jumped, her wings flapped and they were on the Improbable Stair again, dripping wet.

Arthur's breath came whistling back in. He felt like collapsing in relief, but he knew he couldn't. Wearily he pulled Suzy's hand and started up the stairs once again.

"How many of these Landing places do we have to put up with?" asked Suzy. She was flapping her wings a little in an effort to dry them. At least some of the coal dust had come off and they were looking a little whiter. Or at least off-white, rather than grey. "And where are we going anyhow?"

"I don't know," replied Arthur. As he said that, he felt the step under his feet go sort of soft, like butter just out of the fridge, and for a moment he feared he might fall through.

"I mean I know where we're going," he said as quickly and as confidently as he could, at the same time bringing the Will's drawing of Mister Monday's Antechamber clearly into his mind. "I mean I don't know how many Landings there'll be. We're going to Mister Monday's Antechamber, to meet the Will."

The step hardened up as he spoke, feeling like marble once again and not like marshmallow.

"Oh, that's all right, then," said Suzy sarcastically. "My friend the Will. I hope you sticks by your promise, Artie."

"Don't call me Artie," snapped Arthur. "I'll do whatever I can to get you and the other children home."

The steps ahead did a sort of shimmy as he spoke and seemed to curve a little to one side. But it only lasted a second and Arthur wasn't sure what it meant, if anything. Perhaps it was just part of the weirdness of the whole thing.

"Something up ahead!" warned Suzy. "Another one of—"

Once again they came to the Landing far faster than they expected. One moment they were lifting their feet to take a step, in the next moment they were on level ground.

It was dark and cool. Arthur raised the Key, but all he could see were stone walls. Wet stone walls. They were in a cave.

A slight noise made Arthur turn with the Key held high to shed more light. There, in one corner, a group of people grovelled in abject fear. They were naked but covered in thick pelts of hair, and their heads were ridged and bony.

Neanderthals, thought Arthur. *Or Cro-Magnons or something*. He wanted to tell them not to be afraid, but there was no time and they wouldn't understand anyway.

Arthur turned to the wall and quickly scratched some zigzag and very uneven steps with the point of the Key. But before he could start visualising the Stair, Suzy spoke.

"Don't look much like steps to me."

"Shhh!" hissed Arthur. Now he couldn't visualise the Stair at all. He started to panic.

We're going to be trapped in the Stone Age for ever... no! No!

Arthur took a deep breath and scratched some more steps, taking it a little slower, making the lines more geometric. *They did look like steps. They were steps. He was going to jump at them, dragging the ungrateful Suzy with him—*

He jumped at the wall with his eyes open, half expecting to hurt himself and end up on the floor of a cave. But he didn't. The white light exploded around him, welcoming them in. They were back on the Improbable Stair.

They climbed in silence for a while. Then Suzy spoke. "Sorry about wot I said. I'll keep my lips pegged shut now."

Arthur didn't reply at first. Then he said, "It wasn't your fault. I don't think the drawing would have worked anyway. I doubted it before you said a word."

"You won't let go of me?" asked Suzy in a much smaller voice than her usual loud tones. "Leave me behind?"

"No! Of course I won't!" said Arthur. He almost stopped climbing, he was so shocked that Suzy thought he might abandon her.

"Only, I've been remembering things," said Suzy softly. "I remember when I first saw the Piper. I remember my mam taking me out into the country and... and leaving me there. Me a city girl, and I didn't know what to do, and then the Piper came along, with all the children dancing behind..."

Arthur gripped her hand even more tightly. He knew there was nothing he could say.

"Funny how it's all coming back," continued Suzy. She sniffed a little and produced a not very clean handkerchief from her pocket to wipe her nose. "Must be the air or somefing."

"Must be," said Arthur. "Hang on – there's something coming up—"

They were standing by the side of a road, under a hot sun and clear sky, bordered on the horizon by the slightest of clouds. The road was hardly more than a track. It wasn't even cobbled, but simply dirt with occasional patches where irregular paving stones had been laid down. Short, gnarly trees planted in irregular rows ran along one side of the road. The other side, where Arthur and Suzy stood, was a field of short grass, kept down by the goats that were staring at them from the hillside a few hundred yards away.

"Stones!" said Arthur, pointing to a stack piled up under the trees back along the road. "We can make steps out of them."

He pulled Suzy across the road and they ran towards the pile of stones. They had almost reached it when Arthur saw a man running along the road towards them. He was running fast, but with a steady rhythm that proclaimed he would keep up the speed for a long time. The man was thin and sinewy and wore only a loincloth and sandals, the sweat shining on his bare smooth chest.

The runner checked for a moment as he first saw them, then checked again as Suzy absently flapped her wings. He stared at her and made a formal gesture, as if to shield his eyes from the sun and salute at the same time.

"Victory at Marathon!" he shouted. "The Persians are defeated! We thank Nike for the victory!"

He didn't stop, but averted his eyes as he passed, almost stumbling over a flagstone. Arthur and Suzy didn't stop either. They kept on to the pile of stones, then Suzy helped Arthur stack them up into steps and he brandished the Key and imagined the Stair and stepped up on the rocking stones and for once it was easy, and they were immediately on the marble steps and the white light shone all around them.

"I think I know where that was," said Arthur. "I mean, when that was. In our world. In history. I did a project on where some famous trademark names came from. He thought you were Nike, the winged goddess of victory."

"Me!" snorted Suzy. "If I could get these stupid wings off there'd be no confusion, I reckon."

"I wonder if it's possible not to stop at the Landings," mused Arthur. "I bet the Architect never stopped off all over the place without wanting to. Come on!"

They did.

CHAPTER TWENTY

Arthur started to climb at a punishing pace, jumping up several steps at a time.

"Why... why so fast?" asked Suzy.

"Maybe if we go faster then there will be fewer Landings! I don't know! It feels like the right thing to do!"

"But if it isn't, we'll just run into the Landings even faster," said Suzy.

Arthur didn't answer. He did feel that by going faster they would get where he wanted to go more quickly, and that it might somehow cut out some of the Landings. But it was only a feeling. He never managed to find out enough about anything, from the Atlas, from the Will, from the Old One...

"Something up ahead!" shouted Suzy.

Arthur blinked, saw something solid, and then the Key

struck it and he and Suzy tumbled through a light wooden door and out on to a narrow cobbled street. For a brief moment, Arthur thought he was back in the Atrium of the House.

Then a terrible stench hit his nose and he knew that he wasn't.

There were bodies piled all along the street. Lots and lots of corpses that had been quickly covered with lime, the white powder obscuring faces and features so that they might almost be statues or dummies laid out in rows. Save for the smell, and the flies that buzzed around in spirals above the bodies, and the rats that skittered around them and in and out of the open sewer that ran along the far side of the street.

There was no sign of anybody living.

Arthur held his breath and tried not to throw up as he looked around. All the houses were narrow, three-storey buildings that leaned into the street, so it was heavily shadowed despite the bright sun overhead. The houses were built of stone up to about six feet, but wood took over from there, with exposed beams and painted panels. Most of the houses had thatched roofs, though some were shingled in wood or slate. They all had bright painted doors and shutters. In Arthur's time, they would be very old houses, too old to be found outside England or Europe. Here they were, if not new, not that old.

This would have been quite a cheerful street, for its time,

Arthur thought. *Not now.*

Every house had a whitewashed cross crudely painted on its front door and walls. Arthur knew what that meant and what had killed all the people.

"Bubonic plague," he whispered. They were probably in England, sometime in the seventeenth century. There had been a terrible outbreak of the plague there in the 1660s. Or they had come out in an equivalent time in some other world. Once again, Arthur didn't know enough about the House, the Improbable Stair or the Secondary Realms to be sure.

Suzy's grip on his hand suddenly loosened. Too late, Arthur tightened his own hand. For a moment he held her fingers, then she pulled them free and walked away.

"Suzy! We have to keep going!"

She didn't come back. Arthur hurried after her as the girl crossed the street and pushed against a pale blue door. It scraped open a few inches, then thudded against a body that blocked the doorway. She pushed at the door again, then kicked it and started to cry. Tears fell down her cheeks and made dark splashes on her necktie, and her wings hung drab and woebegone upon her back.

"What is it?" asked Arthur. Suzy had always seemed so happy-go-lucky, even when confronted by dinosaurs or sword-waving barbarians. What had happened to her?

"This was my house!" she sobbed. "It's all coming back to me. This was where we lived!"

She turned to the closest pile of bodies and would have rolled the topmost one over to look at it, but Arthur grabbed her wrist and pulled her away.

"You can't do anything!" he said urgently. "And you can't stay here! We have to find some steps!"

"Why, it's Jack Dyer's daughter, Suzy, come back as the Angel of Death," mumbled a voice.

For a terrible instant both Arthur and Suzy froze, thinking one of the corpses had spoken. Then they saw what looked like a bundle of rags rise up from the shadowed doorway of the house next door. It was an old woman wrapped in a fur-lined robe, though the day was warm. She held a wet handkerchief to her face. Arthur smelled the cloves and rose oil mixture it was dampened with, strong even with the stench from the dead bodies.

"So you died anyway," mumbled the old woman. "I told your mother it was stupid to take you out of here. Death knows no parish boundary, I said. Death walks where it will, city or country."

"Is she dead?" asked Suzy quietly.

"Everyone's dead!" The old woman laughed. "Everyone's dead! I'm dead too, only I don't know it yet!"

She started to cackle madly. Arthur pulled at Suzy's hand again. This time she didn't resist. But she didn't help either as he dragged her away.

"Come on!" Arthur insisted. There was a wide-open door in the next house and there had to be a staircase beyond it.

But even with that so near, he worried that they'd stayed here longer than anywhere else, and Suzy had let go of his hand.

"Think of Mister Monday's Antechamber!" shouted Arthur as he dragged Suzy through the open doorway, along a short and very narrow hall and on to a winding stair so tight he banged his head on the steps above. Suzy started to climb without being dragged. "Concentrate on getting back to the House!"

Arthur called that out as he tried to concentrate himself. But he couldn't help thinking about all the dead bodies. He'd never seen a dead person before and he'd always imagined that if he did, it would be in a hospital bed. He couldn't stop thinking about those terrible, haphazard piles of corpses, just covered quickly with lime by the few survivors too frightened to do anything else.

The Sleepy Plague was a modern equivalent of the bubonic plague. The doctors and healers back then hadn't had a clue how it spread or where it came from, and modern doctors were in the same position with the Sleepy Plague. Arthur was the only hope. If he failed, then the Fetchers' disease might kill almost everybody in his city, including everybody he loved and cared about. Just like the last epidemic had killed his parents.

And then it would spread and there would be piles of bodies in the streets like here...

I have to get to Monday's Antechamber, Arthur thought

fiercely. *Monday's Antechamber. Monday's Antechamber.*

The last wooden and plaster step vanished beneath his feet and was replaced by marble. Pearly-white light washed out dingy seventeenth- century walls.

Arthur was back on the Improbable Stair. His left hand was closed, closed so tight he couldn't tell for a moment whether he still had hold of Suzy. Had she made it through, or was she trapped back in her own original time and place, where she would almost certainly have died... would die... of the Black Death?

Arthur looked back – and met Suzy's gaze.

"Guess you're stuck with me," sniffed Suzy. She tried to smile, but it wavered away. "No point in me going home now."

Arthur started up the steps, talking as he kept up a steady pace.

"We could find the records for your family, change them so they lived through the plague," he said.

"No," said Suzy slowly. "I told you. Hundreds of years looking and I never found my own record. None of us ever found a record for even someone we'd heard of. I guess that's it. I'll go back to ink-filling for ever after."

"No you won't," declared Arthur. He tried to inject more confidence and hope in his voice than he could actually feel. "We're going to beat Mister Monday and get everything sorted out in the Lower House. You'll see."

Suzy answered with something that sounded like a snort,

but perhaps she was just blowing her nose. Like she usually did, rather unhygienically across her sleeve.

"I'm going to really concentrate on Monday's Antechamber now," said Arthur. "I think if I focus on it hard enough, we'll get straight there, without another stop."

"Like the one up ahead?" asked Suzy.

Arthur swore and tried to run faster up the steps, as if somehow they could break through the swirling mass of colour that marked another Landing. But they couldn't. Once again, Arthur found himself on the steps one second and somewhere completely different the next.

Only it wasn't the sort of different they'd experienced before. This wasn't the age of dinosaurs, or a cave, or ancient Greece, or plague-ridden Europe. Arthur goggled at the new-model widescreen TV with the sound turned low, which was showing a newsreader going on about something, the leather lounge, the coffee table laden with copies of *Rolling Stone* and *Fortune* and an empty bottle of Coke. This was a typical living room from his own time.

Then he goggled even more as Leaf sat up from where she'd been lying face down on the sofa. Her eyes were red and there were tears on her scrunched-up face. She stared open-mouthed, then screamed.

"Arthur! And... uh... are you an angel?"

"Leaf!"

"No, I'm not a angel," said Suzy. She wiped her eyes and

took a deep breath, then added, "I just can't get my wings off. Name's Suzy Turquoise Blue."

Leaf nodded cautiously and backed up to the other end of the couch, where she stood warily.

"That *is* you, Arthur? Isn't it?"

"Yes, it's me! We can't stop," gabbled Arthur. "Is there another floor here? Some steps, a staircase?"

"Yes, up... up there," said Leaf slowly. She was in shock, Arthur saw. Behind her, on the television, a newsreader was suddenly replaced by a shot of a burning building. His school. "What—"

"We can't wait!" exclaimed Arthur. He headed for the door Leaf had indicated, yanking Suzy away from staring at the television. Leaf hesitated, then rushed after them.

"When is it?" asked Arthur as they ran down a hall. "I mean, when was the school on fire? Yesterday?"

"What? It came on the news fifteen minutes ago," said Leaf. "The whole town's cut off! Quarantine. But what are *you* doing? Is that the clock hand the dog-faces were looking for?"

"Is Ed OK? Your family?" asked Arthur.

"They're sick," sobbed Leaf. "Really sick. In weird comas. They're calling it the Sleepy Plague. Arthur, you have to do—"

Her voice disappeared as Arthur jumped on the first step and jumped again, fiercely visualising the white marble and the light of the Improbable Stair.

"Was that your sister?" asked Suzy. "Or your betrothed?"

"Just a friend," puffed Arthur. "Leaf, her name is. Please... quiet. I have to concentrate. We're coming up to something."

He recognised the weird feeling under his feet, the sensation of an escalator accelerating towards a higher point. There was colour swirling into the white light too, another giveaway.

"Hang on!" Arthur cried.

CHAPTER TWENTY-ONE

The next second Arthur and Suzy fell sprawling across a pile of cushions. They came to rest looking at a small green frog that was seated opposite them, on top of a silver cakestand that had several chocolate eclairs and four macaroons on the other levels.

"An opportune arrival!" boomed the Will, its voice far too loud to come out of the small frog's mouth. "Welcome to Mister Monday's Antechamber."

Arthur looked around. They were inside a silken tent, a round one with a central wooden pole. It couldn't be more than fifteen feet in diameter.

"This is Monday's Antechamber?"

The frog followed Arthur's gaze with one eye while the other eye looked at Suzy.

"No. This is a tent, one of the thousands encamped in

Monday's Antechamber, so it is an excellent place of concealment. Now, I have procured several choices for disguising you and Suzy. Please look in that chest, quickly select some clothes and hair, and put them on. I believe the hair is self-adhesive."

The Will indicated with his tongue a bronze-bound chest in the corner of the tent. Arthur and Suzy went over to it and pulled out at least a dozen different coats, shirts, hats and wigs, including beard-wigs.

"This self-adhesive hair will come off again, won't it?" asked Arthur several minutes later, as he began to gingerly lower a long-haired white wig on to his head. "What are we disguising ourselves for, anyway?"

"Yes, yes, simply say, 'Hair today, gone tomorrow' three times and it will fall off," remarked the Will. It seemed more impatient than usual. "You need to be disguised, as we have to get across a large part of the Antechamber. As your escape from the Coal Cellar has already been reported, there will be many watchers and searchers looking for all of us."

"OK," replied Arthur. He shrugged on a tattered coat that appeared to be made out of three-inch-thick felt. But it was the best fit of the three that he'd swiftly tried on, and it had a thin pocket in the inner sleeve suitable for the Key, so he kept it. There was some sort of label hanging from the sleeve. Arthur grabbed it and was about to cut it off with the Key when the Will cried out. "Don't! Leave the label on. It's your waiting ticket."

Arthur looked at the ticket. It was plain paper with the number 98,564 written in bright blue ink upon it. The ink flashed and changed colour as he twisted the label, moving between red and orange and then back to blue. Suzy looked at the ticket on her coat, which had a similar number.

"Everyone in the Antechamber is waiting for an appointment with Mister Monday in his Dayroom," explained the Will. "To wait, you must have a ticket or you will be thrown out. When your number is called, you can go in and discuss whatever business you have with Monday."

"Big number," said Arthur. "Is it just the last two digits that count? How many people does he see in a day?"

"All the digits count. Mister Monday completes perhaps two appointments with Denizens of the House each year," said the Will. "I got those tickets yesterday, in another guise, of course."

"You mean there are almost a hundred thousand people... Denizens... waiting to see Mister Monday?" asked Arthur.

"Yes," said the Will. "Sloth! I've spoken of it before. That is why there are at least a hundred thousand things wrong with the operations of the Lower House! Nothing can be done without Monday's approval, and Monday does not see the officials who seek approval."

"We can't waste any time in a queue. I have to get a cure!" exclaimed Arthur impatiently.

"We won't be in the queue at all. Now that you are

disguised, we can venture forth out to the Antechamber proper," said the Will. "Some distance from here, an ally will meet us, one who claims to know a weirdway into Mister Monday's Dayroom. We will take that weirdway, you will obtain the Greater Key, and all will be well."

Suzy made a snorting noise.

"Who is this ally?" asked Arthur suspiciously.

"Mmmm, not to put too fine a point on it, it is Monday's Dusk," replied the Will. "After Suzy's departure with my message, he found me. After some minor contretemps, I discovered he was a loyal servant of the Architect."

"Or a particularly clever enemy," said Arthur. "Have you thought about that?"

"He sees the true way," said the Will. "Stand still and I will jump to your shoulder."

Arthur hesitated, then stood still as the frog jumped to his shoulder and settled down by his neck.

"You won't try to get down my throat, will you?"

"It will not be necessary for me to inhabit anyone, thank you," said the Will. "However, please fold up your collar so that I am concealed."

Arthur complied. The frog felt strange against his skin. Cool but not clammy, like a cold glass straight out of the fridge.

"Everyone ready?" Arthur asked, looking back at Suzy. He never would have recognised her or thought she was a child. She looked rather like a dwarf from a fantasy book. She'd kept her usual clothes, but changed her hat to a weird-looking pointy cloth cap with earflaps, and had stuck on a bristling moustache and sideburns that came down to the corners of her mouth.

"Your wings are still on," said Arthur.

"I dunno how to get 'em off," said Suzy. "I've tried everything."

Except soap and water, thought Arthur. Then he felt bad for having mean thoughts. Besides, Suzy looked dirty but she didn't smell at all. And, Arthur suddenly realised, he was pretty filthy himself, from the various Landings of the Improbable Stair.

"Leave them," said the Will. "Up here, it is not uncommon to wear wings. Many petitioners fly from the lesser waiting rooms below up to the Antechamber. Let us go, Arthur. Turn to the right when you leave the tent."

Arthur undid the ties on the tent door and rolled them back. It was light outside, the pseudo-sunlight cast by the bright elevator shafts. Arthur blinked, stepped out of the tent and looked around.

He'd learned not to expect anything like a normal room, but he was still surprised and couldn't help gawping and craning his head.

Monday's Antechamber was an enormous veranda built two-thirds of the way up a mountain. Or actually, a volcano. Arthur could see the lip of the crater several hundred yards up the slope.

The veranda was two or three hundred yards wide, extending straight out from the side of the volcano. Something was supporting it underneath, columns or beams or perhaps unseen magic. It wasn't clear what the veranda itself was made of. It was so crowded with waiting petitioners, who had brought tents and carpets and rugs and straw mats and all manner of furnishings to make themselves more comfortable. Which was quite reasonable, since they might be waiting for centuries.

There was talking, laughter and just plain noise everywhere, even above Arthur's head, where large numbers of winged Denizens were swooping back and forth. They were an odd sight in their Victorian-era clothes, combined with sweeping wings. Though some of them flew very high, Arthur noted that none of them went near the mouth of the volcano.

All around, the place looked rather like a carnival. Unlike the Atrium, where everyone was at least pretending to be busy, the House Denizens here had an excuse to wait or amuse themselves however they wanted, provided they kept their waiting tickets. So just in Arthur's immediate sight, there were people – Arthur felt he had to call them people, even if they weren't – reading, playing board games or cards, practising fencing, juggling, writing, doing strange calisthenics, drinking tea, eating cakes and scones, staring at him...

Arthur stared back at the last fellow. There was something familiar about the way he stood, though he didn't think he'd seen him before. He was well-dressed, in matching pale pink coat, waistcoat and pantaloons, and had long, drooping mustachios.

Seeing Arthur meet his gaze, this pink-clad person ducked his head and scuttled back into the crowd. It was this scuttle that gave him away.

"Pravuil!" exclaimed Arthur. "I think that was Pravuil! From the Coal Cellar!"

"A spy!" growled the Will. "Quickly! Turn right and head for the crimson tent with the golden ball atop the central pole. You see it?"

Arthur nodded as he set off at a quick walk.

"Pravuil said he was working for Dusk," muttered Arthur as he made his way through the crowd, Suzy following close behind.

"He may be," growled the Will. "But we must be careful. Go into the crimson tent, turn to the left and follow the passage around to the back door, go out. We will come out in a passage between stacked crates."

The tent was dark inside and hung with many curtains or dividers. Arthur turned left and followed the side of the tent around. He saw a knife glittering in Suzy's hand and wondered where she had found it.

"I hope you won't need that!" he whispered over his shoulder as they walked around. It was a big tent, perhaps as big as a circus big top, though it hadn't looked that large from the outside.

Suzy looked at the knife in her hand.

"It's for cutting through the tent side if we need to," she explained. "Quickest way out. No point using one on a Denizen. It'd hurt them, but no more than that."

"Quiet," said the Will. But it spoke much more loudly than anyone else, making Arthur wonder why it bothered with the warning. Or perhaps as a jade frog the Will couldn't hear itself properly.

As the Will had said, there was a narrow lane past the back door of the tent, between two huge and precarious-looking stacks of wooden crates. Each one was about the size of an old-fashioned tea chest and there were thousands of them, piled up very dangerously in rows twenty to thirty feet high. Upon closer examination, Arthur saw that they *were* tea chests and had stencilled inscriptions like BEST CEYLON and HIGH GROWN DIMBOLA. Many of them had inscriptions that he couldn't read at first, until he touched the Key in his sleeve. Then the letters blurred from their odd symbols into English letters. They spelled things like TERZIKON MARILOR BLACKWATER and OGGDRIGGLY NO. 3, which Arthur was fairly sure had never been written on tea chests from his own world. At least not tea chests filled with tea.

"Loot from the Secondary Realms," said the Will disapprovingly. "More evidence of Mister Monday's interference!"

At the end of the passage through the stacked tea chests, there was the side of the volcano. Blank grey stone, solidified lava. Arthur reached it, touched its cool, smooth surface and said, "What now?"

"Now you hand over the Key or I will visit whatever torments I can upon you, and many more upon your friends," declared a familiar voice from above, as a shadow of wide-swept wings fell upon Arthur's face.

CHAPTER TWENTY-TWO

As Arthur whipped the Key out of the pocket in his sleeve, Suzy closed in on him and they put their backs against the stony side of the volcano.

Monday's Noon spread his wings wider and dropped to the ground. As he landed, crates were pushed aside further back, starting a landslide all the way along the makeshift passage. Dozens of metal Commissionaires and Commissionaire Sergeants bulled their way through the piled up mess of crates and broken bits of plywood, to form a wedge behind Noon.

Noon raised his hand and a flaming sword appeared in his fist. It crackled and spat, and the flames lengthened. He smiled his bright smile and held out his left hand. "The Key," he said. "Or I shall burn the Ink-Filler."

"It is a trap! What do we do now?" whispered Arthur,

ducking his chin down to talk to the Will.

"All three of you need to step forward a little," replied a voice that was not the Will's. Arthur looked over his shoulder and was surprised to see that a doorway had formed in the lava wall. A dark, shadowed doorway. He could just make out the face of Dusk within it.

Arthur and Suzy stepped forward a pace.

"And be more trusting," added Dusk as he stepped out of the doorway, followed by several of his Midnight Visitors. "Go through the doorway, Arthur. You too, Miss Blue."

Noon's smile had slipped as Dusk appeared and moved in front of Arthur. Now it became a frown as Dusk drew a sword of his own out of the air. Dusk's sword had a blade of darkest night, sprinkled with stars.

"What is this, Dusk?" Noon stormed. "I am to have the Key!"

"No, brother," answered Dusk gently. "We will let them go on their way."

"Traitor!" hissed Noon. "Step aside!"

"No," replied Dusk. "I am loyal to the Architect and Her Will."

Noon screamed and threw his flaming sword straight at Suzy. Arthur saw it and tried to raise the Key to intercept it, but he was too slow. The Key was only halfway up and the sword's point was a few inches from Suzy's throat when Dusk's dark blade batted it away. The sword ricocheted off the volcano and returned to Noon's hand, setting several tea chests alight from its flaming passage.

"Charge!" roared Noon and he ran forward, once again cutting at Suzy. Dusk parried this attack, and he and Noon exchanged a series of blows almost too fast to follow. A thin line of Midnight Visitors rushed to meet the charge of the Commissionaires. Whips flashed with sonic booms as batons and swords crackled with lightning. Tea chests exploded into matchsticks and burst into flame. Smoke began to spread.

"We have to help them," shouted Arthur, brandishing the Key. Noon and Dusk were evenly matched, but there were far fewer Midnight Visitors than Commissionaires.

"No," boomed the Will. "We must go through the weirdway. There's no time!"

Arthur hesitated. At that moment, Dusk ducked under a cut and gripped his brother's arm. Before Noon could break free, he was spun into a somersault and hurled up into the air.

"Go!" shouted Dusk as his black wings burst out of his back and he launched himself up into the sky. "We will hold Noon as long as we can!"

Still Arthur hesitated. He saw Noon streak up like a rocket, then turn and plunge to meet Dusk's ascent. Fire and night met with a terrible shriek as the two tumbled down, trading lightning-fast blows and parries as they fell.

The Will shouted, "Get in the—"

Noon and Dusk struck the ground like a shooting star,

right in the middle of the melee. The force of the impact rocked the entire veranda. Arthur and Suzy were hurled into each other, and it knocked down most of the Commissionaires and the Midnight Visitors – and all of the remaining tea chests.

As Arthur struggled to his feet, he saw Noon burst out of the debris, rage distorting his handsome face. He turned towards Arthur and leaped forward, only to fall as Dusk grabbed his ankle. Then both were on their feet and fighting again.

"Slay the girl!" screamed Noon to his minions as they began to clamber out of the splintered piles of wood and burning wreckage. "Close the weirdway!"

Four Commissionaire Sergeants smashed their way through the thin line of Midnight Visitors and rushed towards Arthur and Suzy.

This time, Arthur didn't wait. He turned and plunged into the dark doorway, once again dragging Suzy by the hand.

The red glow of fire streamed in behind Arthur, followed by the rattling boom of a Visitor's whip. Then the doorway snapped shut, and everything was suddenly quiet and dark save for the glow of the Key in Arthur's hand, which revealed the sides and roof of an upwards-sloping tunnel that was not made of lava. Arthur let go of Suzy and led the way at a swift walk, though he didn't like the feel of the ground underfoot. It rippled and moved, like walking on a trampoline, and the walls of the tunnel were soft as well.

Suzy saw him slide his finger along the wall for the third time and whispered, "Weirdways are all like this. This is a big one, though. Often you have to crawl. And if they close down, you get squelched, cause they're made with Nothing. Or through Nothing."

"Weirdways exploit the interstices of Nothing in the structure of the House," said the Will. "There is little danger provided a weirdway is well made. Now, Arthur. When we come out you must get as close to Mister Monday as possible and then, holding your own Key, recite this incantation: 'Minute by minute, hour by hour, two hands as one, together the power.' Quite simple, really. The Hour Hand will fly to you. You must catch it and then immediately prick your right thumb with the Hour Hand and prick your left thumb with the Minute Hand and smear a drop of blood from your left hand on the Hour Hand and from your right thumb on the Minute Hand. Then hold both Keys together and recite another very simple incantation: 'I, Arthur, anointed Heir to the Kingdom, claim this Key and with it the Mastery of the Lower House. I claim it by blood and bone and contest, out of truth, in testament and against all trouble.' Got that?"

"No," said Arthur, shaking his head. "Which thumb for which hand? And what if Mister Monday is holding on to the Hour Hand?"

"Oh, he won't be," said the Will breezily. "He'll be asleep, or in a steam bath. The Dayroom is full of steaming pools. Let me go over what you need to do—"

"Hang on!" said Arthur. "What if Mister Monday isn't asleep or in a steam bath? What do I do?"

"We shall improvise," said the Will. "I shall instruct you as required."

Silence greeted this remark. Even the Will seemed to recognise "we shall improvise" wasn't a big help to Arthur.

"I reckon you can take on Mister Monday," said Suzy, punching Arthur on the arm quite hard, obviously in an effort to bolster his confidence. "He'll probably be flat out snoring anyway."

"There's no choice," said Arthur. He was thinking once more of the plague. Of the cure. Of his parents. "I have to go through with it."

I will improvise, he thought grimly. *I will do whatever it takes. I will keep on fighting and thinking and trying, no matter what.*

"Excellent!" said the Will and it went over what it had said before. Arthur repeated the instructions. After four repetitions, he was reasonably sure that he could remember what to do. But he couldn't help thinking about everything that might go wrong. Starting with Mister Monday ready and waiting at the other end of the weirdway. Surely Noon would have warned him? Or had Dusk stopped him in time?

"Are you ready?" the Will asked. "The weirdway is

narrowing. We are about to emerge into Monday's Dayroom."

"Can we lose the hair first?" asked Suzy.

"If you must," sighed the Will. It waited as they recited the spell and various heads of hair and beards fell to the floor. "Are you ready *now*?"

"Yes," said Arthur, and Suzy nodded in agreement. "We're ready."

The weirdway was indeed getting much narrower. Arthur had to duck his head and then get down on all fours and crawl the last few yards. He couldn't see an exit as such, but there was a circular patch of darkness ahead that was not lit up by the Key's glow. When Arthur touched it, his hand disappeared. It was similar to Monday's Postern in the wall around the House, as manifested in Arthur's world.

"That is the door," said the Will. "Go through, but not too quickly. The ledge is narrow on the other side."

Arthur crawled through carefully and stopped so suddenly that Suzy ran into his feet.

It was a very narrow ledge he'd come out on. It was not much wider than he was and only extended for about ten feet to either side. Worse than that, it was quite a long way up the crater wall. Arthur looked down and, through billowing clouds of steam, saw a bubbling lake, lit deep within by red and yellow plumes of molten magma. The whole crater was a steaming lake, and Arthur could see nowhere to go and no way to get down off this ledge unless they flew, and Suzy was the only one with wings.

Nevertheless, he knew that first appearances in the House could be misleading. So he crawled to the side and let Suzy emerge. They both huddled on the ledge, staring down into the turbulent waters, watching the great billows of steam that rose up as lava poured out deep below.

Above them, the golden net that prevented flying visitors gleamed, picking up and reflecting the light from the elevators that surrounded the volcano. For the first time, Arthur wondered where those elevators went to. He had always thought Monday's Dayroom must be at the top of the House. But of course, this was only the Lower House, and there were the regions governed by the Morrow Days above. Or so he presumed.

Arthur shook his head. He shouldn't be thinking about stuff like that. He had to concentrate on the immediate problem. It was hard to think because it was much, much hotter than it had been and he was sweating furiously under his heavy coat.

"There's something in the middle," said Suzy, who had continued to stare down. "Look, there!"

She pointed as the steam clouds momentarily parted. There, right in the middle of the bubbling lake, was an island and a sprawling building. A low, spread out, L-shaped house complex with red-tiled roofs that looked kind of familiar to Arthur. He was sure he'd seen it before somewhere. In a book. A Roman villa.

"Monday's Dayroom," said the Will. "There is a fine bridge to it from the other side. But we will have to cross by the spiderwire. It may be a little difficult to see at first. Look by your left foot, Arthur."

Arthur looked down. At first he couldn't see a thing, then he caught the faintest shine of some gossamer thread. He reached down and touched it. It was a taut wire, about as thick as his finger but almost completely translucent. Arthur plucked it and it emitted a soft harmonic note.

"Uh, how do we use this?"

"It will stick to the soles of your feet," said the Will. "You simply walk down it to Monday's Dayroom."

"I think I'll fly," said Suzy.

"No, you—" snapped the Will. "No. Close to the island, fliers attract targeted bursts of steam that will strip the flesh from your bones. The only way down is by spiderwire and there is no time to procrastinate. Arthur, step on."

"What happens if I lose my balance?" asked Arthur. "I mean, my soles might stick, but I'll be hanging upside down."

"Then you will have to walk the whole way upside down," said the Will. "Hurry! It is easier than it sounds."

"What would you know? You're a frog," muttered Suzy. "You haven't even got soles."

"Shhh," said Arthur. He stood up, carefully stowed the Key in his sleeve pocket and tied a handkerchief around the sleeve so it couldn't fall out. Then he spread his arms out for balance, took a deep breath of the humid air and slid one foot out along the spiderwire.

CHAPTER TWENTY-THREE

It was easier than it looked. Arthur slid one foot after the other along the spiderwire. It felt rock solid under his feet and he had no trouble with balance. At least he had no trouble with balance as long as he didn't look down. As soon as he glanced towards his feet, he started to shake and quiver, and that became a general wavering that threatened to send him upside down. But if he looked up and ahead, it stopped again.

Suzy came next, moving quickly. She had no trouble at all and didn't even need to extend her arms, because her wings spread out and easily kept her upright.

Soon she was right behind Arthur and he was all too conscious of his own slow progress.

"Is this perhaps the time to mention that the spiderwire is impermanent?" asked the Will after Arthur had slowly shuffled along another twenty yards.

"No," said Arthur. He made himself go faster and tried not to look down. "What do you mean impermanent?"

"It will disappear in a few minutes."

Arthur started a peculiar running motion. It was very odd to not be able to pick up his feet. It also made balancing more difficult and, though Arthur was making faster progress, he also picked up a wobble that got worse and worse.

"Faster," said the Will when they were halfway down the wire, moving through thick clouds of cooling steam. It wasn't anywhere near as hot as Arthur had feared. It was just like the steam in the bathroom after a shower. "Much faster!"

Arthur tried to comply. The wobble got even worse and Arthur realised he was expending as much energy throwing himself from side to side to try to regain his balance as he was running along the wire.

"Faster! The spiderwire unravels!" called out the Will just as Arthur spotted the island up ahead. It was about two hundred yards away. The bubbling waters were only ten or twenty yards below, the steam was much hotter and the red glow of deeply submerged lava brighter. Arthur was unpleasantly reminded of Suzy telling him the few ways it was possible to be killed in the House. *Fire, if it's hot enough.* Superheated water probably fell into the same category.

Arthur stopped that train of thought and focused all his

energy into a sprint, but it was very difficult to pick up speed. He simply couldn't go any faster without lifting his feet.

Fifty yards... forty yards... thirty... twenty... ten... five...

"We're going to make it!" shouted Arthur as his feet finally left the spiderwire and he threw himself on to the cool green grass of the lawn that surrounded Monday's Roman villa.

But when he turned around, Arthur nearly had a heart attack. Suzy had not only fallen back, she was hanging upside down!

Arthur sprang up and ran to the spiderwire. But when he put his right foot on it and tried to slide along, he slid off and almost fell off the island into the water.

"One-way wire," said the Will. "Leave her. We must get on."

"Stop!" shouted Arthur. "What's wrong with you anyway? She's my friend!"

"Even friends must be sacrificed for the goal—" the Will began.

But Arthur wasn't listening. He undid the handkerchief around his sleeve and pulled out the Key.

"Hurry!" he shouted to Suzy and then said to the Will, "How long before the spiderwire unravels?"

"It is already withdrawing from the far anchor," said the Will. Arthur looked down and saw the little frog staring across the lake into the clouds of steam. "At the current rate of unravelling and the speed of Suzy Blue, she will fall into the water in ten seconds."

Arthur touched the Key to the spiderwire and commanded it fiercely.

"Stop! Do not unravel!"

The Key glowed a little brighter for a second, but Arthur couldn't see any difference.

"That was foolish," complained the Will. "Using the Key may alert Mister Monday—"

"I said to stop!" snapped Arthur. Then, contradicting himself, he added, "Did it work? Will it stay up?"

The Will didn't answer for a second. Then it said mulishly, "It has slowed. The spiderwire was made with the Greater Key and is governed by the schedule laid upon it then. But it has slowed."

Arthur stood back and waved frantically at Suzy, willing her on. She was flapping her wings furiously and was almost upright again.

"Faster!" he screamed. "Go faster!"

Suzy hurled herself forward, her wings beating up a storm. She got closer and closer and Arthur could see the tension and fear in her face. He found himself gripping the Key so tightly that it almost cut him again and left a livid line down his palm.

Closer, closer...

Twenty feet from the island, the wire snapped out from under Suzy's feet. She screamed and flapped with all her might. At the same time, a huge bubble formed in the lake beneath her and Arthur remembered the other danger. Gouts of steam specifically designed to hit free-fliers.

The bubble expanded as Suzy flew. Arthur held his breath. Three seconds. The bubble hadn't burst; Suzy was almost at the island. He suddenly remembered the Key in his hand and pointed it at the bubble—

It burst, sending a great jet of steam straight up like a geyser. Arthur staggered back.

Too slow! Too slow! he thought. *Suzy's been blown to pieces—*

Then she crashed into him and they both rolled across the lawn.

"That was close," said Suzy as they extricated themselves and stood up. "I reckon my shoulders 'ave been pulled up to my ears."

"What were you doing?" yelled Arthur.

"Sorry. I got tired of waiting for you to get out of the way. So I thought I could run along upside down. Only I couldn't get my wings to work properly the wrong way around—"

"Forget it," said Arthur. *Concentrate on what has to be done.* "Sorry I yelled."

He looked across at the villa. Its windows were shuttered, but he could see a door. An unassuming back door of unfinished wood. "I guess we go in there."

"Indeed," said the Will. "Before we enter, I should alert

you that it may be a little confusing inside. I believe Monday has had the entire interior converted to steam rooms and bathing pools, and it is much larger in than it is out. Obviously, Arthur, you must find Monday and speak the incantation. I... ahem... *we* shall assist as best we can."

"Let's do it," said Arthur. He hefted the Key in his hand, ran over the incantations and procedure for joining the Keys, and headed for the door.

Ten paces away, he stopped. There was a deep ditch in front of the door. A dry moat really, about six feet deep and six feet wide. Not much of an obstacle. Except that it was knee-deep in writhing, undulating, coiling, hissing snakes. And not just ordinary-looking snakes. These were patterned in yellow and red flames that flowed from their flat heads to their pointy tails, and their eyes were shiny and blue, as bright as sapphires.

"Bibliophages!" exclaimed the Will, its voice alive with panic. "Step back! Step back!"

Arthur needed no encouragement. He stepped back as the snakes flung themselves at the side of the ditch and tried to get out. He was relieved to see that they couldn't.

"What's a bibliophage?" asked Arthur nervously.

"They are creatures of Nothing," said the Will slowly. "Book eaters. A type of Nithling. They spit a poison that dissolves any writing or type into Nothing. They should not be here. Monday has gone beyond the limits of... of anything!"

"Will they spit on us if we don't have any writing or type?" asked Arthur.

"No," said the Will. "But I am entirely composed of type! I cannot cross!"

"Which is what Monday had in mind, I reckon," said Suzy. "How's the plan looking now?"

"It remains as discussed," said the Will, rallying quickly. "Arthur, you must cross without me. But first you must be sure you have no writing or type of any kind upon you. Labels in clothing. Notes. The bibliophages will detect even a single letter and will spit. Their poison will dissolve you if they do and all will be lost."

"And we'll be dead," added Suzy.

Five minutes later, they were ready. Arthur had to tear labels off all his own clothing. There were some handwritten laundry letters marked in Suzy's clothes, but she just discarded them and was still left wearing three shirts, breeches, two pairs of stockings and her boots.

It wasn't so easy for Arthur. Every item of his regular clothing had multiple labels or printing on the cloth. He even had to tear the waistband out of his underwear, but he was past embarrassment. He was glad he didn't have a tattoo or the habit of writing on his hands with ink.

"You are certain you have no words upon you, no writing?" asked the Will. It had jumped down to sit on top of the discarded clothing. "Not even a single letter? What is that upon your wrist?"

Arthur looked at his watch and gulped as he realised the brand name on the face was type and would attract bibliophage spit.

"Nothing else?" asked the Will again, and they all checked their pockets. Then Arthur glanced down at his jeans and said, "Uh-oh. There are letters on my zip."

Now he was embarrassed as he worked to break off the zipper tag. But then he saw that there was writing down the inside of the zipper as well.

"This isn't going to work," he said slowly. "Uh, I'm going to have to get rid of all my own clothes and just wear the stuff from the Antechamber."

Arthur turned his back, quickly stripped off, then put on the long shirt the Lieutenant Keeper of the Front Door had given him, which was long enough to be like a nightshirt, then his coat. Still, it felt pretty weird and exposed, even with everything buttoned up. He hoped there weren't any Marilyn Monroe-style wind gusts around.

"May you be successful," said the Will. "Let the Will be done."

Arthur nodded. The frog stood on his hind legs and bowed. Suzy gave a rough curtsy back. Arthur nodded, then felt that wasn't enough and gave a kind of salute.

Then he led the way to the ditch and stared down at the bibliophages. There were thousands of them. Snakes. Every one at least four feet long. Arthur felt his mouth drying up as he watched them writhe and coil around one another. He and Suzy would have to literally wade through this mass of snakes. He hadn't even asked if they bit as well as spat.

And he didn't have any underwear on.

For some reason that brought a faint, almost hysterical chuckle to his mouth. He couldn't believe he was in this situation. He was supposed to be some sort of hero, going up against Mister Monday, and here he was without any pants on, worrying about being bitten somewhere very unpleasant by Nithling snakes. Surely no real hero would end up in this predicament.

"No time like the present," he said, and lowered himself over the side.

CHAPTER TWENTY-FOUR

The snakes were unpleasantly warm, almost hot against Arthur's bare legs and feet. He flinched as he lowered himself completely into the writhing mass, and they started to coil around his calves. Their scales, or whatever their skin was, was also raspy, like sandpaper, making the experience even worse.

Arthur tried not to think about it and began to wade across the trench to the sunken door. Bibliophages wound around his waist and were all around his legs and under his coat. Some of them started to hang off his arms as well, and one slithered up and around his neck. But even when they were wound quite tightly, they didn't constrict, and so far they hadn't bitten. Arthur supposed the Key would do something if they did. Or try to.

By the time he was halfway across, Arthur was simply

covered in snakes. They were everywhere, even around his head, hanging down his face, and there had to be dozens of them around his legs. There were so many it was hard to walk and Arthur stumbled a couple of times, allowing even more snakes the opportunity to climb on board.

"Avert! Foul snakelings!" cried out Suzy behind him. Arthur didn't reply as he was afraid a bibliophage would get in his mouth. He didn't turn to look either. He would overbalance for sure, and he didn't think he would be able to get up if he fell. Even though the bibliophages weren't biting, the sheer weight of them would keep him down. He concentrated on pushing his way through.

At last he came to the door. A simple wooden door in the side of the trench, half buried in bibliophages. It had a silver handle. Arthur tried to turn it, but it was locked. Shaking his arm to remove some bibliophages, he touched the handle with the Key and said, "Open!"

The door shivered. The handle turned of its own accord and then the door slowly groaned inwards, letting out a blast of heat and the very unpleasant smell of rotten eggs. The bibliophages that had been piled against the door didn't fall inside as Arthur expected. They stayed suspended, as if there was some invisible barrier as well as the door that kept them out.

If there was, it didn't stop Arthur. Holding his nose against the smell, he stepped inside. As he did so, all the bibliophages fell off him like leaves from a tree suddenly struck by a high wind.

The inside of Monday's lounge was not the interior of a Roman villa. It bore no resemblance to the building outside.

Arthur stood on a platform of old black-brown cast iron, an island in a sea of steam. Through the open diamond weave of the floor, he could see boiling mud about fifteen yards below. Dark yellow mud that bubbled and popped like burning porridge, sending up wafts of stinking steam.

An extremely narrow one-person bridge led out from the platform into the steamy interior. It was iron too and had the monogram MM cast into the diamond weave every few yards. Arthur couldn't see where it led. There was too much steam and the bridge was simply smothered in billowing clouds.

"The stink of the match factory," said Suzy slowly. "I remember it. Father said it was the stench of the—"

"Sulphur dioxide," said Arthur quickly. "From the hot mud. Like in Yellowstone National Park. There'll probably be geysers too."

The words were barely out of Arthur's mouth when a geyser fountained up nearby, spattering droplets of hot mud everywhere. Suzy folded her wings over her head to protect herself, and Arthur found the Key took the heat out of the mud that hit him.

"Come on," said Arthur. He started along the iron walkway. But Suzy didn't follow. Arthur didn't notice at first, but after twenty yards or so, he turned back. Suzy was staring up into the clouds of steam.

"There's something up there," she said quietly, drawing her knife.

Arthur looked up just as a shadowy figure dipped out of the steaming clouds. Not Mister Monday, but someone shorter. Dressed in pink, with yellow wings that shed feathers as he hovered above them.

"Pravuil!"

Arthur's shout of recognition was answered by a crossbow bolt that whistled straight at him. Without conscious effort from its wielder, the Key struck the bolt out of the air, cutting it in two, the separate halves passing to either side of Arthur.

"Nothing personal, sir!" called out Pravuil, hidden in the steam above. "Simply a commercial priority. Now I must sound the alarm. Fare— arrgh!"

The clouds had parted for a moment and Suzy had thrown her knife. It hit Pravuil in the left foot and stuck there, quivering. The Denizen dropped his small crossbow and hunched over to try to pull out the knife, his wings labouring.

Before Pravuil could do anything else, Suzy launched herself up at him.

"Go on, Arthur!" she yelled as she flew. Like a small bird attacking a larger one, she spun in circles around Pravuil's head, kicking and scratching. He hit back, forgetting the knife. They flew higher as they fought, disappearing into the clouds completely.

Arthur craned his head and stood on tiptoe, looking up, the Key held ready. But all he could see were clouds of steam and a single pearly-white feather that came spiralling down. Arthur caught it and saw it was stained with blood. Red blood, not the blue blood of a Denizen.

Arthur stared at the feather. Then he opened his hand and let it fall. Suzy was gone. But her sacrifice would not be in vain. Even if she lost the aerial battle... or had lost it already... she had gained Arthur precious time. He would not waste it.

He held back his fear and ran along the bridge, into the swirling steam, the geysers and the raining mud. He ran faster than he ever had, his footsteps ringing on the iron, until he pointed down with the Key and said, "Silence!"

The bridge went for a very long way, much further than he expected. There were platforms every hundred yards or so, but apart from that, Arthur saw nothing but steam, boiling mud and the occasional geyser that was close enough. He heard a lot more geysers than he saw, and boiling mud fell so often it was like rain, coating Arthur completely. The Key stopped it from doing him any harm, but every now and then he had to slow down to wipe it off his face.

As he ran, Arthur repeated the Will's instructions over and over in his head. Beneath that there was an undercurrent in his head that thought the Will's plan was all very well, but it was unlikely to work. He had to be prepared for anything.

Finally, the bridge changed. It widened a little and inclined down. Arthur slowed, peering ahead into the steam, the Key clutched hard in his hand, ready for action.

There was another platform ahead. A low, broad platform that must be only a foot or two above the mud. Someone was standing there next to a table. Arthur crouched down and crept closer, his heart hammering in his chest. Was this Mister Monday, awake and waiting for him?

The figure turned and Arthur's heart seemed to stop in his chest. He took a breath and opened his mouth to start the incantation. But he didn't speak it, because the steam eddied apart and he saw who it was.

Sneezer. Mister Monday's butler. He looked exactly the same as he had back in Arthur's world, with one very noticeable change. His left wrist was chained to a table leg, which Arthur saw was also cast iron. It was an extremely long chain, coiled up under the table. On top of the table was a silver tray, a methylated spirit burner, two bottles of cognac or whisky or something similar, a saucepan, and a large decanter of colourless fluid, probably water.

Sneezer was mumbling to himself and fiddling with his fingerless gloves. As Arthur watched, he turned around, and the boy saw that his coat and shirt were cut into strips on the back. There were ugly red weals on the jaundiced-looking skin beneath. Given that all House Denizens healed quickly, Arthur knew that no ordinary whip could have inflicted those wounds.

Arthur thought about that. He had to get past Sneezer without the butler giving the alarm. Mister Monday probably wasn't far away. There were steps down from the platform to yet another lower bridge, at the level of the mud. Monday could well be only yards away, concealed by the steam.

Arthur kept watching. Sneezer rearranged his gloves, then aimlessly shifted the bottles and the decanter. After a minute of this, Arthur crept closer, while Sneezer's back was turned. When he was only a few feet away, he could make out Sneezer's mumblings.

"Not my fault. I was only visiting for a card game. How was I to know that the Will would crawl up my nose? I never thought to look in a handkerchief. Who would? Used that handkerchief since Time began, never had anything in it before I sneezed. Not my fault. Always strived to give the best service. Never had the training. Not my fault. I mean, a handkerchief? Not my fault, ulp—"

Sneezer stopped in midsentence as Arthur pressed the sharp point of the Key against his throat and whispered, "Freeze!"

Arthur was quite unprepared for what happened next. Sneezer *did* freeze, but it was a *literal* freeze. Ice flowed from the Key in a softly crackling rush, moving swiftly down

Sneezer's body and arms and up over his head. In a few seconds, the butler was completely encased in shiny blue ice. Frozen solid.

Arthur slowly pulled the Key back. While he hadn't expected it, this was a good result. But would the ice last in this incredible heat? Just to be sure, he touched Sneezer with the Key again and said, "Double freeze!"

More ice gushed from the Key, flowing steadily till it wasn't so much Sneezer that stood in front of Arthur, but a man-sized icicle, the ice so thick that the butler was just a dim shape at its core.

Arthur inspected the icicle. There were a few drops of water sliding off it already, but it should hold for a few hours. Hopefully Arthur would only need a fraction of that time to do what he had to.

Arthur left the platform and trod as quietly as he could down the steps to the low bridge. It was barely above the mud and, in fact, in places the steaming mud flowed across it. Protected by the Key, Arthur had no trouble walking through it.

The steam was even thicker this close to the surface. Arthur slowed down even more and waved the Key in front of him to send the steam swirling apart so he could see. Mister Monday had to be somewhere close, surely?

He was. Steam parted and Arthur saw that the bridge stopped. Ahead there was a pool of bubbling mud that had several iron posts sticking out of it. Hung between the posts was a hammock of silver rope, and in the hammock was Mister Monday.

Arthur stopped, his mouth dry despite the steam. Monday looked asleep. He was wrapped in a thick white bathrobe and had something on his eyes. For a moment Arthur thought they were slices of cucumber like his mother used sometimes, then he saw they were coins. Gold coins.

Arthur edged closer, right up to the end of the bridge. The top rungs of an iron ladder went down from there into the mud. Arthur looked at the ladder, then at Monday again. What was that glint in his pocket on the right-hand side? Was it the Hour Hand, the Greater Key?

Monday moved slightly. Arthur flinched, then calmed himself. It was only a small movement, and Monday's chest continued to rise and fall with the steady motion of a sleeper.

Recite the incantation. The Hour Hand will fly to you. The words of the Will echoed in Arthur's head. *Recite the incantation.*

Arthur raised his own Key and pointed it at Monday. Then he swallowed twice and in a soft voice, little more than a whisper, spoke.

"Minute by minute, hour by hour, two hands as one, together the power!"

CHAPTER TWENTY-FIVE

The gold coins screamed into the air as Monday's eyes flashed open. He made a grab for his pocket, but it was too late. The Hour Hand rocketed away, flying across the mud towards Arthur, a gold and silver streak almost too fast to see.

Somehow, Arthur caught it. One moment it was a flash in the air, then it was in his left hand, the Minute Key in the right. He held both Keys, the attraction between them making his arms shiver with the effort of holding them apart. Now all he had to do was prick his thumbs—

But before he could move, a great gust of wind knocked him back and sent him sprawling across the bridge, almost into the mud. As Arthur scrambled to get up he saw Mister Monday hovering above him, his too-handsome face distorted in rage. Huge golden wings stained with rust spread from his shoulders and he used them to buffet Arthur with another gust of wind, sending the boy rolling along the bridge.

"Foolish mortal! Come to me, my Key!"

Arthur felt the Hour Hand leap in his grip as it tried to return to Mister Monday. He clenched his fist, but his fingers slowly opened and the Hour Hand began to slip free. To stop it, Arthur pressed the Minute Hand against it and pushed both Keys against his chest. At the same time he struggled to his feet and began to run back along the bridge.

"Come to me, my Key!" shouted Monday again, and he flew up above Arthur, into the steam. The Hour Hand wriggled against Arthur's chest. It almost got free, but at the last second Arthur pushed the point of the Minute Hand through the circle of the Hour Hand and held them together, shouting himself.

"Hold fast!"

He kept running as he shouted. If he could just get outside, then the Will could help him, hold Mister Monday off somehow so Arthur could prick his thumbs. But the Hour Key kept trying to break free, and then Arthur found himself losing traction on the bridge. The Hour Hand was rising up to where Mister Monday flew above – and was lifting up Arthur with it!

"Key, make me heavy!" shouted Arthur as he lifted off and only his toes were touching the ground. He could hear Monday shouting something too, but didn't know what.

Then he was crashing down again, crashing so hard that his feet dented the iron bridge. He felt the jar through his bones and knew that ordinarily they would have broken.

Making himself heavy worked for a few minutes. Arthur sprinted like he had never sprinted before, holding both Keys tight. The Hour Hand kept pulling up, but Arthur could hold it down.

At least till it tugged suddenly to the left. Surprised, and going full tilt, Arthur hit the railing of the bridge and went straight over. As he fell, he took a death grip on the two Keys and shouted, "Key, make me fly!"

The last word came out as he hit the mud. Arthur was so heavy that his impact was like a car going into a river. Mud exploded everywhere around them and Arthur went straight down. Mud covered his eyes and filled his nose and mouth. But he didn't breathe it in and he didn't seem to need to breathe. He kept sinking for a few seconds, but even as he sank, he felt a strange itching in his back. Then the muscles on his chest rippled and his shoulder blades got pins and needles. It reminded Arthur of something and in that same instant he knew what it was. The paper wings Noon had made for him.

His wings expanded in the mud and beat with incredible strength. Arthur burst out of the mud like a rocket, catapulting past the hovering Monday. Arthur's wings were pure, pearly white. They shed the mud instantly as he flew straight up – up and up and up into the writhing steam.

A bellow of rage followed Arthur's climb and Monday followed, his golden wings thrusting him up like an avenging missile.

Arthur didn't wait. At the apex of his climb he dived forward, folding his wings for greater speed. Though he couldn't see, somehow he knew exactly where the door was. He dived straight at it, the steam parting before him as he swooped down.

Monday met him halfway, a sword of black fire in his hand, thin as a rapier and much quicker. Arthur jinked sideways as Monday lunged. The black sword pricked him in the leg as they both tumbled down, Arthur twisting to get away, Monday trying to stab him.

They hit the platform together, both shouting, the iron screaming as it buckled. Blood fountained from the wound in Arthur's leg, but congealed a second later as the Key healed him.

Arthur was the first to recover. He flung himself at the door, which was shut again. But before he could open it, Monday was upon him. The black sword stabbed down—

To be met by the Minute Key moving of its own accord in Arthur's hand. The two blades met and drops of molten gold flew in all directions, many of them sizzling on Monday's robe. Monday hissed and stabbed again, with the same result.

"Give me the Keys!" screamed Monday. He stabbed once more, couldn't get through and threw his sword away in disgust. Then he stepped back, raised his arms and shouted something up into the air. Immediately his wings disappeared and Monday began to take on a dull red glow, like metal heating in a forge. Then he started to melt, his head flowing down into his neck and then into his shoulders.

He was turning into something else.

Arthur frantically tried to prick his right thumb with the Hour Hand, but every time he moved the Hour Key even a little, it kicked and bucked. It took all Arthur's strength to drag it back and hold it against his chest.

Panicking, Arthur looked at Monday. He was stretching and thinning as he melted, but horribly his face stayed the same. He snarled at Arthur, his forked tongue flickering.

"Key, know your Master!"

The Hour Hand shook in Arthur's grasp, cutting into his hand. Unlike the boiling mud or the black sword, this actually hurt. Arthur gasped and pressed the Hour Hand even tighter to his chest. It shook again and sliced into him just above his heart.

"Do you think a minute can withstand the hour?" sneered Mister Monday. "Strike, my Key! Strike!"

The Hour Hand leaped in Arthur's grasp and the point drove into him, sliding between his ribs. It only got in half an inch before Arthur managed to twist it aside, but the pain almost made him black out.

Desperately, Arthur flung out his right hand and touched

the door with the Minute Hand, screaming, "Open!"

The door flung open. Arthur pulled the Minute Hand back and used it to try to lever the Hour Hand off his chest. But the Greater Key took advantage of the momentary absence of its lesser half, its point sliding up along his ribs, heading inexorably towards Arthur's heart. He tried to interpose his thumb, but the angle was all wrong, and he couldn't let go of the Minute Hand or he would lose his leverage and be impaled.

Monday laughed. Arthur groaned and turned his head. Monday's transformation was complete. He had turned into a huge snake, coloured gold and red. The flat head of the snake had Monday's face upon it, though it had another mouth underneath where a snake's usually would be.

Monday laughed again. Then he slithered forward, pushed his head under Arthur's legs, ignoring his violent kicking, and started to wind up and around the boy's body.

"Help!" screamed Arthur. But there was no one to answer him.

Monday slithered under him again. Two coils were around Arthur's legs. Arthur couldn't strike at the snake, because he couldn't move either Key. He was going to die. He was trapped. He'd be crushed, or impaled by the Hour Key. The Minute Key might keep him alive for a while, but it was less powerful than the Hour Hand.

It was all over. He had failed. He would die, and everyone else would too, from the plague, or suffer terribly—

Something hit the platform hard, making it ring like a bell. Yellow and white feathers flew everywhere, and out of the feather storm came Suzy. Bloody, but triumphant, with Pravuil cowering and whimpering behind her.

"Hang on, Arthur!"

Suzy pulled her knife from Pravuil's foot and plunged it towards Mister Monday's scaly coils.

The Hour Hand twitched in Arthur's grasp, momentarily turning away from him. At the same time, long crackling sparks of electricity arced out of the snake and hit the descending knife, blasting Suzy back against the railing. She dropped her blade, screaming. Pravuil stopped whimpering and attacked her once again.

Monday coiled around Arthur's waist and squeezed, accompanied by a malignant chuckle.

Arthur shut his eyes. Nothing could hurt Monday. This was the end.

Nothing could hurt Monday?

Arthur's eyes flashed open again. He bucked and wriggled, edging himself forward like a worm towards the doorway.

"Suzy! Ink! Have you got any ink?"

He was answered by a scream as Suzy tripped Pravuil and sent him over the railing into the mud. For an instant it looked like Suzy would go over too, but she regained her balance and in the same movement, drew out a bottle of ink from an inside pocket of her coat.

"Great!" Arthur yelled. "Now drag me across the door!"

"Fool!" hissed Monday. "Die here or there, it makes no matter!"

Suzy ran forward and grabbed Arthur under the shoulders. Monday lunged at her, but couldn't reach without uncoiling from Arthur. He hissed in frustration and pushed his head under the boy, sliding quickly around to add another coil. Suzy used that moment to drag Arthur across the doorway, where they were instantly set upon by a writhing horde of bibliophages.

"Write something on Monday!" screamed Arthur. He could feel the Hour Hand biting into him again, vibrating its way into his flesh as Monday's coils tightened.

Monday's coils suddenly loosened as he heard Arthur's shout. Desperately the huge snake tried to wriggle off, retreating back as the bibliophages coiled around him in turn.

Suzy poured ink across her finger and began to write on Monday's tail. As she formed the first letter, all the bibliophages stopped moving, and everyone felt their sudden focus and concentration. Then, as Suzy completed a downstroke and the letter was complete, every single one of the thousands of bibliophages lunged forward, a tidal wave of snakes falling upon the Master of the Lower House.

"Key! Kill him!" shouted Monday before his voice dissolved into a wordless howl of pain.

The Hour Key struck viciously at Arthur, but he deflected

it, so it drove into him below and to the left of his heart, straight into his lung. Arthur shrieked at the pain and staggered to his feet, the last coils of Monday releasing him as Nothing dissolved the snake's nerves and muscles.

Suzy kept feverishly writing, though she couldn't see what she was doing, there were so many bibliophages biting and attacking the greater snake. Monday was still trying to get back through the doorway and had in fact forced most of himself through.

When there was nowhere left to write, Suzy jumped off and helped Arthur up. She stared aghast at the Hour Hand embedded in his chest, with the Minute Hand wedged under it so it could go in no farther.

"Has it come out the back?" whispered Arthur. The ditch was swimming around him and he knew only the power of the Minute Hand kept him from fainting. The Hour Hand was still shaking back and forth, cutting deeper into his body, despite all he could do.

"Yes, yes, it has!" sobbed Suzy.

Arthur sighed and barely managed to whisper, "Key... hold the Hour Hand for... a minute... a minute..."

He let go of the Hour Hand, reached behind his own back, and pricked his right thumb with the point of the Greater Key, though it was already slick with his own blood. Then he reached around again, held the Minute Key with his right hand, and pricked the thumb of his left hand with the Lesser Key. Then he smeared a drop of blood from his left thumb on to the Hour Key and from his right thumb on to the Minute Key.

Behind him, Monday managed to hurl himself back through the doorway, sending both Suzy and hundreds of bibliophages flying.

Arthur touched the bloodied circle ends of the Keys together and sobbed out, "I, Arthur, anointed Heir to the Kingdom... claim this Key and with it the Mastery of the Lower House... I claim it by blood and bone and contest..."

The Hour Key drove in again, at least an inch. Arthur screamed and the whole world darkened. But he only had a few words left to get out. Just a few words. He could do it. He had to do it.

"Out... out of truth, in testament, and..."

CHAPTER TWENTY-SIX

Against all trouble!"

The Hour Hand eased itself out of Arthur's chest and the two hands twisted in his grasp, until the Hour Hand lay across the Minute Hand. There was a bright flash and the Minute Hand grew longer as the Hour Hand shrank. Then Arthur was holding not two clock hands, but a sword that had some resemblance to what it had been, in the shape of its circular pommel, the circles on each end of the hilt, and the gold chasing down the silver blade.

The wound in Arthur's chest closed over with a *pop* and the pain began to ebb away. Arthur stood straighter and took a long, lingering breath. Suzy stared back at him, her hands and wings shaking.

"I guess," Arthur said, raising the sword, "I guess we've won."

He looked down at the writhing river of bibliophages they were standing in and lowered the sword into the heaving mass.

"Return to Nothing!" commanded Arthur. The sword shone and delicate rivulets of molten gold shot from its point, moving and dividing until a fine network of gold spread all through the ditch. As it spread, the bibliophages faded and became indistinct, until they disappeared and the golden threads went with them.

"Rise up!" said Arthur, touching the bottom of the ditch. The ground rumbled and shook beneath his feet, then slowly began to rise, burying the door. Arthur quickly touched it with the sword and commanded it to rise as well. In a few seconds, the ditch was no more and the door was back in place against the wall of the villa.

"I feel a bit off," said Suzy. She looked very pale and was holding her side. Pravuil had obviously wounded her, and dragging Arthur out hadn't helped. She started to stagger, then collapsed.

Arthur just managed to catch her head as she fell back on the grass. A second later, he touched the sword to her stomach and said, "Heal. Be well."

A glowing nimbus of light spread from the Key and surrounded Suzy's body. As it spread, her hands and wings stopped their violent shivering. Suzy opened her eyes again. When the light faded, she slowly got up. She felt her side and experimentally flexed both her fingers and wings.

"I thought we were done for," she said quietly. Then she smiled and jumped in the air, her wings sending a blast of air in Arthur's face. "But we done it, Arthur! You finished off Mister Monday!"

Arthur stared at her. He knew he should be celebrating but somehow he just didn't feel like jumping up and down. He wasn't in pain, but he felt really tired.

"You have the Key, the First of the Seven Keys to the Kingdom! Well done, Arthur! Very well done!" exclaimed the Will as it came hopping across the lawn, high-jumping in excitement. "Where there's a Will, there's a Way, if I do say so myself. Where is the former Monday?"

Arthur gestured with the sword at the door.

"Summon him forth," instructed the Will. "Let justice be meted out. There is much to do, you know, Arthur."

"You'd think we could 'ave a cup of tea and a biscuit first," muttered Suzy. She stopped jumping and scowled at the Will, who ignored her.

"Monday!" called out Arthur, not very enthusiastically. He waved the sword – the First Key – in the air. "Come out!"

The door opened and a bedraggled figure slowly limped out. It was recognisably Monday, but only just. The bibliophages' Nothing poison had eaten away part of his face, and there were strange holes all over – and completely through – his body. His clothes were ripped and shredded, little more than rags that he clutched around himself.

"Execution," said the Will with some satisfaction. "A tap

on the shoulder will do, Arthur, and just say, 'From Nothing, to Nothing.' That will do the trick."

Monday collapsed on his knees before Arthur and bowed his head. Arthur extended the Key and touched it to Monday's shoulder. But he did not say the words the Will had told him. He remembered what Dusk had said about Mister Monday as they slowly fell into the Coal Cellar. *Monday was not always as he is now.*

"Be healed," said Arthur quietly. "In body and in mind."

Monday looked up in astonishment as the Will jumped up and down angrily, booming out something that Arthur ignored. He watched the holes in Monday shrink into pinpoints as the flesh regrew. Even Monday's clothes restitched and rewove themselves. But they weren't as fine as the ones he'd worn before, and neither was his face so handsome. But Arthur saw that his eyes were also kinder, and there were laughter lines around them. He stared up at Arthur and then bowed his head once more.

"I beg forgiveness, Master," he said. "I do not know why I did what I have done. But I thank you for my new life."

"Charity is a very labour-intensive virtue," said the Will crossly. "And you never know where it will end. But I suppose it was well enough done."

"Indeed," said someone. "I'm sure it will end badly for all concerned."

Everyone swung around just in time to see the door slide shut on a very small, narrow elevator, no larger than a phone booth. A bell rattled, and the elevator shot up and vanished inside a beam of light that easily pierced the golden net above.

"Pravuil!" shouted Suzy. "I thought I finished the little creep off."

"Unfortunately not, it seems," said the Will. "He must be more than he seems. A spy for one of the Morrow Days, curse their treacherous hearts. But they cannot do anything here and now. They are bound by the compact with the former Master of the Lower House. They cannot interfere here, or on any Monday in the Secondary Realms. They are your preserves now, Arthur. In any case, we will deal with the Morrow Days in due course. First we must make a solid beginning here. Ah, here comes our ally, Dusk. And with him Noon and Dawn, come to beg for their miserable existences."

Sure enough, the three principal servants of Mister Monday were coming around the side of the villa. Dusk came first, Noon hangdog at his heels. Both showed no physical signs of their battle. Behind them came a gaggle of Inspectors, Commissionaires and other Denizens, all of them unarmed, save for the Midnight Visitors who marched around them, proudly holding their whips at the salute. Dawn hung close behind.

When the crowd was about twenty feet away and slowing down, fear and apprehension clear on many faces, Arthur raised the Key and they all stopped. He lowered it again and looked out on them.

"I suggest that you reappoint Dusk in his position," said the Will. "As for Noon, I think that I had best take that on for the time being—"

Arthur shook his head. "I'm not staying on as the Master of the Lower House."

A collective gasp went up from everyone except the former Monday, who remained kneeling, his head bent.

"But you have to," expostulated the Will. "You can't just give it up!"

"You mean I'm not allowed or is it actually impossible?" asked Arthur.

"It's impossible!" said the Will. "You are the Heir! Selected by me, proven by challenge. And there is much to be done here!"

"I told you before," said Arthur. "I want a cure for the plague in my world. That's all I want! A cure and to go home."

"You cannot return to the Secondary Realms," said the Will sternly. "Or cure the plague. Remember the Original Law. No interference is allowed, even interference to correct interference."

Arthur stared down at the green frog. Anger swelled up inside him, and he started to raise the Key. He would smash it down on the Will—

No. That's not the way to do anything, he thought. *I have to stay calm. The Will is a manipulator. I have to work around it.*

"You said I could," Arthur said coldly. "Explain."

"No, I merely implied that you could by saying that a great many things were possible if you became the Master. Besides, if you go back to your own time and place without the Key, I expect you'll die."

"But I can change my record, can't I?" said Arthur grimly. "And since no one else seems to follow the Original Law around here, why should I?"

"Even if you happen to be correct about your record and so on," protested the Will, "you can't give up the Key, and as Master you must uphold the Original Law."

Arthur looked at Suzy.

"I dunno," said Suzy, pointing to the undertaker-like Dusk. "Ask Dusk."

Arthur looked at Dusk, who took off his top hat and bowed, extending one leg.

"It is true I have some small knowledge, but it pales to insignificance next to the Will's. Monday had some right to the Key as a Trustee, up until it was claimed by a Rightful Heir. It is possible that now no one else can wield it."

"I don't believe I've been through all this for nothing!" Arthur shouted. "I want a cure for the plague and I want it now."

"The Original Law—" the Will began, but shut up when Arthur turned on it, the Key poised to strike.

"The plague is due to contamination from Fetchers, is it not?" asked Dusk. When Arthur nodded, he continued,

"Then it is a simple matter. With your permission, I shall conjure a Nightsweeper from Nothing. Taken back to the Realm you once inhabited, it will collect any remnants of contamination in a single night and return to Nothing with them. That will remove the effect upon both people and place."

"Well. That's a start," said Arthur.

Dusk bowed again, took out a black-bound book and a quill, dipped the quill in an ink bottle a Midnight Visitor proffered, and wrote quickly. Then he tore off the page, walked over to where the ditch had been, rolled the page into a funnel and plunged it into the dirt.

Nothing happened for a few seconds, then there was a faint whinny from the paper funnel. That was followed by a tiny black horse's head, two hooves and legs, and then a complete horse no more than three inches high. It gave another whinny, stamped its foot and then stood completely still. Dusk picked it up and handed it to Arthur, who took it gingerly and slipped it into the pocket of his coat.

"It must be set on a window ledge shortly before midnight, with the window open," instructed Dusk. "It will then ride forth, setting all to rights by morning."

Arthur nodded and let out a sigh of relief. This was what he wanted. Now all he had to do was figure out how to get back with it. He sensed that the Will wasn't telling him the whole truth. There had to be a way.

A noise at the door distracted him. It opened to reveal

Sneezer, several icicles hanging off his nose. He carried the silver tray, which had a tall, thin bottle upon it and a piece of paper. Sneezer proceeded calmly towards Arthur and offered the tray.

"A drink, milord? A beverage from your native Realm, I believe. Orange juice. Perhaps you are familiar with it? And a document I believe you were looking for?"

CHAPTER TWENTY-SEVEN

Arthur stared and started to slide the sword through his belt. Only then did he realise he didn't have one. He was standing in front of all these people covered in mud and wearing only a coat and what might be a nightshirt. But he didn't care. He stuck the Key point-first in the grass instead. It quivered there as he picked up the glass of juice and the paper.

As he touched the paper, a name appeared on it in golden type.

Arthur Penhaligon.

"My record," said Arthur. "Can I change it so I don't die? What does it say now?"

"I do not know, milord," replied Sneezer. "I cannot read it, now you are Master."

"Can I read it?"

Sneezer didn't answer. Neither did the Will. Arthur looked at Dusk, who shrugged. Arthur shook his head. Why was nothing simple? He drank the juice, gave the glass to Sneezer and examined the paper. But aside from the name on the outside, it seemed to be blank.

"Well, I don't care what it has on there, or if I can change it," Arthur said finally. "I'm going to go back anyway. I have to use the Nightsweeper. Even if I die."

"You won't," said the former Monday. He didn't stand up and kept his head bowed. "No one in the House can read or change their own record, Arthur. But once you survived your own death, the record will have changed to reflect that. You have borne the Lesser Key for some time too, so it will have strengthened your body. You will not die if you go back. At least not from your lung sickness."

"So I can go back," repeated Arthur. "I am going to go back."

He looked down at the Will. It was sulking near his feet.

"I want you to help me, Will. Forget about the Original Law. How can I get back home?"

"You must not go back," said the Will. It puffed itself up to twice its usual size in an effort to impress him with the gravity of its words. "You wield the First Key. You are Master of the Lower House. There are still six imprisoned sections of the Will that must be freed, and six Keys that must be claimed—"

"I'm a boy!" interrupted Arthur. "I want to go home and

grow up normally. Grow up to be a man, not a Lord of the Universe or whatever. I don't want to change into an immortal, like the Old One said I would if I keep the Key. Can't I – I don't know, make someone else look after everything till I'm old enough?"

The Will muttered something inaudible.

"Can't I make someone else look after the Lower House till I'm old enough?" Arthur repeated firmly.

"Yes, yes, you are within your rights to request a delay in your full assumption of power," said the Will grumpily. "I suppose we can allow you five or six years in your own backwater. After ten millennia, it is little enough, and there is a certain amount of preliminary work that will not require your presence. But who knows what the Morrow Days will do if you hand over your powers and return to the Secondary Realms, even temporarily? I do not know the exact terms of their compact, but I think you could be in danger from Grim Tuesday at least, since his powers and authority border your own."

"I don't care!" exclaimed Arthur. "I have to risk it. Maybe the Morrow Days will leave me alone once they know I've passed on my powers. And you can always get another mortal heir if you need one."

"Who shall be your Steward?" asked the Will. "You do realise this is how the present trouble arose with the Trustees? It is very hard to find a trustworthy bearer of power."

"You will be, of course," said Arthur. "But you'll have to choose a more imposing presence than a frog."

"But I'm a facilitator, not an executive," protested the Will. "A mere functionary."

"You were going to be my Noon, weren't you?"

"Yes," replied the Will. It hopped about in agitation. "This is not at all as I planned!"

"Well, tough luck," said Arthur. "Are you going to be the Steward or not?"

The Will did not answer. Everyone stared as it hopped madly backwards and forwards across the lawn for at least a minute. Finally it stopped and knelt near Arthur's feet

"I will be your Steward of the Lower House," croaked the Will.

A single sharp black letter oozed out of the frog's skin, followed by another, and another, until a whole sentence spilled out across the grass. More words followed, and more sentences, like a ribbon unspooling. The words began to spin and tumble and rise up in the air. More and more letters joined them, buzzing backwards and forwards with the sound of a harp strumming. Soft trumpets joined in as the letters moved into set positions and spread out to join in new and constantly changing combinations.

Then the letters all stopped in midair, containing and outlining the shape of a tall manlike figure. The trumpets blared and white light flashed, blinding everyone for a second.

Arthur blinked twice. With the flash of light, the words of the Will had become a woman. A tall winged woman in a plain blue dress that totally paled to insignificance under her arched and shining silver wings. She was not young, nor old, and was imposing rather than beautiful, with serious dark eyebrows and a rather large nose under her tightly pulled-back platinum hair. Her forehead was wrinkled in either exasperation or thought. She bent down, picked up the jade frog, and put it in the small lace-trimmed reticule she carried in her left hand.

"I'll make that into a brooch. It has served me well."

The Will's voice was clear and musical to start with, but disconcertingly lapsed into the deep rasp it... she... had used as a frog.

The Will curtsied to Arthur. He bowed back, suddenly much more nervous. It had been easier to deal with the Will as a frog.

"I will be your Steward," repeated the Will. "But who shall be your... our... Dawn, Noon and Dusk?"

"Dusk," said Arthur slowly. "Do you want to keep your job?"

"No, my lord," said Dusk. He smiled and bowed. "I would step out of the shadows and stand in the sun to serve you and your Steward, my lord, as either Dawn or Noon. Many of my Midnight Visitors would also like a change of employment, if you see fit to allow them. They grow weary of wearing black."

"You shall be Noon, then," said Arthur. He looked at the Will and added nervously, "And if it's all right with you, Will, then the old Noon shall be the new Dusk."

"Hummph!" exclaimed the imposing lady. Her tongue was still green, Arthur noticed. The pale green of fine jade. "On probation! I shall be keeping a careful eye on everyone! What about Dawn?"

"I guess she can keep her job too, for now," said Arthur slowly. Dawn smiled gratefully at him and swept a very low curtsy that sent small sunbeams sparkling across the lawn. "But there is one other appointment I'd like to make. Can Noon have an assistant?"

"Of course," replied the Old Dusk, now the New Noon.

Arthur turned to Suzy.

"I know you can't go back," he said haltingly. "I'm sorry... I'm very sorry I can't change that. But you don't need to be an Ink-Filler any more. Would you like to be Noon's Assistant? Then you can help the other children the Piper brought here and keep an eye on things for me in general. A mortal eye."

Suzy looked at the ground and shuffled one foot back and forth.

"That'd make me Monday's Morning Tea or something stupid, wouldn't it?" she said gruffly. "I s'pose I could give it a go."

"The post is Tierce, the hour halfway between Dawn and Noon," intoned the Will. "Monday's Morning Tea indeed!"

"Monday's Tierce," repeated Suzy softly. She sniffed and wiped her sleeve across her nose and face before looking up at Arthur.

"I hope your family... I hope they all... you know... they're all right."

She rushed forward and gave him an embarrassed hug. Before Arthur could hug her back, she let him go and retreated to stand by Dawn and Noon and Dusk.

"Do I have to do anything else?" Arthur asked the Will quietly. "Can I go back now?"

"You must grant me use of the Key," said the Will. "It is quite simple. You need to hand it to me hilt-first and repeat a few words."

Arthur drew the Key out of the grass. It felt good in his hand. Right. As if it belonged there. He could feel power from it surging into him, lending him strength. It would be so easy to keep it. To be Master in truth and not concern himself with the petty matters of the Secondary Realms...

Arthur shuddered and quickly reversed the Key, holding it by the blade towards the Will, who took it.

"Now repeat, 'I, Arthur, Master of the Lower House and Wielder of the First and Least of the Seven Keys of the Kingdom...'"

Arthur repeated the words dully. He felt exhausted. Worn out by his battle with Monday, by everything.

"'I grant my faithful servant, the First Part of the Great Will of the Architect, all my powers, possessions and appurtenances, to exercise on my behalf as Steward, until such time as I shall require them rendered unto me once more.'"

Arthur gabbled out the words as quickly as he could, fighting the desire to stop and snatch back the Key. Then he finally let go, and would have fallen over if the Will had not swept him up under one powerful arm.

"Home," whispered Arthur. "I want to go home."

CHAPTER TWENTY-EIGHT

I'm still not sure I approve," said the Will. "Sneezer, is Seven Dials still located within the Dayroom, or has it moved?"

"I believe it is still there, milady," said Sneezer. The butler had undergone a rapid transformation and was much cleaner and better groomed. His fingerless, falling-apart gloves had become spotless, complete and white. His teeth were no longer curved and yellow and his nose was no longer crisscrossed with broken blood vessels.

"There are two main ways to enter the Secondary Realms from the Lower House," explained the Will to Arthur. "Seven Dials is certainly the easiest, if you know how to set the dials. The Door, of course, is the other."

"I don't want to go through that dark void again," said Arthur, thinking back to Monday's Postern.

"Oh, you wouldn't have to do that," said the Will, her voice once again disconcerting Arthur by shifting between melodic female tones and gravelly frog-in-the-throat. "You would go out the Front Door all the way. Though as that is almost certainly watched more carefully by the Morrow Days, it would be wiser to avoid their interest for as long as possible. So, I think Seven Dials will be best. Come along."

Arthur nodded and yawned. He turned back to say goodbye, mainly to Suzy, and was surprised to see everyone kneeling on the grass.

"Goodbye!" Arthur called out. He hesitated, then bowed. They all bent their heads while remaining on one knee. Arthur's heart sank. He didn't want to say goodbye like this. Then he saw Suzy raise her head. She winked and smiled and rolled her eyes at the company she was in.

"Goodbye, Monday's Tierce," said Arthur quietly.

"See you," said Suzy. "Watch out for them Morrow Days."

"Goodbye, everyone!"

"Goodbye, sir!" chorused Dawn, Noon and Dusk, and all the assembled Denizens behind them.

Arthur waved again, then turned and followed the Will back through the door into Monday's Dayroom. All the steaming mud had disappeared. Now it looked like the interior of an old house, or maybe a museum.

"This way, please," said Sneezer, taking them up a stairway and down a very long corridor. Arthur and the Will followed the butler into a library, a very comfortable-looking one, about as big as the one at Arthur's school, but with old wooden shelves and several thickly unholstered leather armchairs.

"I have taken the liberty of placing your clothes behind that shelf, milord," said Sneezer as he rapidly applied a cloth and a brush to Arthur, magically removing the mud.

"Oh, yeah, thanks," said Arthur. He looked down at his strange clothing and a faint smile crossed his face. He didn't want to go back in a nightshirt without underpants.

It only took Arthur a minute to get dressed. Though his school clothes were pressed and cleaned, the labels and the waistband from his underpants were still missing. That would be a tough one to explain to his mum, he thought.

He took special care to take the Nightsweeper from his coat and put it in his shirt pocket, wedging it tightly so it could not fall out. The little horse whinnied quietly, but seemed quite comfortable.

When Arthur emerged, Sneezer was waiting.

"I believe this is yours, milord," said Sneezer, and he plucked a volume from a small ivory-fronted shelf next to one of the chairs. He gave the book to Arthur, then went to pull on a bell rope in the corner. A bell boomed in the distance as he tugged the rope. A few seconds later, it was answered by a deep rumbling. The floor shivered under Arthur's feet, and one entire wall of bookshelves rolled back to reveal a strange seven-sided room. In the centre of the room seven grandfather clocks were set facing one another, their pendulums making a collective swimmy sort of *thrum* that was like listening to your own heartbeat with your fingers in your ears.

Distracted for a moment, Arthur didn't look at the book. When he did, he realised it was the *Compleat Atlas of the House*.

"But this isn't mine," he protested to the Will. "You should have this. I can't even open it without the Key."

"It is yours," boomed the Will. "You have borne the Key long enough that some pages will open to your hand. You will also need this."

She reached into her sleeve again and pulled out not a handkerchief, but a red lacquered container about the same size as a shoe box. Arthur took it and tucked it under his arm.

"What is it?"

"A telephone," said the Will. "You may have need to speak to me, should the Morrow Days prove less kind than we might hope. Or if I need your counsel."

"I don't want it," said Arthur stubbornly. "You said I could have five or six years!"

"The telephone will not be used save in the most dire emergency," replied the Will. "It is insurance against perfidious fate, nothing more."

"Oh, all right!" said Arthur. He tucked the box under his arm and paced angrily next to the Will. "Now, can I finally go home?"

"I do beg your pardon, milord," said Sneezer. He had gone inside the room and was moving the hands of the clocks around. "This is rather complicated, but it will only take a moment."

Arthur stopped pacing. Once again he checked his pocket to make sure the tiny black horse was still there.

"Ready!" pronounced Sneezer. "Quickly, quickly, get in before the clocks strike!"

"Goodbye, Master," said the Will. "You have shown great fortitude and proved, as I fully expected, to be a most excellent choice."

She gave Arthur what was clearly meant to be a small push towards the clocks, but actually sent him flying across the room and almost into them. Sneezer caught him, spun him around and set him in the middle, caught between the clocks. Then the butler leaped out of the circle.

The clocks began to strike. The room wavered around Arthur, as if a heat haze had sprung up. Arthur dimly saw the Will waving her handkerchief and Sneezer saluting. The clocks continued to strike, and a familiar white glow spread all around.

Just like the Improbable Stair, thought Arthur.

He stood for a while, wondering what was going to happen next and where... and when he was going to come out.

I guess I should have told Sneezer exactly what I wanted. Not that it matters. As long as I can get the Nightsweeper going...

The white light pulsed and began to close in around Arthur on three sides. But on the fourth side, it stretched out, making a kind of narrow corridor. Arthur hesitated, but as the light continued to press in, started along it.

He seemed to walk for a long time and was starting to get worried. He even briefly contemplated opening the red lacquer box and calling the Will. What if something had gone wrong with the Seven Dials? What if Sneezer was a traitor like Pravuil, in the employ of the Morrow Days?

Arthur fought back his fears once again and kept walking. Eventually the white light began to fade and he could make something out. A different sort of light. Yellow, not white. He could hear things too, distant sounds coming into the silence. A helicopter, far off, and distant sirens. And he was having a little trouble breathing. Not a lot, just a little, a minor catch to his breath.

The white light disappeared completely. Sunshine hit, and the sound of the city under quarantine. Arthur screwed up his eyes and shielded his face with his hand. He was standing on a suburban street. Outside a house with a newly painted garage door.

Arthur dropped his hand and looked. The House had disappeared, and once again he could see the normal buildings that had been there before. In the distance, a plume of black smoke rose to the sky, with helicopters buzzing around it. Sirens wailed in symphony all around.

He saw a car approaching fast down the road and

crouched down behind a small shrub, which offered very little camouflage. But the car was coming too quickly to find a better hiding place. Even if it was the police, Arthur hoped they would simply take him to East Area Hospital and he would still be able to send the Nightsweeper out from there.

Then he recognised the car. It was his brother Eric's old blue clunker, heading fast for home.

Arthur stood up and waved. For a second it looked like Eric hadn't seen him, then the car screeched to a halt, blowing smoke from its rear tyres. Eric didn't normally drive like that, but then this was no normal time.

"Arthur! What are you doing here?" shouted Eric, sticking his handsome blond head out the window. "Get in!"

"Going home," said Arthur as he ran across and climbed in. "What are you doing here?"

"I was at a one-on-one master class at the city gym," said Eric as he put his foot down again. "Then we heard there was a fire at the school. I headed over there right away but got turned back and told to get home within thirty minutes. They're going to shoot all unauthorised vehicles and pedestrians after two o'clock! It's total quarantine!"

"Is Mum OK?" asked Arthur. "The others? What time is it?"

"I don't know," said Eric, shaking his head. He was in shock, Arthur saw. He hadn't even asked how Arthur got out of school. "Time? Uh, one thirty-five. We'll make it easily."

Arthur settled back in his seat and tightened the seat belt

as Eric zoomed the car around the second-to-last corner before home. He checked the Nightsweeper in his pocket. He couldn't use it for at least ten hours.

A lot could happen in that time. People could die and the Nightsweeper would not bring them back. Arthur hadn't thought of that in his desire to get home. He'd thought it was all over. But defeating Monday wasn't the end. There was still more to do.

Arthur's breath caught and he instinctively reached for his inhaler. But it wasn't there. Panic rose, then was forced back as Arthur realised he didn't really need it. He wasn't breathing as free and easy as he had in the House, but his lungs weren't totally tightening up either. There was a catch to his breath and his lungs felt strangely lopsided, as if more air was getting in his left lung. But he was OK.

Eric didn't so much park the car as stop it near the front door. They both jumped out and rushed upstairs. Bob and Michaeli met them at the door, themselves rushing down to see who it was. After quick hugs, they all retreated into Bob's studio. Wherever they'd lived, that was always the place of family conferences and important events.

"Emily's all right," was the first thing Bob said. "But this is a bad one. A real outbreak. They don't know what it is, where it came from, or even what it can do."

"Mum'll work it out," said Michaeli. Eric nodded in agreement.

Bob noticed that Arthur didn't. He reached out and

clapped his youngest son on the shoulder. "She'll be OK," he said. "We'll all be OK."

"Yeah," said Arthur. He touched his pocket again. Why, oh why hadn't he asked for something that would stop the plague right away? Anything could happen in the next ten hours. He could get the plague himself and fall asleep.

CHAPTER TWENTY-NINE

The next ten hours were the longest of Arthur's life. He sat within the studio for a while, listening to Bob play the same tune over and over again on the piano. He watched the news on television with Michaeli for a much shorter time, but couldn't bear to hear of the many new cases or the attempts to break quarantine. And on the hour, every hour, some of the patients were dying. So far, it was all very old people, but that was no comfort to Arthur. He felt responsible for their deaths.

Finally he retreated to his room and lay on his bed. The red lacquer box was on his desk, and the Atlas with it. Arthur didn't even feel like looking at that. Instead he just held the Nightsweeper on the palm of his hand. It mostly stood still, but every now and then would take a few steps, or lower its head and nibble at his palm.

Eventually, without meaning to, or wanting to, Arthur fell asleep. One moment he was awake, the next he was suddenly aware that he was asleep.

Asleep! Every alarm in his brain went off as he struggled to wake up.

What if I've missed midnight? What if I have to wait a whole day till tomorrow night? More people will die! Mum might die!

Arthur woke thrashing and crying out. It was pitch black, save for the glow of his digital clock. He stared at it, sleep clogging his senses.

11:56! There was still time!

Then he had another panic. He was under a quilt. Bob must have found him asleep and thrown the quilt over him. The Nightsweeper was gone from his hand!

Arthur hurled himself out of bed and turned on every light. Then he ripped the quilt from the bed. The Nightsweeper had to be there somewhere.

What if Bob took it downstairs? Or if Michaeli had been the one who—

Then Arthur saw it, standing easily on top of the lacquer box. The Nightsweeper was prancing now, eager to be at its work.

Arthur let out the longest sigh he had ever made, reached over and picked it up. It reared in his hand and gave an excited neigh.

Arthur took it to the window. It became even more restive as he raised the sash.

"Go on," said Arthur softly, opening his palm.

The black horse leaped into the night. Arthur saw it grow as it flew up to the sky. Grow and grow and grow, till its hooves alone were larger than the house. It neighed, and its neigh was like thunder, rattling the windows, shaking the house. It circled high in the air, then dived back down, great gusts of cold wind jetting from its flared nostrils.

The wind blew Arthur back on to the bed. It was cold, but a delicious cold, beautifully brisk. He felt it wake him up completely, sending a jolt through his entire body. It was the breath of pure, excited life, of raw energy, of the simple joy of running as hard as you can.

Arthur rushed back to the window in time to see the Nightsweeper gallop high over the town beyond, its fresh, invigorating breath blowing the leaves from trees, shaking signs and sweeping up anything loose upon the streets. Car alarms came on everywhere it passed, and lights flicked on in waves beneath it.

The Nightsweeper was waking everything... and everyone... up.

Downstairs, Arthur heard the phone ringing. He ran out to see Michaeli and Eric already in the corridor. Together they tumbled down the stairs, down to the main living room. Bob was there, fully dressed and weary. He slowly put the phone down and smiled at his children.

"That was Emily. They've identified the genetic structure," he said, relief evident in every word and gesture. "There will be a vaccine within days. But it seems the virus is less fatal than everyone first thought. Lots of patients are waking up."

Arthur smiled then, relief washing through him. Finally it was over.

Then he heard another telephone ring. No one else reacted and for a second Arthur thought he was imagining it. But the sound got even louder, though Bob, Michaeli and Eric still paid it no attention. It was an old-fashioned chattering bell, not an electronic beep. Arthur had only heard something like it in the House...

It had to be the phone in the red lacquer box.

Arthur looked at the clock on the wall. It ticked, and the minute hand moved a fraction.

It was one minute past twelve.

On Tuesday morning.

About the author

Garth Nix was born on a Saturday in Melbourne, Australia, and got married on a Saturday, to his publisher wife, Anna. So Saturday is a good day. Garth used to write every Sunday afternoon because he has had a number of day jobs over the years that nearly always started on a Monday, usually far too early. These jobs have included being a bookseller, an editor, a PR consultant and a literary agent. Tuesday has always been a lucky day for Garth, when he receives good news, like the telegram (a long time ago, in the days of telegrams) that told him he had sold his first short story, or when he heard his novel *Abhorsen* had hit *The New York Times* bestseller list.

Wednesday can be a letdown after Tuesday, but it was important when Garth served as a part-time soldier in the Australian Army Reserve, because that was a training night.

Thursday is now particularly memorable because Garth and Anna's son, Thomas, was born on a Thursday afternoon. Friday is a very popular day for most people, but since Garth has become a full-time writer it has no longer marked the end of the work week. On any day, Garth may generally be found near Coogee Beach in Sydney, where he and his family live.

THE **KEYS** TO THE **KINGDOM** series

Seven days. Seven keys.
One mysterious book.
One strange house filled with secrets.

GRIM TUESDAY

When Arthur left the strange house that had almost
killed him on Monday, he didn't expect to be called
back there the very next day.

DROWNED WEDNESDAY

An invitation to lunch leads to a stormy voyage,
Nothing-laced gunpowder and pirates, landing
Arthur in very hot water indeed!

SIR THURSDAY

Arthur is trapped in the House, drafted into
Sir Thursday's army for a hundred years. Meanwhile,
a doppelganger has assumed his identity at home.

HarperCollins *Children's Books*

www.garthnix.co.uk